TYPHOON
AND OTHER STORIES

JOSEPH CONRAD

with an introduction, commentaries and notes by
RICHARD ADAMS

LONGMAN

LONGMAN GROUP LIMITED
Longman House,
Burnt Mill, Harlow, Essex CM20 2JE, England
and Associated Companies throughout the World.

This edition first published 1980
Fourth impression 1986
ISBN 0 582 31524 7

Produced by Longman Singapore Publishers Pte Ltd
Printed in Singapore

The Heritage of Literature Series

TYPHOON AND OTHER STORIES

CONTENTS

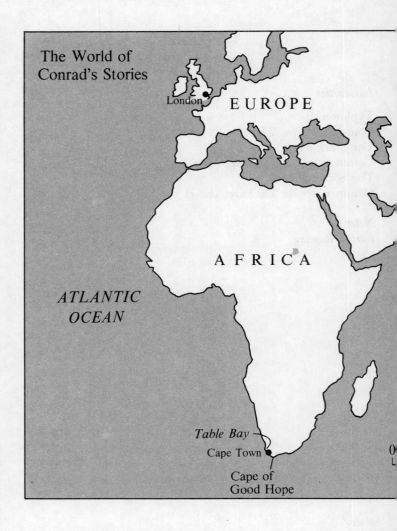

The World of
Conrad's Stories

London

EUROPE

AFRICA

ATLANTIC
OCEAN

Table Bay
Cape Town
Cape of
Good Hope

The ship, this ship, our ship, the ship we serve, is the moral
symbol of our life. A ship has to be respected, actually and
ideally; her merit, her innocence, are sacred things. Of all

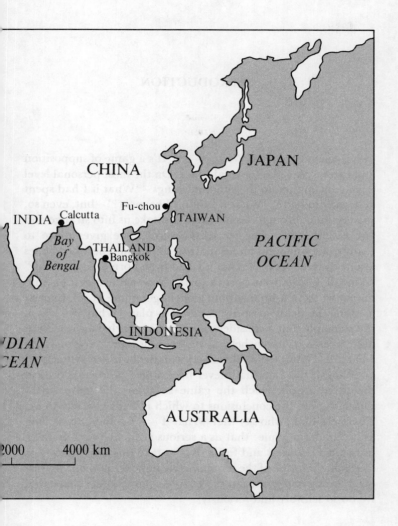

the creations of man she is the closest partner of his toil and
courage . . . mute and compelling, she claims not only your
fidelity, but your respect.

INTRODUCTION

What if –?

Have you ever played 'What if – ?'? It's a game of supposition
and can be played on several levels. On the most personal level
it may be applied to the simplest things – 'What if I had spent
yesterday in bed?', 'What if I didn't like meat?' – but, even so,
the thinking through of such ideas can take us into strange and
fascinating areas. The straightforward game gives place to
really quite profound philosophizing about our cherished hopes
or our dearest beliefs. 'What if I had been born an only child?'
'What if I had been born a girl?' Now we are getting into
deeper water; the implications loom huger, more awful. Experts
in different fields of study sometimes play 'What if – ?' on
the principle that a consideration of what nearly happened but
didn't can very often help us in focusing more accurately on
what did: 'What if Napoleon had won the battle of Waterloo?'
or 'What if the atom had never been split?' The more critical
the situation on which the game is based, the more earth-
shattering are the conclusions to which it leads us likely to be.
There are those who say that 'What if – ?' is valid only so long
as it remains a game; that as a serious academic exercise it is,
in the end, fruitless and futile. But to take this line is surely to
overlook the value of the discipline we impose upon our powers
of reasoning in playing out the game – assuming, of course, that
we do so sensibly and seriously.

'Conrad blessé envoyez argent – arrivez'

It was 1878.

He was twenty years of age, Polish by nationality but living in the French port of Marseilles. His parents had been dead for some years and he had been brought up by an uncle who was still in Poland. Indeed, if his uncle had had his way, he too would still have been living there. But from his early years the young man had shown a romantic longing for life at sea, and so it was that, by dint of his persistent demands and pleas to his guardians, he had at last, in 1874, wrung from them their reluctant agreement that he should go to Marseilles in order to join the French merchant navy.

Though he had not at first been successful in his attempt, he had at least seen some colourful adventures. His uncle had settled on him an annual allowance of 2,000 francs and had arranged introductions to several French contacts, so that he had soon learned to enjoy the comforts of his new independence with adolescent relish. He had been taken into the homes of hospitable and friendly Marseillaises and had been initiated into the spirited bohemian café life of the city. He had, in particular, become associated with a band of royalists working to secure the Spanish throne for Don Carlos de Bourbon, and had even taken a hand in their gun-running activities. He had made a number of sea voyages, though on the first of these, to Martinique, it had been as a passenger and at his own expense rather than as a member of the crew. He had also begun to spend his allowance more wildly and extravagantly than was wise, so that his letters home had been perforce punctuated with requests for more funds. His activities had become more and more shady and dangerous: he had been involved in a smuggling ring organized by a woman called Rita de Lastaola, with whom, to make matters more complicated, he had also fallen in love. He and his fellow smugglers had come close to being taken prisoner and their ship had had to be sunk in order to avoid capture. Moreover, he had lost the 3,000 francs that he had invested in the crazy venture. More disasters had followed his return to France. For one thing, his affair with Rita had come to an end; for another, he had failed to secure a position on a ship on which he had been anxious to serve. What is more, because of an irregularity in his papers and his foreign status, he had been reprimanded by the authorities and forbidden to enlist in the future on any French vessel. And he had got deeper and deeper into debt. In a determined effort to extricate himself from his many troubles he had borrowed 800 francs from his friend Richard Fecht and gone off to the port of Villefranche in the hope of being able to join the American navy. Once again, however, he had been unsuccessful, and in a wild, hopeless attempt to recoup some of his financial losses he had gone along the coast to Monte Carlo to try his luck at the gaming tables.

He had lost everything.

So here he was, back in Marseilles in February 1878 – ruined, desperate and lonely. One fine, mild evening, he invited Richard Fecht to join him for tea in his room. Shortly before his guest was due to arrive, he took out a pistol that was normally kept hidden among his belongings, pointed it at his heart and shot himself.

The young man was Joseph Conrad. Fortunately, the bullet missed its target. Fecht, finding him wounded, immediately sent for help and, luckily finding the appropriate address, cabled his friend's uncle: 'Conrad blessé envoyez argent – arrivez' (Conrad wounded send money – come).

Playing out the game . . .

The most obvious question to ask is, of course, 'What if Joseph Conrad had succeeded in committing suicide in 1878?' Well, the answers are easy: few people would ever have heard of him, I would not be writing this introduction and no one would have had a chance to read his stories. But let us be a little more subtle: 'What if Conrad's suicide attempt in 1878 had left him an invalid, a cripple for the rest of his life?' Now the possibilities become more informative. Certainly, a semi-paralysed Conrad might never have pursued his sea-going career any further, would very likely never have come to England and learned our language, would – even if he had still become a writer – probably not have been an English writer with a direct appeal to the English imagination. And this brings us back to what really happened: he recovered fully, joined the English merchant service, travelled the world for twenty more years and finally settled in this country. When he took to writing he drew on the vast fund of experience of people, places and events which he had amassed in his years as a wanderer and at sea. But, just for a moment, let us go back to the beginning of his story . . .

The early years

Conrad was born in 1857 in a part of Poland which was then under Russian occupation. His real name was Józef Teodor Konrad Korzeniowski. His was a noble family whose members had owned large estates in Poland for many generations. As an aristocrat, his father Apollo Korzeniowski was acutely aware of his country's subservience to a foreign power and subscribed vigorously to the growing nationalist movement which sought to throw off the Russian yoke. To the authorities he was indeed a dangerous figure, and it would be quite wrong to minimize the strength of his determination to see his homeland free and independent of Russian influence. He was no quaint, gentlemanly patriot of the old school, but a blood-red revolutionary extremist who did all in his power to stir up resistance to the Russian authorities. He opened his house in Warsaw as a meeting place for those who shared his views, he paraded publicly in peasant costume, symbolic for him of the grass-roots nature of his struggle; he formed a secret resistance committee, and he led public demonstrations. His wife, Evelina, openly defied police regulations by wearing tokens of mourning for those who had died as a result of the government's harsh repressive measures.

The danger in which Conrad's parents were placing themselves can best be illustrated by recalling that the Russians were perfectly prepared to subdue such manifestations of nationalism with force. Public rallies were broken up with cavalry charges, Polish politicians were summarily executed or exiled. Indeed, Apollo himself was arrested and, together with his wife and year-old son, was later sent into banishment in a remote northerly part of Russia. Their property, lands and money were confiscated. They were, in a way, lucky; some of the relatives and friends they left behind in Poland 'disappeared' in a new spate of cruel repression. They were not so lucky, however, in another respect. The strain of exile and their enforced movement from one part of the Russian Empire to another during the next few years sapped the strength of both parents. Eva died in 1865; four years later her husband followed her to the grave.

Thus, at the age of eleven, Conrad became an orphan. His childhood had been one of isolation, of constant movement, of instability; it had been coloured with bitterness and misery and recurring illness. Now he became the ward of his mother's brother, Thaddeus Bobrowski, a kindly but sensible man who had managed to keep his own nationalistic feelings in check and who had managed to remain on reasonable terms with the authorities. Under his influence, Conrad's formal education was completed. The boy had already shown considerable promise and in particular had revealed a love of books (especially adventure stories and books about the sea) and creative writing. He had also revealed a taste for poring in studied fascination over maps of the distant places of the earth. In 1872 he first announced to his uncle his wish to follow a career at sea. It took, as we have seen, two years before he was able to realize his ambition, and there is no doubt that Thaddeus Bobrowski was both alarmed and worried at the prospect of his charge striking out alone in life in the fashion he proposed. In the end, two principal factors must have influenced the granting of his permission: first, the genuine passion for the sea and exploration which had been fostered by Conrad's reading; second, the fact that Poland was still a dangerous place for the young man, who, as the son of a convicted revolutionary, was liable to serve for up to twenty-five years in the Russian army. So far as Conrad himself was concerned, the sea meant leaving Poland, which had no sea coast in those days, and breaking away from the carefully structured and supervised life which he had been obliged to lead under his uncle's influence.

Thus it was that Conrad came to Marseilles in 1874 and that the events that we have already discussed took place. We may well ask ourselves whether things might have turned out very differently had he not been the son of his particular parents and had he not experienced the sort of childhood and adolescence that he had. The child is father of the man. How vividly our early experiences in life colour the ultimate canvas of our lives. Perhaps that restless, excitable young man might never have turned the pistol on his own heart? 'What if – ?' Anyway, Uncle Thaddeus duly arrived in response to Richard Fecht's telegram in late February 1878 to find his nephew already recovering from his self-inflicted wound. It was clearly time to take stock of the situation.

New departures

The immediate result of these events was the decision that Conrad should try to join the British merchant service, because in doing so he was unlikely to experience the sort of problems he had encountered in his efforts to sail under either the French or the American flag. He therefore joined the crew of the coal-freighter *Mavis* in which eventually, in mid-June 1878, he arrived at the east coast port of Lowestoft.

It was a momentous decision with far-reaching consequences. Here was a young expatriate Pole, who by his own admission knew at the time only 'six words of English', setting out on what to the impartial observer might have appeared yet another reckless adventure. But this time destiny was on his side. Over the next eight years he served in a succession of mainly British ships (though he seems to have quarrelled all too frequently with their captains), gradually working his way up the ladder of promotion and qualification, until in November 1886 he was awarded his master mariner's certificate. In the same year Conrad became a naturalized British subject. He continued his career at sea on and off until the autumn of 1894, when the acceptance for publication of his first novel, *Almayer's Folly*, prompted his determination to settle down to the life of a writer and to forsake the ocean world that had fascinated him for so long. The significance of his 1878 decision and his joining of the *Mavis* is reflected in the twin facts that his novel, on which he had been working spasmodically for five years, was written in English, and that from 1894 onwards England was to become his permanent home. Though as a writer he made several extended trips to various parts of Europe and to America, he spent the rest of his days in the south of England. He died on 3 August 1924, having achieved an enormous and well-deserved reputation as a novelist in a language not his by birth, against a bourgeois background remote from his aristocratic origins, in an island country far removed from his native Poland, at the end of a life a large proportion of which had been spent wandering the earth.

Conrad the voyager

It is not my intention here to recount in detail the events of Conrad's wandering years from 1878 until 1894. Sufficient to say that, characteristically, they were neither plain-sailing nor free from the moments of frustration and hankering after new horizons that had punctuated his years in France. He started very much at the bottom of the ladder as an ordinary seaman – demanding enough for a young man of a background such as his – on a coaster in home waters plying between Lowestoft and Newcastle. His first extended cruise during this period was aboard a wool-clipper bound for Australia. But he appears never to have stayed long in any ship, usually because of those differences of opinion with his superiors. Nor was he utterly committed to the particular brand of seafaring in which he found himself, and from time to time he investigated the possibilities of going into business or becoming a whaler. Later in his career he was to put money into and work for a firm of shipping-agents and to consider his prospects as a Suez Canal pilot or in the Australian pearl-fisheries.

His next notable voyage was in 1882–3 as second mate in the barque *Palestine* – a voyage which ended in shipwreck off the coast of Sumatra (part of present-day Indonesia), and which he was to immortalize in his short novel *Youth*. He was to return to this part of the world in ensuing years and, as we shall see, it forms the background to a number of his works. The *Palestine* was a steam-assisted vessel, the *Narcissus*, in which he served in 1884 on a voyage from Bombay to Dunkirk and which was to be the inspiration for his important story *The Nigger of the 'Narcissus'*, was a sailing ship. The period during which Conrad served in the merchant fleet marked the transition from sail to steam and we are fortunate that his stories reflect so accurately and in such detail what life aboard both types of vessel must have been like.

Another watershed in his career came about 1885–6 when, although he was close to qualifying as a master mariner, Conrad was again becoming disenchanted with the sea and contemplated giving it up for good. It is perhaps significant that at about the same time he appears to have written his first story, *The Black Mate*. Fortunately for us, he was to continue his sea travels for a further eight years, during which time he not only visited and revisited areas of the world which were to feature prominently in his later writing – notably the (then) Belgian Congo, the setting for what many regard as his masterpiece, *Heart of Darkness*, Malaysia and Thailand, whose capital

Bangkok is the starting point for *The Secret Sharer* – but also met many of the men and women – seamen, traders, explorers, settlers – on whom the principal characters of his stories were to be modelled.

For our purposes, the most remarkable of these encounters took place in 1887 when Conrad signed on in Amsterdam as first mate on the sailing ship *Highland Forest*. He was not the only new member of the crew:

> The day after we had finished loading [he writes], on the very eve of the day of sailing our new captain arrived. I first beheld him on the quay, a complete stranger to me, obviously not a Hollander, in a black bowler and a short drab overcoat, ridiculously out of tone with the winter aspect of the waste lands, bordered by the brown fronts of houses with their roofs dripping with melting snow.

This new captain's name was John McWhirr: the voyage of the *Highland Forest* was to be notable for a very rough patch of weather. Here were some of the seeds from which *Typhoon* was to grow.

Conrad was also, during this period, given his first captaincy, of the barque *Otago*, which he took to the Indian Ocean, the Far East and Australia. His experiences were to be of great value in the understanding depiction in his writing of the psychology of command. Between 1887 and his last professional landfall in 1894, he suffered recurring bouts of sickness which may have contributed towards his final decision to give up the life of a voyager.

Conrad the writer

When in 1894 Conrad gave up the sea in order to become a full-time writer he almost certainly did so because promise of publication of *Almayer's Folly* had given him sufficient confidence to make the break with a way of life which was becoming more and more exacting the older he grew. He was in his late thirties: he had seen and experienced as much of life as one man could hope or desire. Now he needed detachment and quiet to ponder those experiences, to allow his creative imagination to shape them into satisfying literary form. Is it surprising, that as many as nine major characters in his books commit suicide, while three others go to certain death in a spirit of self-sacrifice? That his novels *Nostromo*, *The Secret Agent* and *Under Western Eyes* all have to do with activities of revolutionaries? That he should have confessed that most of the characters portrayed in *The Nigger of the 'Narcissus'* 'actually belonged to the crew of the real *Narcissus*?' That he knew a real Captain McWhirr? What might *Youth* or *Heart of Darkness* have been like, assuming they were written at all, if Conrad had never seen the Malay Archipelago or travelled up the Congo River and met the men and women who had made their homes in those remote regions? Moreover, when he was not depicting characters and events from his personal experience he could call on a vast fund of sea-lore – stories about incidents on board vessels other than his own, picked up from those who served on them, such as that concerning the chief mate of the famous clipper *Cutty Sark* who accidentally killed an insubordinate seaman but managed to slip away from his ship and live for a time as a fugitive from the law and the consequences of his action. The man, in fact, who was to become Leggatt in *The Secret Sharer*. And even when he was not using events and characters from his own past or from what he had gleaned from other people, he could and did give his stories the stamp of authority by setting them in real places, conjuring up the atmosphere of the great rivers and cities, islands and settlements he had visited during his career. By examining in them, too, the passions and emotions which we all have in common, such as loneliness – the loneliness of flight, of command, or the loneliness of those who are without warning pitched by destiny into strange surroundings, like the young shipwrecked sailor in *Amy Foster*. It is this recurring reference to real people, places, events and feelings which gives

Conrad's writing the same ring of truth today that it had when his stories and novels first appeared.

Conrad's method of working was slow and painstaking. He was, after all, not merely spinning a good yarn or entertaining an audience hungry for adventure. He was practising an art, the object of which was the true and faithful revelation of the human soul. In order to live up to so high an ideal, he once told a young writer who had sought his advice, of the necessity for working with unflagging intensity:

> You must squeeze out of yourself every sensation, every thought, every image – mercilessly, without reserve and without remorse: you must search the darkest corners of your heart, the most remote recesses of your brain ... you must do it sincerely, at any cost: you must do it so that at the end of your day's work you should feel exhausted, emptied of every sensation and every thought, with a blank mind and an aching heart, with the notion that there is nothing – nothing left in you.

Not that his thirty years as a writer were by any means years of pure triumph. It was not until the last decade of his life that he achieved any lasting popularity with the English public, though he received early recognition from a number of fellow-writers and critics. Even after the publication of his first books, he felt the need to strive after constant improvement. He knew that there were things he still had to learn. For one thing he had to pare down his style. H.G. Wells pointed out in a review of one of his stories that he must avoid wordiness and the accusation that his narrative line could only be perceived 'intermittently through a haze of sentences'. Happily, none of the three pieces included in the present volume, not even *The Black Mate* which he reworked for publication in 1908 (it appears here in its revised form), can be accused of falling short in this respect. Indeed, *Typhoon* and *The Secret Sharer* stand out as fine examples of his art in its most accomplished and polished form.

Something of the spirit in which Conrad approached his

task as a writer is reflected in the words of Jessie George, the girl he married in 1896 and who bore him two sons: 'My marriage ...' she tells us, 'had ... an added element of high adventure ... I had to endeavour to adapt myself to the moods of a man whose mind had been occupied with the meaning of life, with its difficulties, joys and sorrows, long before he had met me ...' This absorption on her husband's part with the essential significance of the human condition is corroborated in his assertion that he wrote in order to stir up in his audience that sense of oneness, that 'unavoidable solidarity ... which binds men to each other and all mankind to the whole world'. That he should find such solidarity most evident among those who spend their lives sailing the world's oceans, pitting their courage and skill against the inscrutable treachery of wind and wave, is scarcely surprising. For Conrad the sea is a metaphor of the sum total of success and failure, of lasting triumph and sudden disaster, of which our earthly existence is capable. While the ship, to quote the words with which it has seemed fitting to preface this collection, 'this ship, our ship, the ship we serve, is the moral symbol of our life'. Her solitary ploughed path across the sea's great wastes bears constant witness to man's eternal insignificance in the face of a boundless and hostile universe. Here is a world where a man's spirit and determination may be thrown into sharp relief, his inner qualities revealed, where physical danger will take the measure of this true character; a world where sacrifice is called for but not always recognised, where greatness sometimes does not receive its due; a world where routine and self-discipline are the most certain hedges against anarchy and disorder. These are just a few of the themes which recur in Conrad's writing. They, and others like them, are examined more fully in the commentaries which follow each of the three stories in this book.

The voice of Conrad

Conrad wrote in a language not his by birth. He learned it, as he learned so much of his seamanship, from the sailors 'of the Norfolk shore' on the Lowestoft to Newcastle run, and from the men he encountered on his world-wide voyaging. Yet he became one of our greatest novelists. He retained a noticeable Polish accent in his speech throughout his life; but little evidence of his origins is to be found in his writing, even in his early work. Indeed, R.B. Cunninghame Graham in his preface to the *Tales of Hearsay* comments that in *The Black Mate* (which was published as part of that collection) Conrad's English 'is as perfect, perhaps more perfect, than in his latest work'. He goes on:

> This is not so curious as it appears, for as the years roll on, a language that we have acquired in youth, when all our faculties are keen, and with the first impact that a strange tongue makes on the brain, gradually fades, and the speech that we learned at our mother's knee subconsciously reasserts itself. . . . Such : . . was the case with Conrad. Although his flow of vigorous and idiomatic English never failed and his vocabulary only got richer as the years passed by, his accent, on the contrary, that years ago was slight, became more marked, and certain turns of phrase appeared that, though they were not English, yet gave his English grace.

But perhaps the best appreciation of the unique contribution made to our literary heritage by this expatriate Polish sea-captain comes from his own pen, in his description of the way in which two very different foreigners express themselves in the language which he too had adopted. The first is Yanko Goorall, the shipwrecked sailor in *Amy Foster*:

> He told me this story of his adventure . . . as he acquired the language, with great fluency, but always with that singing, soft, and at the same time vibrating intonation that instilled a strangely penetrating power into the sound of the most familiar English words, as if they had been the words of an unearthly language.

The second is the mysterious Kurtz in *Heart of Darkness*:

> The point was in his being a gifted creature, and that of all his gifts the one that stood out pre-eminently, that carried with it a sense of real presence, was his ability to talk, his words – the gift of expression, the bewildering, the illuminating, the most exalted and the most contemptible, the pulsating stream of light, or the deceitful flow from the heart of an impenetrable darkness.

Read the stories in this book carefully, listen intently and you will not fail to catch that 'sense of real presence' which marks Joseph Conrad out as a writer of true genius.

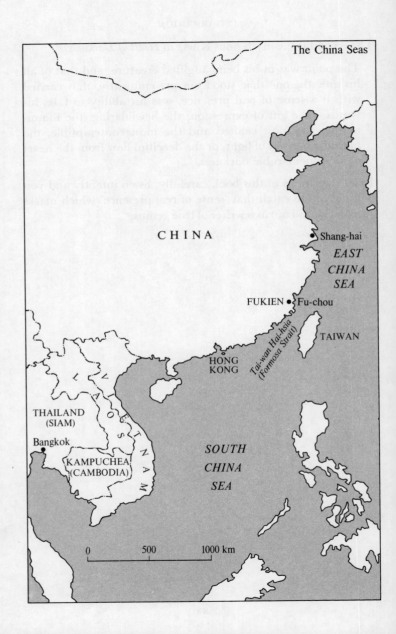

The China Seas

CHINA

Shang-hai

EAST
CHINA
SEA

FUKIEN ● Fu-chou

TAIWAN

HONG
KONG

*Tai-wan Hai-hsia
(Formosa Strait)*

THAILAND
(SIAM)

Bangkok

KAMPUCHEA
(CAMBODIA)

SOUTH
CHINA
SEA

0   500   1000 km

TYPHOON

I

Captain MacWhirr, of the steamer *Nan-Shan*, had a physiognomy that, in the order of material appearances, was the exact counterpart of his mind: it presented no marked characteristics of firmness or stupidity; it had no pronounced characteristics whatever; it was simply ordinary, irresponsive, and unruffled.

The only thing his aspect might have been said to suggest, at times, was bashfulness; because he would sit, in business offices ashore, sunburnt and smiling faintly, with downcast eyes. When he raised them, they were perceived to be direct in their glance and of blue colour. His hair was fair and extremely fine, clasping from temple to temple the bald dome of his skull in a clamp as of fluffy silk. The hair of his face, on the contrary, carroty and flaming, resembled a growth of copper wire clipped short to the line of the lip; while, no matter how close he shaved, fiery metallic gleams passed, when he moved his head, over the surface of his cheeks. He was rather below the medium height, a bit round-shouldered, and so sturdy of limb that his clothes always looked a shade too tight for his arms and legs. As if unable to grasp what is due to the difference of latitudes, he wore a brown bowler hat, a complete suit of a brownish hue, and clumsy black boots. These harbour togs gave to his thick figure an air of stiff and uncouth smartness. A thin silver watch-chain looped his waistcoat, and he never left his ship for the shore without clutching in his powerful, hairy fist an elegant umbrella of the very best quality, but generally unrolled. Young Jukes, the chief mate, attending his commander to the gangway, would sometimes venture to say, with the greatest gentleness, 'Allow me, sir,' – and possessing himself of the umbrella deferentially, would elevate the ferrule, shake the folds, twirl a neat furl in a jiffy, and hand it back; going through the performance with a face of such portentous gravity, that Mr Solomon Rout, the chief engineer, smoking his morning cigar over the skylight, would turn away his head in order to hide a smile. 'Oh! aye! The blessed gamp . . . Thank 'ee, Jukes, thank 'ee,' would mutter Captain MacWhirr heartily, without looking up.

Having just enough imagination to carry him through each successive day, and no more, he was tranquilly sure of himself; and from the very same cause he was not in the least conceited. It is your imaginative superior who is touchy, overbearing, and difficult to please; but every ship Captain MacWhirr commanded was the floating abode of harmony and peace. It was, in truth, as impossible for him to take a flight of fancy as it would be for a watchmaker to put together a chronometer with nothing except a two-pound hammer and a whip-saw in the way of tools. Yet the uninteresting lives of men so entirely given to the actuality of the bare existence have their mysterious side. It was impossible in Captain MacWhirr's case, for instance, to understand what under heaven could have induced that perfectly satisfactory son of a petty grocer in Belfast to run away to sea. And yet he had done that very thing at the age of fifteen. It was enough, when you thought it over, to give you the idea of an immense, potent, and invisible hand thrust into the ant-heap of the earth, laying hold of shoulders, knocking heads together, and setting the unconscious faces of the multitude towards inconceivable goals and in undreamt-of directions.

His father never really forgave him for this undutiful stupidity. 'We could have got on without him,' he used to say later on, 'but there's the business. And he an only son too!' His mother wept very much after his disappearance. As it had never occurred to him to leave word behind, he was mourned over for dead till, after eight months, his first letter arrived from Talcahuano. It was short, and contained the statement: 'We had very fine weather on our passage out.' But evidently, in the writer's mind, the only important intelligence was to the

2

effect that his captain had, on the very day of writing, entered him regularly on the ship's articles as Ordinary Seaman. 'Because I can do the work,' he explained. The mother again wept copiously, while the remark, 'Tom's an ass,' expressed the emotions of the father. He was a corpulent man, with a gift for sly chaffing, which to the end of his life he exercised in his intercourse with his son, a little pityingly, as if upon a halfwitted person.

MacWhirr's visits to his home were necessarily rare, and in the course of years he despatched other letters to his parents, informing them of his successive promotions and of his movements upon the vast earth. In these missives could be found sentences like this: 'The heat here is very great.' Or: 'On Christmas day at 4 p.m. we fell in with some icebergs.' The old people ultimately became acquainted with a good many names of ships, and with the names of the skippers who commanded them – with the names of Scots and English shipowners – with the names of seas, oceans, straits, promontories – with outlandish names of lumber ports, of rice-ports, of cotton-ports – with the names of islands – with the name of their son's young woman. She was called Lucy. It did not suggest itself to him to mention whether he thought the name pretty. And then they died.

The great day of MacWhirr's marriage came in due course, following shortly upon the great day when he got his first command.

All these events had taken place many years before the morning when, in the chart-room of the steamer *Nan-Shan*, he stood confronted by the fall of a barometer he had no reason to distrust. The fall – taking into account the excellence of the instrument, the time of the year, and the ship's position on the terrestrial globe – was of a nature ominously prophetic; but the red face of the man betrayed no sort of inward disturbance. Omens were as nothing to him, and he was unable to discover the message of a prophecy till the fulfilment had brought it home to his very door. 'That's a fall, and no mistake,' he thought. 'There must be some uncommonly dirty weather knocking about.'

The *Nan-Shan* was on her way from the southward to the treaty port of Fu-chau, with some cargo in her lower holds, and two hundred Chinese coolies returning to their village homes in the province of Fo-kien, after a few years of work in various tropical colonies. The morning was fine, the oily sea heaved without a sparkle, and there was a queer white misty patch in the sky like a halo of the sun. The fore-deck, packed with Chinamen, was full of sombre clothing, yellow faces, and pigtails, sprinkled over with a good many naked shoulders, for there was no wind, and the heat was close. The coolies lounged, talked, smoked, or stared over the rail; some, drawing water over the side, sluiced each other; a few slept on hatches, while several small parties of six sat on their heels surrounding iron trays with plates of rice and tiny teacups; and every single Celestial of them was carrying with him all he had in the world – a wooden chest with a ringing lock and brass on the corners, containing the savings of his labours: some clothes of ceremony, sticks of incense, a little opium maybe, bits of nameless rubbish of conventional value, and a small hoard of silver dollars, toiled for in coal lighters, won in gambling-houses or in petty trading, grubbed out of the earth, sweated out in mines, on railway lines, in deadly jungle, under heavy burdens – amassed patiently, guarded with care, cherished fiercely.

A cross swell had set in from the direction of Formosa Channel about ten o'clock, without disturbing these passengers much, because the *Nan-Shan*, with her flat bottom, rolling chocks on bilges, and great breadth of beam, had the reputation of an exceptionally steady ship in a sea-way. Mr Jukes, in moments of expansion on shore, would proclaim loudly that the 'old girl was as good as she was pretty'. It would never have occurred to Captain MacWhirr to express his favourable opinion so loud or in terms so fanciful.

She was a good ship, undoubtedly, and not old either. She had been built in Dumbarton less than three years before, to the order of a firm of merchants in Siam – Messrs Sigg and Son. When she lay afloat, finished in every detail and ready to take

4

up the work of her life, the builders contemplated her with pride.

'Sigg has asked us for a reliable skipper to take her out,' remarked one of the partners; and the other, after reflecting for a while, said, 'I think MacWhirr is ashore just at present.' 'Is he? Then wire him at once. He's the very man,' declared the senior, without a moment's hesitation.

Next morning MacWhirr stood before them unperturbed, having travelled from London by the midnight express after a sudden but undemonstrative parting with his wife. She was the daughter of a superior couple who had seen better days.

'We had better be going together over the ship, Captain,' said the senior partner; and the three men started to view the perfections of the *Nan-Shan* from stem to stern, and from her keelson to the trucks of her two stumpy polemasts.

Captain MacWhirr had begun by taking off his coat, which he hung on the end of a steam windlass embodying all the latest improvements.

'My uncle wrote of you favourably by yesterday's mail to our good friends – Messrs Sigg, you know – and doubtless they'll continue you out there in command,' said the junior partner. 'You'll be able to boast of being in charge of the handiest boat of her size on the coast of China, Captain,' he added.

'Have you? Thank 'ee,' mumbled vaguely MacWhirr, to whom the view of a distant eventuality could appeal no more than the beauty of a wide landscape to a purblind tourist; and his eyes happening at the moment to be at rest upon the lock of the cabin door, he walked up to it, full of purpose, and began to rattle the handle vigorously, while he observed, in his low, earnest voice, 'You can't trust the workmen nowadays. A brand new lock, and it won't act at all. Stuck fast. See? See?'

As soon as they found themselves alone in their office across the yard, 'You praised that fellow up to Sigg. What is it you see in him?' asked the nephew, with faint contempt.

'I admit he has nothing of your fancy skipper about him, if that's what you mean,' said the elder man curtly. 'Is the foreman of the joiners on the *Nan-Shan* outside? ... Come in, Bates. How is it that you let Tait's people put us off with a defective lock on the cabin door? The Captain could see directly he set eye on it. Have it replaced at once. The little straws, Bates ... the little straws. ...'

The lock was replaced accordingly, and a few days afterwards the *Nan-Shan* steamed out to the East, without MacWhirr having offered any further remark as to her fittings, or having been heard to utter a single word hinting at pride in his ship, gratitude for his appointment, or satisfaction at his prospects.

With a temperament neither loquacious nor taciturn, he found very little occasion to talk. There were matters of duty, of course – directions, orders, and so on; but the past being to his mind done with, and the future not there yet, the more general actualities of the day required no comment – because facts can speak for themselves with overwhelming precision.

Old Mr Sigg liked a man of few words, and one that 'you could be sure would not try to improve upon his instructions'. MacWhirr satisfying these requirements, was continued in command of the *Nan-Shan*, and applied himself to the careful navigation of his ship in the China seas. She had come out on a British register, but after some time Messrs Sigg judged it expedient to transfer her to the Siamese flag.

At the news of the contemplated transfer Jukes grew restless, as if under a sense of personal affront. He went about grumbling to himself, and uttering short scornful laughs. 'Fancy having a ridiculous Noah's Ark elephant in the ensign of one's ship,' he said once at the engine-room door. 'Dash me if I can stand it: I'll throw up the billet. Don't it make *you* sick Mr Rout?' The chief engineer only cleared his throat with the air of a man who knows the value of a good billet.

The first morning the new flag floated over the stern of the *Nan-Shan* Jukes stood looking at it bitterly from the bridge. He struggled with his feelings for a while, and then remarked, 'Queer flag for a man to sail under, sir.'

'What's the matter with the flag?' inquired Captain Mac-

Whirr. 'Seems all right to me.' And he walked across to the end of the bridge to have a good look.

'Well, it looks queer to me,' burst out Jukes, greatly exasperated, and flung off the bridge.

Captain MacWhirr was amazed at these manners. Afer a while he stepped quietly into the chart-room, and opened his International Signal Code book at the plate where the flags of all the nations are correctly figured in gaudy rows. He ran his finger over them, and when he came to Siam he contemplated with great attention the red field and the white elephant. Nothing could be more simple; but to make sure he brought the book out on the bridge for the purpose of comparing the coloured drawing with the real thing at the flagstaff astern. When next Jukes, who was carrying on the duty that day with a sort of suppressed fierceness, happened on the bridge, his commander observed:

'There's nothing amiss with that flag.'

'Isn't there?' mumbled Jukes, falling on his knees before a deck locker and jerking therefrom viciously a spare lead line.

'No. I looked up the book. Length twice the breadth and the elephant exactly in the middle. I thought the people ashore would know how to make the local flag. Stands to reason. You were wrong, Jukes . . .'

'Well, sir,' began Jukes, getting up excitedly, 'all I can say——' He fumbled for the end of the coil of line with trembling hands.

'That's all right.' Captain MacWhirr soothed him, sitting heavily on a little canvas folding stool he greatly affected. 'All you have to do is to take care they don't hoist the elephant upside down before they get quite used to it.'

Jukes flung the new lead line over on the fore deck with a loud 'Here you are, bos'n – don't forget to wet it thoroughly,' and turned with immense resolution towards his commander; but Captain MacWhirr spread his elbows on the bridge-rail, comfortably.

'Because it would be, I suppose, understood as a signal of

distress,' he went on. 'What do you think? That elephant there, I take it, stands for something in the nature of the Union Jack in the flag . . .'

'Does it!' yelled Jukes, so that every head on the *Nan-Shan's* decks looked towards the bridge. Then he sighed, and with sudden resignation, 'It would certainly be a dam' distressful sight,' he said meekly.

Later in the day he accosted the chief engineer with a confidential 'Here, let me tell you the old man's latest.'

Mr Solomon Rout (frequently alluded to as Long Sol, Old Sol, or Father Rout), from finding himself almost invariably the tallest man on board every ship he joined, had acquired the habit of a stooping, leisurely condescension. His hair was scant and sandy, his fat cheeks were pale, his bony wrists and long scholarly hands were pale too, as though he had lived all his life in the shade.

He smiled from on high at Jukes, and went on smoking and glancing about quietly, in the manner of a kind uncle lending an ear to the tale of an excited schoolboy. Then, greatly amused but impassive, he asked:

'And did you throw up the billet?'

'No,' cried Jukes, raising a weary, discouraged voice above the harsh buzz of the *Nan-Shan's* friction winches. All of them were hard at work, snatching slings of cargo, high up, to the end of long derricks, only, as it seemed, to let them rip down recklessly by the run. The cargo chains groaned in the gins, clinked on coamings, rattled over the side; and the whole ship quivered with her long grey flanks smoking in wreaths of steam. 'No,' cried Jukes, 'I didn't. What's the good? I might just as well fling my resignation at this bulkhead. I don't believe you can make a man like that understand anything. He simply knocks me over.'

At that moment Captain MacWhirr, back from the shore, crossed the deck, umbrella in hand, escorted by a mournful, self-possessed Chinaman, walking behind in paper-soled silk shoes, and who also carried an umbrella.

The master of the *Nan-Shan*, speaking just audibly and gazing at his boots as his manner was, remarked that it would be necessary to call at Fu-chau this trip, and desired Mr Rout to have steam up to-morrow afternoon at one o'clock sharp. He pushed back his hat to wipe his forehead, observing at the same time that he hated going ashore anyhow; while overtopping him Mr Rout, without deigning a word, smoked austerely, nursing his right elbow in the palm of his left hand. Then Jukes was directed in the same subdued voice to keep the forward 'tween-deck clear of cargo. Two hundred coolies were going to be put down there. The Bun Hin Company were sending that lot home. Twenty-five bags of rice would be coming off in a sampan directly, for stores. All seven-years'-men they were, said Captain MacWhirr, with a camphor-wood chest to every man. The carpenter should be set to work nailing three-inch battens along the deck below, fore and aft, to keep these boxes from shifting in a sea-way. Jukes had better look to it at once. 'D'ye hear, Jukes?' This Chinaman here was coming with the ship as far as Fu-chau – a sort of interpreter he would be. Bun Hin's clerk he was, and wanted to have a look at the space. Jukes had better take him forward. 'D'ye hear, Jukes?'

Jukes took care to punctuate these instructions in proper places with the obligatory 'Yes, sir,' ejaculated without enthusiasm. His brusque 'Come along, John; make look see,' set the Chinaman in motion at his heels.

'Wanchee look see, all same look see can do,' said Jukes, who having no talent for foreign languages mangled the very pidgin-English cruelly. He pointed at the open hatch. 'Catchee number one piecie place to sleep in. Eh?'

He was gruff, as became his racial superiority, but not unfriendly. The Chinaman, gazing sad and speechless into the darkness of the hatchway, seemed to stand at the head of a yawning grave.

'No catchee rain down there – savee?' pointed out Jukes. 'Suppose all 'ee same fine weather, one piecie coolie-man come topside,' he pursued, warming up imaginatively. 'Make so –

Phooooo!' He expanded his chest and blew out his cheeks. 'Savee, John? Breathe – fresh air. Good. Eh? Washee him piecie pants, chow-chow top-side – see, John?'

With his mouth and hands he made exuberant motions of eating rice and washing clothes; and the Chinaman, who concealed his distrust of this pantomime under a collected demeanour tinged by a gentle and refined melancholy, glanced out of his almond eyes from Jukes to the hatch and back again. 'Velly good,' he murmured, in a disconsolate undertone, and hastened smoothly along the decks, dodging obstacles in his course. He disappeared, ducking low under a sling of ten dirty gunny-bags full of some costly merchandise and exhaling a repulsive smell.

Captain MacWhirr meantime had gone on the bridge, and into the chart-room, where a letter, commenced two days before, awaited termination. These long letters began with the words, 'My darling wife,' and the steward, between the scrubbing of the floors and the dusting of chronometer-boxes, snatched at every opportunity to read them. They interested him much more than they possibly could the woman for whose eye they were intended; and this for the reason that they related in minute detail each successive trip of the *Nan-Shan*.

Her master, faithful to facts, which alone his consciousness reflected, would set them down with painstaking care upon many pages. The house in a northern suburb to which these pages were addressed had a bit of garden before the bow-windows, a deep porch of good appearance, coloured glass with imitation lead frame in the front door. He paid five-and-forty pounds a year for it, and did not think the rent too high, because Mrs MacWhirr (a pretentious person with a scraggy neck and a disdainful manner) was admittedly ladylike, and in the neighbourhood considered as 'quite superior'. The only secret of her life was her abject terror of the time when her husband would come home to stay for good. Under the same roof there dwelt also a daughter called Lydia and a son, Tom. These two were but slightly acquainted with their father.

Mainly, they knew him as a rare but privileged visitor, who of an evening smoked his pipe in the dining-room and slept in the house. The lanky girl, upon the whole, was rather ashamed of him; the boy was frankly and utterly indifferent in a straight-forward, delightful, unaffected way manly boys have.

And Captain MacWhirr wrote home from the coast of China twelve times every year, desiring queerly to be 'remembered to the children', and subscribing himself 'your loving husband', as calmly as if the words so long used by so many men were, apart from their shape, worn-out things, and of a faded meaning.

The China seas north and south are narrow seas. They are seas full of everyday, eloquent facts, such as islands, sandbanks, reefs, swift and changeable currents – tangled facts that never-theless speak to a seaman in clear and definite language. Their speech appealed to Captain MacWhirr's sense of realities so forcibly that he had given up his state-room below and practi-cally lived all his days on the bridge of his ship, often having his meals sent up, and sleeping at night in the chart-room. And he indited there his home letters. Each of them, without exception, contained the phrase, 'The weather has been very fine this trip', or some other form of a statement to that effect. And this statement, too, in its wonderful persistence, was of the same perfect accuracy as all the others they contained.

Mr Rout likewise wrote letters; only no one on board knew how chatty he could be pen in hand, because the chief engineer had enough imagination to keep his desk locked. His wife relished his style greatly. They were a childless couple, and Mrs Rout, a big, high-bosomed, jolly woman of forty, shared with Mr Rout's toothless and venerable mother a little cottage near Teddington. She would run over her correspondence, at breakfast, with lively eyes, and scream out interesting passages in a joyous voice at the deaf old lady, prefacing each extract by the warning shout, 'Solomon says!' She had the trick of firing off Solomon's utterances also upon strangers, astonishing them easily by the unfamiliar text and the unexpectedly jocular vein of these quotations. On the day the new curate called for the

first time at the cottage, she found occasion to remark, 'As
Solomon says: "the engineers that go down to the sea in ships
behold the wonders of sailor nature";' when a change in the
visitor's countenance made her stop and stare.

'Solomon ... Oh! ... Mrs Rout,' stuttered the young man,
very red in the face, 'I must say ... I don't ...'

'He's my husband,' she announced in a great shout, throwing
herself back in the chair. Perceiving the joke, she laughed
immoderately with a handkerchief to her eyes, while he sat
wearing a forced smile, and from his experience of jolly women,
fully persuaded that she must be deplorably insane. They were
excellent friends afterwards; for, absolving her from irreverent
intention, he came to think she was a very worthy person
indeed; and he learned in time to receive without flinching
other scraps of Solomon's wisdom.

'For my part,' Solomon was reported by his wife to have said
once, 'give me the dullest ass for a skipper before a rogue. There
is a way to take a fool; but a rogue is smart and slippery.' This
was an airy generalisation drawn from the particular case of
Captain MacWhirr's honesty, which, in itself, had the heavy
obviousness of a lump of clay. On the other hand, Mr Jukes,
unable to generalize, unmarried, and unengaged, was in the
habit of opening his heart after another fashion to an old chum
and former shipmate, actually serving as second officer on board
an Atlantic liner.

First of all he would insist upon the advantages of the Eastern
trade, hinting at its superiority to the Western ocean service.
He extolled the sky, the seas, the ships, and the easy life of the
Far East. The *Nan-Shan*, he affirmed, was second to none as
a sea-boat.

'We have no brass-bound uniforms, but then we are like
brothers here,' he wrote. 'We all mess together and live like
fighting-cocks ... All the chaps of the black-squad are as decent
as they make that kind, and old Sol, the Chief, is a dry stick.
We are good friends. As to our old man, you could not find
a quieter skipper. Sometimes you would think he hadn't sense

enough to see anything wrong. And yet it isn't that. Can't be. He has been in command for a good few years now. He doesn't do anything actually foolish, and gets his ship along all right without worrying anybody. I believe he hasn't brains enough to enjoy kicking up a row. I don't take advantage of him. I would scorn it. Outside the routine of duty he doesn't seem to understand more than half of what you tell him. We get a laugh out of this at times; but it is dull, too, to be with a man like this – in the long-run. Old Sol says he hasn't much conversation. Conversation! O Lord! He never talks. The other day I had been yarning under the bridge with one of the engineers, and he must have heard us. When I came up to take my watch, he steps out of the chart-room and has a good look all round, peeps over at the sidelights, glances at the compass, squints upwards at the stars. That's his regular performance. By-and-by he says, "Was that you talking just now in the port alley-way?" "Yes, sir." "With the third engineer?" "Yes, sir." He walks off to starboard, and sits under the dodger on a little camp-stool of his, and for half an hour perhaps he makes no sound except that I heard him sneeze once. Then after a while I hear him getting up over there, and he strolls across to port, where I was. "I can't understand what you can find to talk about," says he. "Two solid hours. I am not blaming you. I see people ashore at it all day long, and then in the evening they sit down and keep at it over the drinks. Must be saying the same things over and over again. I can't understand."

'Did you ever hear anything like that? And he was so patient about it. It made me quite sorry for him. But he is exasperating too sometimes. Of course one would not do anything to vex him even if it were worth while. But it isn't. He's so jolly innocent that if you were to put your thumb to your nose and wave your fingers at him he would only wonder gravely to himself what got into you. He told me once quite simply that he found it very difficult to make out what made people always act so queerly. He's too dense to trouble about, and that's the truth.'

Thus wrote Mr Jukes to his chum in the Western ocean trade, out of the fullness of his heart and the liveliness of his fancy.

He had expressed his honest opinion. It was not worth while trying to impress a man of that sort. If the world had been full of such men, life would have probably appeared to Jukes an unentertaining and unprofitable business. He was not alone in his opinion. The sea itself, as if sharing Mr Jukes' good-natured forbearance, had never put itself out to startle the silent man, who seldom looked up, and wandered innocently over the waters with the only visible purpose of getting food, raiment, and house-room for three people ashore. Dirty weather he had known, of course. He had been made wet, uncomfortable, tired in the usual way, felt at the time and presently forgotten. So that upon the whole he had been justified in reporting fine weather at home. But he had never been given a glimpse of immeasurable strength and of immoderate wrath, the wrath that passes exhausted but never appeased – the wrath and fury of the passionate sea. He knew it existed, as we know that crime and abominations exist; he had heard of it as a peaceable citizen in a town hears of battles, famines, and floods, and yet knows nothing of what these things mean – though, indeed, he may have been mixed up in a street row, have gone without his dinner once, or been soaked to the skin in a shower. Captain MacWhirr had sailed over the surface of the oceans as some men go skimming over the years of existence to sink gently into a placid grave, ignorant of life to the last, without ever having been made to see all it may contain of perfidy, of violence, and of terror. There are on sea and land such men thus fortunate – or thus disdained by destiny or by the sea.

2

Observing the steady fall of the barometer, Captain Mac-Whirr thought, 'There's some dirty weather knocking about.' This is precisely what he thought. He had had an experience of moderately dirty weather – the term dirty as applied to the weather implying only moderate discomfort to the seaman. Had he been informed by an indisputable authority that the end of the world was to be finally accomplished by a catastrophic disturbance of the atmosphere, he would have assimilated the information under the simple idea of dirty weather, and no other, because he had no experience of cataclysms, and belief does not necessarily imply comprehension. The wisdom of his country had pronounced by means of an Act of Parliament that before he could be considered as fit to take charge of a ship he should be able to answer certain simple questions on the subject of circular storms such as hurricanes, cyclones, typhoons; and apparently he had answered them, since he was now in command of the *Nan-Shan* in the China seas during the season of typhoons. But if he had answered he remembered nothing of it. He was, however, conscious of being made uncomfortable by the clammy heat. He came out on the bridge, and found no relief to this oppression. The air seemed thick. He gasped like a fish, and began to believe himself greatly out of sorts.

The *Nan-Shan* was ploughing a vanishing furrow upon the circle of the sea that had the surface and the shimmer of an undulating piece of grey silk. The sun, pale and without rays, poured down leaden heat in a strangely indecisive light, and the Chinamen were lying prostrate about the decks. Their bloodless, pinched, yellow faces were like the faces of bilious invalids. Captain MacWhirr noticed two of them especially, stretched out on their backs below the bridge. As soon as they had closed their eyes they seemed dead. Three others, however, were quarrelling barbarously away forward; and one big fellow, half-naked, with herculean shoulders, was hanging limply over a winch; another, sitting on the deck, his knees up and his head drooping sideways in a girlish attitude, was plaiting his pigtail with infinite languor depicted in his whole person and in the very movement of his fingers. The smoke struggled with difficulty out of the funnel, and instead of streaming away spread itself out like an infernal sort of cloud, smelling of sulphur and raining soot all over the decks.

'What the devil are you doing there, Mr Jukes?' asked Captain MacWhirr.

This unusual form of address, though mumbled rather than spoken, caused the body of Mr Jukes to start as though it had been prodded under the fifth rib. He had had a low bench brought on the bridge, and sitting on it, with a length of rope curled about his feet and a piece of canvas stretched over his knees, was pushing a sail-needle vigorously. He looked up, and his surprise gave to his eyes an expression of innocence and candour.

'I am only roping some of that new set of bags we made last trip for whipping up coals,' he remonstrated gently. 'We shall want them for the next coaling, sir.'

'What became of the others?'

'Why, worn out of course, sir.'

Captain MacWhirr, after glaring down irresolutely at his chief mate, disclosed the gloomy and cynical conviction that more than half of them had been lost overboard, 'if only the truth was known', and retired to the other end of the bridge. Jukes, exasperated by this unprovoked attack, broke the needle at the second stitch, and dropping his work got up and cursed the heat in a violent undertone.

The propeller thumped, the three Chinamen forward had given up squabbling very suddenly, and the one who had been plaiting his tail clasped his legs and stared dejectedly over his knees. The lurid sunshine cast faint and sickly shadows. The swell ran higher and swifter every moment, and the ship lurched heavily in the smooth, deep hollows of the sea.

'I wonder where that beastly swell comes from,' said Jukes aloud, recovering himself after a stagger.

'North-east,' grunted the literal MacWhirr, from his side of the bridge. 'There's some dirty weather knocking about. Go and look at the glass.'

When Jukes came out of the chart-room, the cast of his countenance had changed to thoughtfulness and concern. He caught hold of the bridge-rail and stared ahead.

The temperature in the engine-room had gone up to a hundred and seventeen degrees. Irritated voices were ascending through the skylight and through the fiddle of the stokehold in a harsh and resonant uproar, mingled with angry clangs and scrapes of metal, as if men with limbs of iron and throats of bronze had been quarrelling down there. The second engineer was falling foul of the stokers for letting the steam go down. He was a man with arms like a blacksmith, and generally feared; but that afternoon the stokers were answering him back recklessly, and slammed the furnace doors with the fury of despair. Then the noise ceased suddenly, and the second engineer appeared, emerging out of the stokehold streaked with grime and soaking wet like a chimney-sweep coming out of a well. As soon as his head was clear of the fiddle he began to scold Jukes for not trimming properly the stokehold ventilators: and in answer Jukes made with his hands deprecatory soothing signs meaning: No wind – can't be helped – you can see for yourself. But the other wouldn't hear reason. His teeth flashed angrily in his dirty face. He didn't mind, he said, the trouble of punching their blanked heads down there, blank his soul, but did the condemned sailors think you could keep steam up in the God-forsaken boilers simply by knocking the blanked stokers about? No, by George! You had to get some draught too – may he be everlastingly blanked for a swab-headed deck-hand if you didn't! And the chief, too, rampaging before the steam-gauge and carrying on like a lunatic up and down the engine-room ever since noon. What did Jukes think he was stuck up there for, if he couldn't get one of his decayed, good-for-nothing deck-cripples to turn the ventilators to the wind?

The relations of the 'engine-room' and the 'deck' of the *Nan-Shan* were, as is known, of a brotherly nature; therefore Jukes leaned over and begged the other in a restrained tone not to make a disgusting ass of himself; the skipper was on the other side of the bridge. But the second declared mutinously that he didn't care a rap who was on the other side of the bridge, and Jukes, passing in a flash from lofty disapproval into a state of exaltation, invited him in unflattering terms to come up and twist the beastly things to please himself, and catch such wind as a donkey of his sort could find. The second rushed up to the fray. He flung himself at the port ventilator as though he meant to tear it out bodily and toss it overboard. All he did was to move the cowl round a few inches, with an enormous expenditure of force, and seemed spent in the effort. He leaned against the back of the wheel-house, and Jukes walked up to him.

'Oh, Heavens!' ejaculated the engineer in a feeble voice. He lifted his eyes to the sky, and then let his glassy stare descend to meet the horizon that, tilting up to an angle of forty degrees, seemed to hang on a slant for a while and settled down slowly. 'Heavens! Phew! What's up, anyhow?'

Jukes, straddling his long legs like a pair of compasses, put on an air of superiority. 'We're going to catch it this time,' he said. 'The barometer is tumbling down like anything, Harry. And you trying to kick up that silly row . . .'

The word 'barometer' seemed to revive the second engineer's mad animosity. Collecting afresh all his energies, he directed Jukes in a low and brutal tone to shove the unmentionable instrument down his gory throat. Who cared for his crimson barometer? It was the steam – the steam – that was going down; and what between the firemen going faint and the chief going silly, it was worse than a dog's life for him; he didn't care a tinker's curse how soon the whole show was blown out of the water. He seemed on the point of having a cry, but after regaining his breath he muttered darkly, 'I'll faint them,' and dashed off. He stopped upon the fiddle long enough to shake his fist at the unnatural daylight, and dropped into the dark hole with a whoop.

When Jukes turned, his eyes fell upon the rounded back and the big red ears of Captain MacWhirr, who had come across. He did not look at his chief officer but said at once, 'That's a very violent man, that second engineer.'

'Jolly good second, anyhow,' grunted Jukes. 'They can't

keep up steam,' he added rapidly, and made a grab at the rail against the coming lurch.

Captain MacWhirr, unprepared, took a run and brought himself up with a jerk by an awning stanchion.

'A profane man,' he said obstinately. 'If this goes on, I'll have to get rid of him the first chance.'

'It's the heat,' said Jukes. 'The weather's awful. It would make a saint swear. Even up here I feel exactly as if I had my head tied up in a woollen blanket.'

Captain MacWhirr looked up. 'D'ye mean to say, Mr Jukes, you ever had your head tied up in a blanket? What was that for?'

'It's a manner of speaking, sir,' said Jukes stolidly.

'Some of you fellows do go on! What's that about saints swearing? I wish you wouldn't talk so wild. What sort of saint would that be that would swear? No more saint than yourself, I expect. And what's a blanket got to do with it – or the weather either ... The heat does not make me swear – does it? It's filthy bad temper. That's what it is. And what's the good of your talking like this?'

Thus Captain MacWhirr expostulated against the use of images in speech, and at the end electrified Jukes by a contemptuous snort, followed by words of passion and resentment, 'Damme! I'll fire him out of the ship if he don't look out.'

And Jukes, incorrigible, thought: 'Goodness me! Somebody's put a new inside to my old man. Here's temper, if you like. Of course it's the weather; what else? It would make an angel quarrelsome – let alone a saint.'

All the Chinamen on deck appeared at their last gasp.

At its setting the sun had a diminished diameter and an expiring brown, rayless glow, as if millions of centuries elapsing since the morning had brought it near its end. A dense bank of cloud became visible to the northward; it had a sinister dark olive tint, and lay low and motionless upon the sea, resembling a solid obstacle in the path of the ship. She went floundering towards it like an exhausted creature driven to its death. The coppery twilight retired slowly, and the darkness brought out overhead a swarm of unsteady big stars, that, as if blown upon, flickered exceedingly and seemed to hang very near the earth. At eight o'clock Jukes went into the chart-room to write up the ship's log.

He copied neatly out of the rough-book the number of miles, the course of the ship, and in the column for 'wind' scrawled the word 'calm' from top to bottom of the eight hours since noon. He was exasperated by the continuous, monotonous rolling of the ship. The heavy inkstand would slide away in a manner that suggested perverse intelligence in dodging the pen. Having written in the large space under the head of 'Remarks' 'Heat very oppressive', he stuck the end of the penholder in his teeth, pipe fashion, and mopped his face carefully.

'Ship rolling heavily in a high cross swell,' he began again, and commented to himself, 'Heavily, is no word for it.' Then he wrote, 'Sunset threatening, with a low bank of clouds to N. and E. Sky clear overhead.'

Sprawling over the table with arrested pen, he glanced out of the door, and in that frame of his vision he saw all the stars flying upwards between the teakwood jambs on a black sky. The whole lot took flight together and disappeared, leaving only a blackness flecked with white flashes, for the sea was as black as the sky and speckled with foam afar. The stars that had flown to the roll came back on the return swing of the ship, rushing downwards in their glittering multitude, not of fiery points, but enlarged to tiny discs brilliant with a clear wet sheen.

Jukes watched the flying big stars for a moment, and then wrote, '8 p.m. Swell increasing. Ship labouring and taking water on her decks. Battened down the coolies for the night. Barometer still falling.' He paused and thought to himself, 'Perhaps nothing whatever'll come of it.' And then he closed resolutely his entries: 'Every appearance of a typhoon coming on.'

On going out he had to stand aside, and Captain MacWhirr

strode over the doorstep without saying a word or making a sign.

'Shut the door, Mr Jukes, will you?' he cried from within.

Jukes turned back to do so, muttering ironically, 'Afraid to catch cold, I suppose.' It was his watch below, but he yearned for communion with his kind; and he remarked cheerily to the second mate, 'Doesn't look so bad, after all – does it?'

The second mate was marching to and fro on the bridge, tripping down with small steps one moment, and the next climbing with difficulty the shifting slope of the deck. At the sound of Jukes' voice he stood still, facing forward, but made no reply.

'Hallo! That's a heavy one,' said Jukes, swaying to meet the long roll till his lowered hand touched the planks. This time the second mate made in his throat a noise of an unfriendly nature.

He was an oldish, shabby little fellow, with bad teeth and no hair on his face. He had been shipped in a hurry to Shanghai, that trip when the second officer brought from home had delayed the ship three hours in port by contriving (in some manner Captain MacWhirr could never understand) to fall overboard into an empty coal-lighter lying alongside, and had to be sent ashore to the hospital with concussion of the brain and a broken limb or two.

Jukes was not discouraged by the unsympathetic sound. 'The Chinamen must be having a lovely time of it down there,' he said. 'It's lucky for them the old girl has the easiest roll of any ship I've ever been in. There now! This one wasn't so bad.'

'You wait,' snarled the second mate.

With his sharp nose, red at the tip, and his thin pinched lips, he always looked as though he were raging inwardly; and he was concise in his speech to the point of rudeness. All his time off duty he spent in his cabin with the door shut, keeping so still in there that he was supposed to fall asleep as soon as he had disappeared; but the man who came in to wake him for his watch on deck would invariably find him with his eyes wide open, flat on his back in the bunk, and glaring irritably from a soiled pillow. He never wrote any letters, did not seem to hope for news from anywhere; and though he had been heard once to mention West Hartlepool, it was with extreme bitterness, and only in connection with the extortionate charges of a boarding-house. He was one of those men who are picked up at need in the ports of the world. They are competent enough, appear hopelessly hard up, show no evidence of any sort of vice, and carry about them all the signs of manifest failure. They come aboard on an emergency, care for no ship afloat, live in their own atmosphere of casual connection amongst their shipmates who know nothing of them and make up their minds to leave at inconvenient times. They clear out with no words of leave-taking in some God-forsaken port other men would fear to be stranded in, and go ashore in company of a shabby sea-chest, corded like a treasure-box, and with an air of shaking the ship's dust off their feet.

'You wait,' he repeated, balanced in great swings with his back to Jukes, motionless and implacable.

'Do you mean to say we are going to catch it hot?' asked Jukes with boyish interest.

'Say? . . . I say nothing. You don't catch me,' snapped the little second mate, with a mixture of pride, scorn, and cunning, as if Jukes' question had been a trap cleverly detected. 'Oh no! None of you here shall make a fool of me if I know it,' he mumbled to himself.

Jukes reflected rapidly that this second mate was a mean little beast, and in his heart he wished poor Jack Allen had never smashed himself up in the coal-lighter. The far-off blackness ahead of the ship was like another night seen through the starry night of the earth – the starless night of the immensities beyond the created universe, revealed in its appalling stillness through a low fissure in the glittering sphere of which the earth is the kernel.

'Whatever there might be about,' said Jukes, 'we are steaming straight into it.'

'*You've* said it,' caught up the second mate, always with his back to Jukes. 'You've said it, mind – not I.'

'Oh, go to Jericho!' said Jukes frankly; and the other emitted a triumphant little chuckle.

'You've said it,' he repeated.

'And what of that?'

'I've known some real good men get into trouble with their skippers for saying a dam' sight less,' answered the second mate feverishly. 'Oh no! You don't catch me.'

'You seem deucedly anxious not to give yourself away,' said Jukes, completely soured by such absurdity. 'I wouldn't be afraid to say what I think.'

'Aye, to me! That's no great trick. I am nobody, and well I know it.'

The ship, after a pause of comparative steadiness, started upon a series of rolls, one worse than the other, and for a time Jukes, preserving his equilibrium, was too busy to open his mouth. As soon as the violent swinging had quieted down somewhat, he said, 'This is a bit too much of a good thing. Whether anything is coming or not I think she ought to be put head on to that swell. The old man is just gone in to lie down. Hang me if I don't speak to him.'

But when he opened the door of the chart-room he saw his captain reading a book. Captain MacWhirr was not lying down: he was standing up with one hand grasping the edge of the bookshelf and the other holding open before his face a thick volume. The lamp wriggled in the gimbals, the loosened books toppled from side to side on the shelf, the long barometer swung in jerky circles, the table altered its slant every moment. In the midst of all this stir and movement Captain MacWhirr, holding on, showed his eyes above the upper edge, and asked,

'What's the matter?'

'Swell getting worse, sir.'

'Noticed that in here,' muttered Captain MacWhirr. 'Anything wrong?'

Jukes, inwardly disconcerted by the seriousness of the

eyes looking at him over the top of the book, produced an embarrassed grin.

'Rolling like old boots,' he said sheepishly.

'Aye! Very heavy – very heavy. What do you want?'

At this Jukes lost his footing and began to flounder.

'I was thinking of our passengers,' he said, in the manner of a man clutching at a straw.

'Passengers?' wondered the captain gravely. 'What passengers?'

'Why, the Chinamen, sir,' explained Jukes, very sick of this conversation.

'The Chinamen! Why don't you speak plainly? Couldn't tell what you meant. Never heard a lot of coolies spoken of as passengers before. Passengers, indeed! What's come to you?'

Captain MacWhirr, closing the book on his forefinger, lowered his arm and looked completely mystified. 'Why are you thinking of the Chinamen, Mr Jukes?' he inquired.

Jukes took a plunge, like a man driven to it. 'She's rolling her decks full of water, sir. Thought you might put her head on perhaps – for a while. Till this goes down a bit – very soon, I dare say. Head to the eastward. I never knew a ship roll like this.'

He held on in the doorway, and Captain MacWhirr, feeling his grip on the shelf inadequate, made up his mind to let go in a hurry, and fell heavily on the couch.

'Head to the eastward?' he said, struggling to sit up. 'That's more than four points off her course.'

'Yes, sir. Fifty degrees. . . . Would just bring her head far enough round to meet this . . .'

Captain MacWhirr was now sitting up. He had not dropped the book, and he had not lost his place.

'To the eastward?' he repeated, with dawning astonishment. 'To the . . . Where do you think we are bound to? You want me to haul a full-powered steamship four points off her course to make the Chinamen comfortable! Now, I've heard more than enough of mad things done in the world – but this . . . If

I didn't know you, Jukes, I would think you were in liquor. Steer four points off. . . . And what afterwards? Steer four points over the other way, I suppose, to make the course good. What put it into your head that I would start to tack a steamer as if she were a sailing ship?'

'Jolly good thing she isn't,' threw in Jukes, with bitter readiness. 'She would have rolled every blessed stick out of her this afternoon.'

'Aye! And you just would have had to stand and see them go,' said Captain MacWhirr, showing a certain animation. 'It's a dead calm, isn't it?'

'It is, sir. But there's something out of the common coming, for sure.'

'Maybe. I suppose you have a notion I should be getting out of the way of that dirt,' said Captain MacWhirr, speaking with the utmost simplicity of manner and tone, and fixing the oilcloth on the floor with a heavy stare. Thus he noticed neither Jukes' discomfiture nor the mixture of vexation and astonished respect on his face.

'Now, here's this book,' he continued with deliberation, slapping his thigh with the closed volume. 'I've been reading the chapter on the storms there.'

This was true. He had been reading the chapter on the storms. When he had entered the chart-room, it was with no intention of taking the book down. Some influence in the air – the same influence, probably, that caused the steward to bring without orders the captain's sea-boots and oilskin coat up to the chart-room – had as it were guided his hand to the shelf; and without taking the time to sit down he had waded with a conscious effort into the terminology of the subject. He lost himself amongst advancing semicircles, left- and right-hand quadrants, the curves of the tracks, the probable bearing of the centre, the shifts of wind and the readings of barometer. He tried to bring all these things into a definite relation to himself, and ended by becoming contemptuously angry with such a lot of words and with so much advice, all head-work and supposition, without a glimmer of certitude.

'It's the damnedest thing, Jukes,' he said. 'If a fellow was to believe all that's in there, he would be running most of his time all over the sea trying to get behind the weather.'

Again he slapped his leg with the book; and Jukes opened his mouth, but said nothing.

'Running to get behind the weather! Do you understand that, Mr Jukes? It's the maddest thing!' ejaculated Captain MacWhirr, with pauses, gazing at the floor profoundly. 'You would think an old woman had been writing this. It passes me. If that thing means anything useful, then it means that I should at once alter the course away, away to the devil somewhere, and come booming down on Fu-chau from the northward at the tail of this dirty weather that's supposed to be knocking about in our way. From the north! Do you understand, Mr Jukes? Three hundred extra miles to the distance, and a pretty coal bill to show. I couldn't bring myself to do that if every word in there was gospel truth, Mr Jukes. Don't you expect me . . .'

And Jukes, silent, marvelled at this display of feeling and loquacity.

'But the truth is that you don't know if the fellow is right anyhow. How can you tell what a gale is made of till you get it? He isn't aboard here, is he? Very well. Here he says that the centre of them things bears eight points off the wind; but we haven't got any wind, for all the barometer falling. Where's his centre now?'

'We will get the wind presently,' mumbled Jukes.

'Let it come, then,' said Captain MacWhirr, with dignified indignation. 'It's only to let you see, Mr Jukes, that you don't find everything in books. All these rules for dodging breezes and circumventing the winds of heaven, Mr Jukes, seem to me the maddest thing, when you come to look at it sensibly.'

He raised his eyes, saw Jukes gazing at him dubiously, and tried to illustrate his meaning.

'About as queer as your extraordinary notion of dodging the

ship head to sea, for I don't know how long, to make the Chinamen comfortable; whereas all we've got to do is to take them to Fu-chau, being timed to get there before noon on Friday. If the weather delays me – very well. There's your log-book to talk straight about the weather. But suppose I went swinging off my course and came in two days late, and they asked me, "Where have you been all that time, Captain?" What could I say to that? "Went around to dodge the bad weather," I would say. "It must've been dam' bad," they would say. "Don't know," I would have to say; "I've dodged clear of it." See that, Jukes? I have been thinking it all out this afternoon.'

He looked up again in his unseeing, unimaginative way. No one had ever heard him say so much at one time. Jukes, with his arms open in the doorway, was like a man invited to behold a miracle. Unbounded wonder was the intellectual meaning of his eye, while incredulity was seated in his whole countenance.

'A gale is a gale, Mr Jukes,' resumed the captain, 'and a full-powered steam-ship has got to face it. There's just so much dirty weather knocking about the world, and the proper thing is to go through it with none of what old Captain Wilson of the *Melita* calls "storm strategy". The other day ashore I heard him hold forth about it to a lot of shipmasters who came in and sat at a table next to mine. It seemed to me the greatest nonsense. He was telling them how he – out-manœuvred, I think he said, a terrific gale, so that it never came nearer than fifty miles to him. A neat piece of head-work he called it. How he knew there was a terrific gale fifty miles off beats me altogether. It was like listening to a crazy man. I would have thought Captain Wilson was old enough to know better.'

Captain MacWhirr ceased for a moment, then said, 'It's your watch below, Mr Jukes?'

Jukes came to himself with a start. 'Yes, sir.'

'Leave orders to call me at the slightest change,' said the Captain. He reached up to put the book away, and tucked his legs upon the couch. 'Shut the door so that it don't fly open, will you? I can't stand a door banging. They've put a lot of rubbishy locks into this ship, I must say.'

Captain MacWhirr closed his eyes.

He did so to rest himself. He was tired, and he experienced that state of mental vacuity which comes at the end of an exhaustive discussion that had liberated some belief matured in the course of meditative years. He had indeed been making his confession of faith, had he only known it; and its effect was to make Jukes, on the other side of the door, stand scratching his head for a good while.

Captain MacWhirr opened his eyes.

He thought he must have been asleep. What was that loud noise? Wind? Why had he not been called? The lamp wriggled in its gimbals, the barometer swung in circles, the table altered its slant every moment: a pair of limp seaboots with collapsed tops went sliding past the couch. He put out his hand instantly, and captured one.

Jukes' face appeared in a crack of the door: only his face, very red, with staring eyes. The flame of the lamp leaped, a piece of paper flew up, a rush of air enveloped Captain Mac-Whirr. Beginning to draw on the boot, he directed an expectant gaze at Jukes' swollen, excited features.

'Came on like this,' shouted Jukes, 'five minutes ago . . . all of a sudden.'

The head disappeared with a bang, and a heavy splash and patter of drops swept past the closed door as if a pailful of melted lead had been flung against the house. A whistling could be heard now upon the deep vibrating noise outside. The stuffy chart-room seemed as full of draughts as a shed. Captain MacWhirr collared the other sea-boot on its violent passage along the floor. He was not flustered, but he could not find at once the opening for inserting his foot. The shoes he had flung off were scurrying from end to end of the cabin, gambolling playfully over each other like puppies. As soon as he stood up he kicked at them viciously, but without effect.

He threw himself into the attitude of a lunging fencer, to

reach after his oilskin coat; and afterwards he staggered all over the confined space while he jerked himself into it. Very grave, straddling his legs far apart, and stretching his neck, he started to tie deliberately the strings of his sou'-wester under his chin, with thick fingers that trembled slightly. He went through all the movements of a woman putting on her bonnet before a glass, with a strained, listening attention, as though he had expected every moment to hear the shout of his name in the confused clamour that had suddenly beset his ship. Its increase filled his ears while he was getting ready to go out and confront whatever it might mean. It was tumultuous and very loud – made up of the rush of the wind, the crashes of the sea, with that prolonged deep vibration of the air, like the roll of an immense and remote drum beating the charge of the gale.

He stood for a moment in the light of the lamp, thick, clumsy, shapeless in his panoply of combat, vigilant and red-faced.

'There's a lot of weight in this,' he muttered.

As soon as he attempted to open the door the wind caught it. Clinging to the handle, he was dragged out over the doorstep, and at once found himself engaged with the wind in a sort of personal scuffle whose object was the shutting of that door. At the last moment a tongue of air scurried in and licked out the flame of the lamp.

Ahead of the ship he perceived a great darkness lying upon a multitude of white flashes; on the starboard beam a few amazing stars drooped, dim and fitful, above an immense waste of broken seas, as if seen through a mad drift of smoke.

On the bridge a knot of men indistinct and toiling, were making great efforts in the light of the wheel-house windows that shone mistily on their heads and backs. Suddenly darkness closed upon one pane, then on another. The voices of the lost group reached him after the manner of men's voices in a gale, in shreds and fragments of forlorn shouting snatched past the ear. All at once Jukes appeared at his side, yelling, with his head down.

'Watch – put in – wheelhouse shutters – glass – afraid – blow in.'

Jukes heard his commander upbraiding.

'This – come – anything – warning – call me.'

He tried to explain, with the uproar pressing on his lips.

'Light air – remained – bridge – sudden – north-east – could turn – thought – you – sure – hear.'

They had gained the shelter of the weather-cloth, and could converse with raised voices, as people quarrel.

'I got the hands along to cover up all the ventilators. Good job I had remained on deck. I didn't think you would be asleep, and so. . . . What did you say, sir? What?'

'Nothing,' cried Captain MacWhirr. 'I said – all right.'

'By all the powers! We've got it this time,' observed Jukes in a howl.

'You haven't altered her course?' inquired Captain Mac-Whirr, straining his voice.

'No, sir. Certainly not. Wind came out right ahead. And here comes the head sea.'

A plunge of the ship ended in a shock as if she had landed her forefoot upon something solid. After a moment of stillness a lofty flight of sprays drove hard with the wind upon their faces.

'Keep her at it as long as we can,' shouted Captain Mac-Whirr.

Before Jukes had squeezed the salt water out of his eyes all the stars had disappeared.

3

Jukes was as ready a man as any half-dozen young mates that may be caught by casting a net upon the waters; and though he had been somewhat taken aback by the startling viciousness of the first squall, he had pulled himself together on the instant, had called out the hands and had rushed them along to secure such openings about the deck as had not been already battened down earlier in the evening. Shouting in his fresh, stentorian voice, 'Jump, boys, and bear a hand!' he led in the work, telling himself the while that he had 'just expected this'.

But at the same time he was growing aware that this was rather more than he had expected. From the first stir of the air felt on his cheek the gale seemed to take upon itself the accumulated impetus of an avalanche. Heavy sprays enveloped the *Nan-Shan* from stem to stern, and instantly in the midst of her regular rolling she began to jerk and plunge as though she had gone mad with fright.

Jukes thought, 'This is no joke.' While he was exchanging explanatory yells with his captain, a sudden lowering of the darkness came upon the night, falling before their vision like something palpable. It was as if the masked lights of the world had been turned down. Jukes was uncritically glad to have his captain at hand. It relieved him as though that man had, by simply coming on deck, taken most of the gale's weight upon his shoulders. Such is the prestige, the privilege, and the burden of command.

Captain MacWhirr could expect no relief of that sort from anyone on earth. Such is the loneliness of command. He was trying to see, with that watchful manner of a seaman who stares into the wind's eye as if into the eye of an adversary, to penetrate the hidden intention and guess the aim and force of the thrust. The strong wind swept at him out of a vast obscurity; he felt under his feet the uneasiness of his ship, and he could not even discern the shadow of her shape. He wished it were not so; and very still he waited, feeling stricken by a blind man's helplessness.

To be silent was natural to him, dark or shine. Jukes, at his elbow, made himself heard yelling cheerily in the gusts, 'We must have got the worst of it at once, sir.' A faint burst of lightning quivered all round, as if flashed into a cavern – into a black and secret chamber of the sea, with a floor of foaming crests.

It unveiled for a sinister, fluttering moment a ragged mass of clouds hanging low, the lurch of the long outlines of the ship, the black figures of men caught on the bridge heads forward, as if petrified in the act of butting. The darkness palpitated down upon all this, and then the real thing came at last.

It was something formidable and swift, like the sudden smashing of a vial of wrath. It seemed to explode all round the ship with an overpowering concussion and a rush of great waters, as if an immense dam had been blown up to windward. In an instant the men lost touch of each other. This is the disintegrating power of a great wind: it isolates one from one's kind. An earthquake, a landslip, an avalanche, overtake a man, incidentally, as it were – without passion. A furious gale attacks him like a personal enemy, tries to grasp his limbs, fastens upon his mind, seeks to rout his very spirit out of him.

Jukes was driven away from his commander. He fancied himself whirled a great distance through the air. Everything disappeared – even, for a moment, his power of thinking; but his hand had found one of the rail-stanchions. His distress was by no means alleviated by an inclination to disbelieve the reality of this experience. Though young, he had seen some bad weather, and had never doubted his ability to imagine the worst; but this was so much beyond his powers of fancy that it appeared incompatible with the existence of any ship whatever. He would have been incredulous about himself in the same way, perhaps, had he not been so harassed by the necessity of exerting a wrestling effort against a force trying to tear him away from his hold. Moreover, the conviction of not being utterly destroyed returned to him through the sensations of being half-drowned, bestially shaken, and partly choked.

It seemed to him he remained there precariously alone with the stanchion for a long, long time. The rain poured on him, flowed, drove in sheets. He breathed in gasps: and sometimes the water he swallowed was fresh and sometimes it was salt. For the most part he kept his eyes shut tight, as if suspecting his sight might be destroyed in the immense flurry of the elements. When he ventured to blink hastily, he derived some moral support from the green gleam of the starboard light shining feebly upon the flight of rain and sprays. He was actually looking at it when its ray fell upon the uprearing sea which put it out. He saw the head of the wave topple over, adding the mite of its crash to the tremendous uproar raging around him, and almost at the same instant the stanchion was wrenched away from his embracing arms. After a crushing thump on his back he found himself suddenly afloat and borne upwards. His first irresistible notion was that the whole China Sea had climbed on the bridge. Then, more sanely, he concluded himself gone overboard. All the time he was being tossed, flung, and rolled in great volumes of water, he kept on repeating mentally, with the utmost precipitation, the words, 'My God! My God! My God! My God!'

All at once, in a revolt of misery and despair, he formed the crazy resolution to get out of that. And he began to thresh about with his arms and legs. But as soon as he commenced his wretched struggles he discovered that he had become somehow mixed up with a face, an oilskin coat, somebody's boots. He clawed ferociously all these things in turn, lost them, found them again, lost them once more, and finally was himself caught in the firm clasp of a pair of stout arms. He returned the embrace closely round a thick solid body. He had found his captain.

They tumbled over and over, tightening their hug. Suddenly the water let them down with a brutal bang; and, stranded against the side of the wheelhouse, out of breath and bruised, they were left to stagger up in the wind and hold on where they could.

Jukes came out of it rather horrified, as though he had escaped somed unparalleled outrage directed at his feelings. It weakened his faith in himself. He started shouting aimlessly to to the man he could feel near him in that fiendish blackness, 'Is it you, sir? Is it you, sir?' till his temples seemed ready to burst. And he heard in answer a voice, as if crying far away, as if screaming to him fretfully from a very great distance, the

33

one word 'Yes!' Other seas swept again over the bridge. He received them defencelessly right over his bare head, with both his hands engaged in holding.

The motion of the ship was extravagant. Her lurches had an appalling helplessness: she pitched as if taking a header into a void, and seemed to find a wall to hit every time. When she rolled she fell on her side headlong, and she would be righted back by such a demolishing blow that Jukes felt her reeling as a clubbed man reels before he collapses. The gale howled and scuffled about gigantically in the darkness, as though the entire world were one black gully. At certain moments the air streamed against the ship as if sucked through a tunnel with a concentrated solid force of impact that seemed to lift her clean out of the water and keep her up for an instant with only a quiver running through her from end to end. And then she would begin her tumbling again as if dropped back into a boiling cauldron. Jukes tried hard to compose his mind and judge things coolly.

The sea, flattened down in the heavier gusts, would uprise and overwhelm both ends of the *Nan-Shan* in snowy rushes of foam, expanding wide, beyond both rails, into the night. And on this dazzling sheet, spread under the blackness of the clouds and emitting a bluish glow, Captain MacWhirr could catch a desolate glimpse of a few tiny specks black as ebony, the tops of the hatches, the battened companions, the heads of the covered winches, the foot of a mast. This was all he could see of his ship. Her middle structure, covered by the bridge which bore him, his mate, the closed wheelhouse where a man was steering shut up with the fear of being swept overboard together with the whole thing in one great crash – her middle structure was like a half-tide rock awash upon a coast. It was like an out-lying rock with the water boiling up, streaming over, pouring off, beating round – like a rock in the surf to which shipwrecked people cling before they let go – only it rose, it sank, it rolled continuously, without respite and rest, like a rock that should have miraculously struck adrift from a coast

34

and gone wallowing upon the sea.

The *Nan-Shan* was being looted by the storm with a senseless, destructive fury; trysails torn out of the extra gaskets, double-lashed awnings blown away, bridge swept clean, weather-cloths burst, rails twisted, light-screens smashed – and two of the boats had gone already. They had gone unheard and unseen, melting, as it were, in the shock and smother of the wave. It was only later, when upon the white flash of another high sea hurling itself amidships, Jukes had a vision of two pairs of davits leaping black and empty out of the solid blackness, with one overhauled fall flying and an iron-bound block capering in the air, that he became aware of what had happened within about three yards of his back.

He poked his head forward, groping for the ear of his commander. His lips touched it – big, fleshy, very wet. He cried in an agitated tone, 'Our boats are going now, sir.'

And again he heard that voice, forced and ringing feebly but with a penetrating effect of quietness in the enormous discord of noises, as if sent out from some remote spot of peace beyond the black wastes of the gale; again he heard a man's voice – the frail and indomitable sound that can be made to carry an infinity of thought, resolution and purpose, that shall be pronouncing confident words on the last day, when heavens fall, and justice is done – again he heard it, and it was crying to him, as if from very, very far – 'All right.'

He thought he had not managed to make himself understood. 'Our boats – I say boats – the boats, sir! Two gone!'

The same voice, within a foot of him and yet so remote, yelled sensibly, 'Can't be helped.'

Captain MacWhirr had never turned his face, but Jukes caught some more words on the wind.

'What can – expect – when hammering through – such – Bound to leave – something behind – stands to reason.'

Watchfully Jukes listened for more. No more came. This was all Captain MacWhirr had to say; and Jukes could picture to himself rather than see the broad squat back before him.

An impenetrable obscurity pressed down upon the ghostly glimmers of the sea. A dull conviction seized upon Jukes that there was nothing to be done.

If the steering-gear did not give way, if the immense volumes of water did not burst the deck in or smash one of the hatches, if the engines did not give up, if way could be kept on the ship against this terrific wind, and she did not bury herself in one of these awful seas, of whose white crests alone, topping high above her bows, he could now and then get a sickening glimpse – then there was a chance of her coming out of it. Something within him seemed to turn over, bringing uppermost the feeling that the *Nan-Shan* was lost.

'She's done for,' he said to himself, with a surprising mental agitation, as though he had discovered an unexpected meaning in this thought. One of these things was bound to happen. Nothing could be prevented now, and nothing could be remedied. The men on board did not count, and the ship could not last. This weather was too impossible.

Jukes felt an arm thrown heavily over his shoulders; and to this overture he responded with great intelligence by catching hold of his captain round the waist.

They stood clasped thus in the blind night, bracing each other against the wind, cheek to cheek and lip to ear, in the manner of two hulks lashed stem to stern together.

And Jukes heard the voice of his commander hardly any louder than before, but nearer, as though, starting to march athwart the prodigious rush of the hurricane, it had approached him, bearing that strange effect of quietness like the serene glow of a halo.

'D'ye know where the hands got to?' it asked, vigorous and evanescent at the same time, overcoming the strength of the wind, and swept away from Jukes instantly.

Jukes didn't know. They were all on the bridge when the real force of the hurricane struck the ship. He had no idea where they had crawled to. Under the circumstances they were nowhere, for all the use that could be made of them. Somehow the captain's wish to know distressed Jukes.

'Want the hands, sir?' he cried apprehensively.

'Ought to know,' asserted Captain MacWhirr. 'Hold hard.'

They held hard. An outburst of unchained fury, a vicious rush of the wind absolutely steadied the ship; she rocked only, quick and light like a child's cradle, for a terrific moment of suspense, while the whole atmosphere, as it seemed, streamed furiously past her, roaring away from the tenebrous earth.

It suffocated them, and with eyes shut they tightened their grasp. What from the magnitude of the shock might have been a column of water running upright in the dark, butted against the ship, broke short, and fell on her bridge, crushingly, from on high, with a dead burying weight.

A flying fragment of that collapse, a mere splash, enveloped them in one swirl from their feet over their heads, filling violently their ears, mouths and nostrils with salt water. It knocked out their legs, wrenched in haste at their arms, seethed away swiftly under their chins; and opening their eyes, they saw the piled-up masses of foam dashing to and fro amongst what looked like the fragments of a ship. She had given way as if driven straight in. Their panting hearts yielded too before the tremendous blow; and all at once she sprang up again to her desperate plunging, as if trying to scramble out from under the ruins.

The seas in the dark seemed to rush from all sides to keep her back where she might perish. There was hate in the way she was handled, and a ferocity in the blows that fell. She was like a living creature thrown to the rage of a mob: hustled terribly, struck at, borne up, flung down, leaped upon. Captain MacWhirr and Jukes kept hold of each other, deafened by the noise, gagged by the wind; and the great physical tumult beating about their bodies, brought, like an unbridled display of passion, a profound trouble to their souls. One of these wild and appalling shrieks that are heard at times passing mysteriously overhead in the steady roar of a hurricane, swooped, as if borne on wings, upon the ship, and Jukes tried to outscream it.

'Will she live through this?'

The cry was wrenched out of his breast. It was as un-intentional as the birth of a thought in the head, and he heard nothing of it himself. It all became extinct at once – thought, intention, effort – and of his cry the inaudible vibration added to the tempest waves of the air.

He expected nothing from it. Nothing at all. For indeed what answer could be made? But after a while he heard with amazement the frail and resisting voice in his ear, the dwarf sound, unconquered in the giant tumult.

'She may!'

It was a dull yell, more difficult to seize than a whisper. And presently the voice returned again, half submerged in the vast crashes, like a ship battling against the waves of an ocean.

'Let's hope so!' it cried – small, lonely and unmoved, a stranger to the visions of hope or fear; and it flickered into disconnected words: 'Ship . . . This . . . Never – Anyhow . . . for the best.' Jukes gave it up.

Then, as if it had come suddenly upon the one thing fit to withstand the power of a storm, it seemed to gain force and firmness for the last broken shouts:

'Keep on hammering . . . builders . . . good men. . . . And chance it . . . engines . . . Rout . . . good man.'

Captain MacWhirr removed his arm from Jukes shoulders, and thereby ceased to exist for his mate, so dark it was; Jukes, after a tense stiffening of every muscle, would let himself go limp all over. The gnawing of profound discomfort existed side by side with an incredible disposition to somnolence, as though he had been buffeted and worried into drowsiness. The wind would get hold of his head and try to shake it off his shoulders; his clothes, full of water, were as heavy as lead, cold and dripping like an armour of melting ice: he shivered – it lasted a long time; and with his hands closed hard on his hold, he was letting himself sink slowly into the depths of bodily misery. His mind became concentrated upon himself in an aimless, idle way, and when something pushed lightly at the back of his knees he nearly, as the saying is, jumped out of his skin.

In the start forward he bumped the back of Captain Mac-Whirr, who didn't move; and then a hand gripped his thigh. A lull had come, a menacing lull of the wind, the holding of a stormy breath – and he felt himself pawed all over. It was the boatswain. Jukes recognized these hands, so thick and enormous that they seemed to belong to some new species of man.

The boatswain had arrived on the bridge, crawling on all fours against the wind, and had found the chief mate's legs with the top of his head. Immediately he crouched and began to explore Jukes' person upwards, with prudent, apologetic touches, as became an inferior.

He was an ill-favoured, undersized, gruff sailor of fifty, coarsely hairy, short-legged, long-armed, resembling an elderly ape. His strength was immense; and in his great lumpy paws, bulging like brown boxing-gloves on the end of furry forearms, the heaviest objects were handled like playthings. Apart from the grizzled pelt on his chest, the menacing demeanour and the hoarse voice, he had none of the classical attributes of his rating. His good nature almost amounted to imbecility: the men did what they liked with him, and he had not an ounce of initiative in his character, which was easy-going and talkative. For these reasons Jukes disliked him; but Captain MacWhirr, to Jukes' scornful disgust, seemed to regard him as a first-rate petty officer.

He pulled himself up by Jukes' coat, taking that liberty with the greatest moderation, and only so far as it was forced upon him by the hurricane.

'What is it, bos'n, what is it?' yelled Jukes, impatiently. What could that fraud of a bos'n want on the bridge? The typhoon had got on Jukes' nerves. The husky bellowings of the other, though unintelligible, seemed to suggest a state of lively satisfaction. There could be no mistake. The old fool was pleased with something.

The boatswain's other hand had found some other body for

in a changed tone he began to inquire, 'Is it you, sir? Is it you, sir?' The wind strangled his howls.

'Yes!' cried Captain MacWhirr.

4

All that the boatswain, out of a superabundance of yells, could make clear to Captain MacWhirr was the bizarre intelligence that 'All them Chinamen in the fore 'tween deck have fetched away, sir.'

Jukes to leeward could hear these two shouting within six inches of his face, as you may hear on a still night half a mile away two men conversing across a field. He heard Captain MacWhirr's exasperated 'What? What?' and the strained pitch of the other's hoarseness. 'In a lump . . . seen them myself . . . Awful sight, sir . . . thought . . . tell you.'

Jukes remained indifferent, as if rendered irresponsible by the force of the hurricane, which made the very thought of action utterly vain. Besides, being very young, he had found the occupation of keeping his heart completely steeled against the worst so engrossing that he had come to feel an over-powering dislike towards any other form of activity whatever. He was not scared; he knew this because, firmly believing he would never see another sunrise, he remained calm in that belief.

These are the moments of do-nothing heroics to which even good men surrender at times. Many officers of ships can no doubt recall a case in their experience when just such a trance of confounded stoicism would come all at once over a whole ship's company. Jukes, however, had no wide experience of men or storms. He conceived himself to be calm – inexorably calm; but as a matter of fact he was daunted; not abjectly, but only so far as a decent man may, without becoming loathsome to himself.

It was rather like a forced-on numbness of spirit. The long, long stress of a gale does it; the suspense of the interminably culminating catastrophe; and there is a bodily fatigue in the mere holding on to existence within the excessive tumult; a searching and insidious fatigue that penetrates deep into a man's breast to cast down and sadden his heart, which is incorrigible, and of all the gifts of the earth – even before life itself – aspires to peace.

Jukes was benumbed much more than he supposed. He held on very wet, very cold, stiff in every limb; and in a momentary hallucination of swift visions (it is said that a drowning man thus reviews all his life) he beheld all sorts of memories altogether unconnected with his present situation. He remembered his father, for instance: a worthy business man, who at an unfortunate crisis in his affairs went quietly to bed and died forthwith in a state of resignation. Jukes did not recall these circumstances, of course, but remaining otherwise unconcerned he seemed to see distinctly the poor man's face; a certain game of nap played when quite a boy in Table Bay on board a ship, since lost with all hands; the thick eyebrows of his first skipper; and without any emotion, as he might years ago have walked listlessly into her room and found her sitting there with a book, he remembered his mother – dead, too, now – the resolute woman, left badly off, who had been very firm in his bringing up.

It could not have lasted more than a second, perhaps not so much. A heavy arm had fallen about his shoulders; Captain MacWhirr's voice was speaking his name into his ear.

'Jukes! Jukes!'

He detected the tone of deep concern. The wind had thrown its weight on the ship, trying to pin her down amongst the seas. They made a clean breach over her, as over a deep-swimming log; and the gathered weight of crashes menaced monstrously from afar. The breakers flung out of the night with a ghostly light on their crests – the light of sea-foam that in a ferocious, boiling-up pale flash showed upon the slender body of the ship the toppling rush, the downfall, and the seething mad scurry of each wave. Never for a moment could she shake herself clear

41

of the water; Jukes, rigid, perceived in her motion the ominous sign of haphazard floundering. She was no longer struggling intelligently. It was the beginning of the end; and the note of busy concern in Captain MacWhirr's voice sickened him like an exhibition of blind and pernicious folly.

The spell of the storm had fallen upon Jukes. He was penetrated by it, absorbed by it; he was rooted in it with a rigour of dumb attention. Captain MacWhirr persisted in his cries, but the wind got between them like a solid wedge. He hung round Jukes' neck as heavy as a millstone, and suddenly the sides of their heads knocked together.

'Jukes! Mr Jukes, I say!'

He had to answer that voice that would not be silenced. He answered in the customary manner: '. . . Yes, sir.'

And directly, his heart, corrupted by the storm that breeds a craving for peace, rebelled against the tyranny of training and command.

Captain MacWhirr had his mate's head fixed firm in the crook of his elbow, and pressed it to his yelling lips mysteriously. Sometimes Jukes would break in, admonishing hastily, 'Look out, sir!' or Captain MacWhirr would bawl an earnest exhortation to 'Hold hard, there!' and the whole black universe seemed to reel together with the ship. They paused. She floated yet. And Captain MacWhirr would resume his shouts. '. . . Says . . . whole lot . . . fetched away. . . . Ought to see . . . what's the matter.'

Directly the full force of the hurricane had struck the ship, every part of her deck became untenable; and the sailors, dazed and dismayed, took shelter in the port alleyway under the bridge. It had a door aft, which they shut; it was very black, cold, and dismal. At each heavy fling of the ship they would groan all together in the dark, and tons of water could be heard scuttling about as if trying to get at them from above. The boatswain had been keeping up a gruff talk, but a more unreasonable lot of men, he said afterwards, he had never been with. They were snug enough there, out of harm's way, and not wanted to do anything, either; and yet they did nothing but grumble and complain peevishly like so many sick kids. Finally, one of them said that if there had been at least some light to see each other's noses by, it wouldn't be so bad. It was making him crazy, he declared, to lie there in the dark waiting for the blamed hooker to sink.

'Why don't you step outside, then, and be done with it at once?' the boatswain turned on him.

This called up a shout of execration. The boatswain found himself overwhelmed with reproaches of all sorts. They seemed to take it ill that a lamp was not instantly created for them out of nothing. They would whine after a light to get drowned by – anyhow! And though the unreason of their revilings was patent – since no one could hope to reach the lamp-room, which was forward – he became greatly distressed. He did not think it was decent of them to be nagging at him like this. He told them so, and was met by general contumely. He sought refuge, therefore, in an embittered silence. At the same time their grumbling and sighing and muttering worried him greatly, but by-and-by it occurred to him that there were six globe lamps hung in the 'tween-deck, and that there could be no harm in depriving the coolies of one of them.

The *Nan-Shan* had an athwartship coal-bunker, which, being at times used as cargo space, communicated by an iron door with the fore 'tween-deck. It was empty then, and its manhole was the foremost one in the alleyway. The boatswain could get in, therefore, without coming out on deck at all; but to his great surprise he found he could induce no one to help him in taking off the manhole cover. He groped for it all the same, but one of the crew lying in his way refused to budge.

'Why, I only want to get you that blamed light you are crying for,' he expostulated, almost pitifully.

Somebody told him to go and put his head in a bag. He regretted he could not recognize the voice, and that it was too dark to see, otherwise, as he said, he would have put a head on *that* son of a sea-cook, anyway, sink or swim. Nevertheless, he had made up his mind to show them he could get a light, if he were to die for it.

Through the violence of the ship's rolling, every movement was dangerous. To be lying down seemed labour enough. He nearly broke his neck dropping into the bunker. He fell on his back, and was sent shooting helplessly from side to side in the dangerous company of a heavy iron bar – a coal-trimmer's slice probably – left down there by somebody. This thing made him as nervous as though it had been a wild beast. He could not see it, the inside of the bunker coated with coal-dust being perfectly and impenetrably black; but he heard it sliding and clattering, and striking here and there, always in the neighbourhood of his head. It seemed to make an extraordinary noise, too – to give heavy thumps as though it had been as big as a bridge girder. This was remarkable enough for him to notice while he was flung from port to starboard and back again, and clawing desperately the smooth sides of the bunker in the endeavour to stop himself. The door into the 'tween-deck not fitting quite true, he saw a thread of dim light at the bottom.

Being a sailor, and a still active man, he did not want much of a chance to regain his feet; and as luck would have it, in scrambling up he put his hand on the iron slice, picking it up as he rose. Otherwise he would have been afraid of the thing breaking his legs, or at least knocking him down again. At first he stood still. He felt unsafe in this darkness that seemed to make the ship's motion unfamiliar, unforeseen, and difficult to counteract. He felt so much shaken for a moment that he dared not move for fear of 'taking charge again'. He had no mind to get battered to pieces in that bunker.

He had struck his head twice; he was dazed a little. He seemed to hear yet so plainly the clatter and bangs of the iron slice flying about his ears that he tightened his grip to prove to himself he had it there safely in his hand. He was vaguely amazed at the plainness with which down there he could hear the gale raging. Its howls and shrieks seemed to take on, in the emptiness of the bunker, something of the human character, of human rage and pain – being not vast but infinitely poignant. And there were, with every roll, thumps too – profound, ponderous thumps, as if a bulky object of five-ton weight or so had got play in the hold. But there was no such thing in the cargo. Something on deck? Impossible. Or alongside? Couldn't be.

He thought all this quickly, clearly, competently, like a seaman, and in the end remained puzzled. This noise, though, came deadened from outside, together with the washing and pouring of water on deck above his head. Was it the wind? Must be. It made down there a row like the shouting of a big lot of crazed men. And he discovered in himself a desire for a light too – if only to get drowned by – and a nervous anxiety to get out of that bunker as quickly as possible.

He pulled back the bolt: the heavy iron plate turned on its hinges; and it was as though he had opened the door to the sounds of the tempest. A gust of hoarse yelling met him: the air was still; and the rushing of water overhead was covered by a tumult of strangled, throaty shrieks that produced an effect of desperate confusion. He straddled his legs the whole width of the doorway and stretched his neck. And at first he perceived only what he had come to seek: six small yellow flames swinging violently on the great body of the dusk.

It was stayed like the gallery of a mine, with a row of stanchions in the middle, and cross-beams overhead, penetrating into the gloom ahead – indefinitely. And to port there loomed, like the caving in of one of the sides, a bulky mass with a slanting outline. The whole place, with the shadows and the shapes, moved all the time. The boatswain glared: the ship lurched to starboard, and a great howl came from that mass that had the slant of fallen earth.

Pieces of wood whizzed past. Planks, he thought, inexpressibly startled, and flinging back his head. At his feet a man went sliding over, open-eyed, on his back, straining with uplifted arms for nothing: and another came bounding like a detached stone with his head between his legs and his hands clenched. His pigtail whipped in the air; he made a grab at the boatswain's legs, and from his opened hand a bright white disc rolled against the boatswain's foot. He recognized a silver dollar, and yelled at it with astonishment. With a precipitated sound of trampling and shuffling of bare feet, and with guttural cries, the mound of writhing bodies piled up to port detached itself from the ship's side and shifted to starboard, sliding, inert and struggling to a dull, brutal thump. The cries ceased. The boatswain heard a long moan through the roar and whistling of the wind; he saw an inextricable confusion of heads and shoulders, naked soles kicking upwards, fists raised, tumbling backs, legs, pigtails, faces.

'Good Lord!' he cried, horrified, and banged-to the iron door upon this vision.

This was what he had come on the bridge to tell. He could not keep it to himself; and on board ship there is only one man to whom it is worth while to unburden yourself. On his passage back the hands in the alleyway swore at him for a fool. Why didn't he bring that lamp? What the devil did the coolies matter to anybody? And when he came out, the extremity of the ship made what went on inside of her appear of little moment.

At first he thought he had left the alleyway in the very moment of her sinking. The bridge ladders had been washed away, but an enormous sea filling the after-deck floated him up. After that he had to lie on his stomach for some time, holding to a ring-bolt, getting his breath now and then, and swallowing salt water. He struggled farther on his hands and knees, too frightened and distracted to turn back. In this way he reached the after-part of the wheelhouse. In that comparatively sheltered spot he found the second mate. The boatswain was pleasantly surprised – his impression being that everybody on deck must have been washed away a long time ago. He asked eagerly where the captain was.

The second mate was lying low, like a malignant little animal under a hedge.

'Captain? Gone overboard, after getting us into this mess.'

The mate, too, for all he knew or cared. Another fool. Didn't matter. Everybody was going by-and-by.

The boatswain crawled out again into the strength of the wind; not because he much expected to find anybody, he said, but just to get away from 'that man'. He crawled out as outcasts go to face an inclement world. Hence his great joy at finding Jukes and the captain. But what was going on in the 'tween-deck was to him a minor matter by that time. Besides, it was difficult to make yourself heard. But he managed to convey the idea that the Chinamen had broken adrift together with their boxes, and that he had come up on purpose to report this. As to the hands, they were all right. Then, appeased, he subsided on the deck in a sitting posture, hugging with his arms and legs the stand of the engine-room telegraph – an iron casting as thick as a post. When that went, why, he expected he would go too. He gave no more thought to the coolies.

Captain MacWhirr had made Jukes understand that he wanted him to go down below – to see.

'What am I to do then, sir?' And the trembling of his whole wet body caused Jukes' voice to sound like bleating.

'See first . . . Bos'n . . . says . . . adrift.'

'That bos'n is a confounded fool,' howled Jukes shakily.

The absurdity of the demand made upon him revolted Jukes. He was as unwilling to go as if the moment he had left the deck the ship were sure to sink.

'I must know . . . can't leave . . .'

'They'll settle, sir.'

'Fight . . . bos'n says they fight . . . Why? Can't have . . . fighting . . . board ship . . . Much rather keep you here . . . case . . . I should . . . washed overboard myself. . . . Stop it . . . some way. You see and tell me . . . through engine-room tube. Don't want you . . . come up here . . . too often. Dangerous . . . moving about . . . deck.'

Jukes, held with his head in chancery, had to listen to what seemed horrible suggestions.

'Don't want . . . you get lost . . . so long . . . ship isn't. . . . Rout . . . Good man . . . Ship . . . may . . . through this . . . all right yet.'

All at once Jukes understood he would have to go.

'Do you think she may?' he screamed.

But the wind devoured the reply, out of which Jukes heard only the one word, pronounced with great energy ' . . . Always . . .'

Captain MacWhirr released Jukes, and bending over the boatswain, yelled, 'Get back with the mate.' Jukes only knew that the arm was gone off his shoulders. He was dismissed with his orders – to do what? He was exasperated into letting go his hold carelessly, and on the instant was blown away. It seemed to him that nothing could stop him from being blown right over the stern. He flung himself down hastily, and the boatswain, who was following, fell on him.

'Don't you get up yet, sir,' cried the boatswain. 'No hurry!'

A sea swept over. Jukes understood the boatswain to splutter that the bridge ladders were gone. 'I'll lower you down, sir, by your hands,' he screamed. He shouted also something about the smoke-stack being as likely to go overboard as not. Jukes thought it very possible, and imagined the fires out, the ship helpless. . . . The boatswain by his side kept on yelling. 'What? What is it?' Jukes cried distressfully; and the other repeated, 'What would my old woman say if she saw me now?'

In the alleyway, where a lot of water had got in and splashed in the dark, the men were still as death, till Jukes stumbled against one of them and cursed him savagely for being in the way. Two or three voices then asked, eager and weak, 'Any chance for us, sir?'

'What's the matter with you fools?' he said brutally. He felt as though he could throw himself down amongst them and never move any more. But they seemed cheered; and in the midst of obsequious warnings, 'Look out! Mind that manhole lid, sir,' they lowered him into the bunker. The boatswain tumbled down after him, and as soon as he had picked himself up he remarked, 'She would say, 'Serve you right, you old fool, for going to sea.'

The boatswain had some means, and made a point of alluding to them frequently. His wife – a fat woman – and two grown-up daughters kept a greengrocer's shop in the East-end of London.

In the dark, Jukes, unsteady on his legs, listened to a faint thunderous patter. A deadened screaming went on steadily at his elbow, as it were; and from above the louder tumult of the storm descended upon these near sounds. His head swam. To him, too, in that bunker, the motion of the ship seemed novel and menacing, sapping his resolution as though he had never been afloat before.

He had half a mind to scramble out again; but the remembrance of Captain MacWhirr's voice made this impossible. His orders were to go and see. What was the good of it, he wanted to know. Enraged, he told himself he would see – of course. But the boatswain, staggering clumsily, warned him to be careful how he opened that door; there was a blamed fight going on. And Jukes, as if in great bodily pain, desired irritably to know what the devil they were fighting for.

'Dollars! Dollars, sir. All their rotten chests got burst open. Blamed money skipping all over the place, and they are tumbling after it head over heels – tearing and biting like anything. A regular little hell in there.'

Jukes convulsively opened the door. The short boatswain peered under his arm.

One of the lamps had gone out, broken perhaps. Rancorous, guttural cries burst out loudly on their ears, and a strange panting sound, the working of all these straining breasts. A hard blow hit the side of the ship: water fell above with a stunning shock, and in the forefront of the gloom, where the air was reddish and thick, Jukes saw a head bang the deck violently, two thick calves waving on high, muscular arms twined round a naked body, a yellow face, open-mouthed and with a set wild stare, look up and slide away. An empty chest clattered turning over; a man fell head first with a jump, as if lifted by a kick; and farther off, indistinct, others streamed like a mass of rolling stones down a bank, thumping the deck with their feet and flourishing their arms wildly. The hatchway ladder was loaded with coolies swarming on it like bees on a branch. They hung on the steps in a crawling, stirring cluster, beating madly with their fists the underside of the battened hatch, and the headlong rush of the water above was heard in the intervals of their yelling. The ship heeled over more, and they began to drop off; first one, then two, then all the rest went away together, falling straight off with a great cry.

Jukes was confounded. The boatswain, with gruff anxiety begged him, 'Don't you go in there, sir.'

The whole place seemed to twist upon itself, jumping incessantly the while; and when the ship rose to a sea Jukes fancied that all these men would be shot upon him in a body. He backed out, swung the door to, and with trembling hands pushed at the bolt . . .

As soon as his mate had gone Captain MacWhirr, left alone on the bridge, sidled and staggered as far as the wheelhouse. Its door being hinged forward, he had to fight the gale for admittance, and when at last he managed to enter, it was with an instantaneous clatter and a bang, as though he had been fired through the wood. He stood within, holding on to the handle.

The steering-gear leaked steam, and in the confined space the glass of the binnacle made a shiny oval of light in a thin white fog. The wind howled, hummed, whistled with sudden booming gusts that rattled the doors and shutters in the vicious patter of sprays. Two coils of lead-line and a small canvas bag hung on a long lanyard, swung wide off, and came back clinging to the bulkheads. The gratings underfoot were nearly afloat; with every sweeping blow of a sea, water squirted violently through the cracks all round the door, and the man at the helm had flung down his cap, his coat, and stood propped against the gear-casing in a striped cotton shirt open on his breast. The little brass wheel in his hands had the appearance of a bright and fragile toy. The cords of his neck stood hard and lean, a dark patch lay in the hollow of his throat, and his face was still and sunken as in death.

Captain MacWhirr wiped his eyes. The sea that had nearly taken him overboard had, to his great annoyance, washed his sou'-wester hat off his bald head. The fluffy, fair hair, soaked and darkened, resembled a mean skein of cotton threads festooned round his bare skull. His face, glistening with sea-water, had been made crimson with the wind, with the sting of sprays. He looked as though he had come off sweating from before a furnace.

'You here?' he muttered heavily.

The second mate had found his way into the wheel-house some time before. He had fixed himself in a corner with his knees up, a fist pressed against each temple; and this attitude suggested rage, sorrow, resignation, surrender, with a sort of concentrated unforgiveness. He said mournfully and defiantly, 'Well, it's my watch below now: ain't it?'

The steam gear clattered, stopped, clattered again; and the helmsman's eyeballs seemed to project out of a hungry face as if the compass card behind the binnacle glass had been meat. God knows how long he had been left there to steer, as if forgotten by all his shipmates. The bells had not been struck; there had been no reliefs; the ship's routine had gone down wind; but he was trying to keep her head north-north-east. The rudder might have been gone for all he knew, the fires out, the engines broken down, the ship ready to roll over like a corpse. He was anxious not to get muddled and lose control of her head, because the compass-card swung far both ways, wriggling on the pivot, and sometimes seemed to whirl right round. He suffered from mental stress. He was horribly afraid, also, of the wheel-house going. Mountains of water kept on tumbling against it. When the ship took one of her desperate dives the corners of his lips twitched.

Captain MacWhirr looked up at the wheel-house clock. Screwed to the bulkhead, it had a white face on which the black hands appeared to stand quite still. It was half-past one in the morning.

'Another day,' he muttered to himself.

The second mate heard him, and lifting his head as one grieving amongst ruins, 'You won't see it break,' he exclaimed. His wrists and his knees could be seen to shake violently. 'No, by God! You won't . . .'

He took his face again between his fists.

The body of the helmsman had moved slightly, but his head didn't budge on his neck – like a stone head fixed to look one way from a column. During a roll that all but took his booted legs from under him, and in the very stagger to save himself, Captain MacWhirr said austerely, 'Don't you pay any attention to what that man says.' And then, with an indefinable change of tone, very grave, he added, 'He isn't on duty.'

The sailor said nothing.

The hurricane boomed, shaking the little place, which seemed air-tight; and the light of the binnacle flickered all the time.

'You haven't been relieved,' Captain MacWhirr went on, looking down. 'I want you to stick to the helm, though, as long as you can. You've got the hang of her. Another man coming here might make a mess of it. Wouldn't do. No child's play. And the hands are probably busy with a job down below . . . Think you can?'

The steering-gear leaped into an abrupt short clatter, stopped smouldering like an ember; and the still man, with a motionless gaze, burst out, as if all the passion in him had gone into his lips, 'By Heavens, sir! I can steer for ever if nobody talks to me.'

'Oh! aye! All right, . . .' The captain lifted his eyes for the first time to the man, '. . . Hackett.'

And he seemed to dismiss this matter from his mind. He stooped to the engine-room speaking-tube, blew in, and bent his head. Mr Rout below answered, and at once Captain MacWhirr put his lips to the mouthpiece.

With the uproar of the gale around him he applied alternately his lips and his ear, and the engineer's voice mounted to him, harsh and as if out of the heat of an engagement. One of the stokers was disabled, the others had given in, the second engineer and the donkey-man were firing up. The third engineer was standing by the steam-valve. The engines were being tended by hand. How was it above?

'Bad enough. It mostly rests with you,' said Captain Mac-Whirr. Was the mate down there yet? No? Well, he would be presently. Would Mr Rout let him talk through the speaking-tube? – through the deck speaking-tube, because he – the captain – was going out again on the bridge directly. There was some trouble amongst the Chinamen. They were fighting, it seemed. Couldn't allow fighting anyhow . . .

Mr Rout had gone away, and Captain MacWhirr could feel against his ear the pulsation of the engines, like the beat of the ship's heart. Mr Rout's voice down there shouted something distantly. The ship pitched headlong, the pulsation leaped with a hissing tumult, and stopped dead. Captain MacWhirr's face was impassive, and his eyes were fixed aimlessly on the crouching shape of the second mate. Again Mr Rout's voice cried out in the depths, and the pulsating beats recommenced, with slow strokes – growing swifter.

Mr Rout had returned to the tube. 'It don't matter much what they do,' he said hastily; and then, with irritation, 'She takes these dives as if she never meant to come up again.'

'Awful sea,' said the captain's voice from above.

'Don't let me drive her under,' barked Solomon Rout up the pipe.

'Dark and rain. Can't see what's coming,' uttered the voice. 'Must – keep – her – moving – enough to steer – and chance it,' it went on to state distinctly.

'I am doing as much as I dare.'

'We are – getting – smashed up – a good deal up here,' proceeded the voice mildly. 'Doing – fairly well – though. Of course, if the wheel-house should go . . .'

Mr Rout, bending an attentive ear, muttered peevishly

something under his breath.

But the deliberate voice up there became animated to ask, 'Jukes turned up yet?' Then, after a short wait, 'I wish he would bear a hand. I want him to be done and come up here in case of anything. To look after the ship. I am all alone. The second mate's lost. . . . '

'What?' shouted Mr Rout into the engine-room, taking his head away. Then up the tube he cried, 'Gone overboard?' and clapped his ear to.

'Lost his nerve,' the voice from above continued in a matter-of-fact tone. 'Damned awkward circumstance.'

Mr Rout, listening with bowed neck, opened his eyes wide at this. However, he heard something like the sounds of a scuffle and broken exclamations coming down to him. He strained his hearing; and all the time Beale, the third engineer, with his arms uplifted, held between the palms of his hands the rim of a little black wheel projecting at the side of a big copper pipe. He seemed to be poising it above his head, as though it were a correct attitude in some sort of game.

To steady himself, he pressed his shoulder against the white bulkhead, one knee bent, and a sweat-rag tucked in his belt hanging on his hip. His smooth cheek was begrimed and flushed, and the coal-dust on his eyelids, like the black pencilling of a make-up, enhanced the liquid brilliance of the whites, giving to his youthful face something of a feminine, exotic and fascinating aspect. When the ship pitched he would with hasty movements of his hands screw hard at the little wheel.

'Gone crazy,' began the captain's voice suddenly in the tube. 'Rushed at me. . . . Just now. Had to knock him down. . . . This minute. You heard, Mr Rout?'

'The devil!' muttered Mr Rout. 'Look out, Beale!'

His shout rang out like the blast of a warning trumpet, between the iron walls of the engine-room. Painted white, they rose high into the dusk of the skylight, sloping like a roof; and the whole lofty space resembled the interior of a monument, divided by floors of iron grating, with lights flickering at different levels, and a mass of gloom lingering in the middle, within the columnar stir of machinery under the motionless swelling of the cylinders. A loud and wild resonance, made up of all the noises of the hurricane, dwelt in the still warmth of the air. There was in it the smell of hot metal, of oil, and a slight mist of steam. The blows of the sea seemed to traverse it in an unringing, stunning shock, from side to side.

Gleams, like pale long flames, trembled upon the polish of metal; from the flooring below the enormous crank-heads emerged in their turns with a flash of brass and steel – going over; while the connecting-rods, big-jointed, like skeleton limbs, seemed to thust them down and pull them up again with an irresistible precision. And deep in the half-light other rods dodged deliberately to and fro, crossheads nodded, discs of metal rubbed smoothly against each other, slow and gentle, in a commingling of shadows and gleams.

Sometimes all those powerful and unerring movements would slow down simultaneously, as if they had been the functions of a living organism, stricken suddenly by the blight of languor; and Mr Rout's eyes would blaze darker in his long sallow face. He was fighting this fight in a pair of carpet slippers. A short shiny jacket barely covered his loins, and his white wrists protruded far out of the tight sleeves, as though the emergency had added to his stature, had lengthened his limbs, augmented his pallor, hollowed his eyes.

He moved, climbing high up, disappearing low down, with a restless, purposeful industry, and when he stood still, holding the guard-rail in front of the starting-gear, he would keep glancing to the right at the steam-gauge, at the water-gauge, fixed upon the white wall in the light of a swaying lamp. The mouths of two speaking-tubes gaped stupidly at his elbow, and the dial of the engine-room telegraph resembled a clock of large diameter, bearing on its face curt words instead of figures. The grouped letters stood out heavily black, around the pivot-head of the indicator, emphatically symbolic of loud excla-mations: AHEAD, ASTERN, SLOW, HALF, STAND BY; and the fat black hand pointed downwards to the word FULL, which thus singled out, captured the eye as a sharp cry secures attention.

The wood-encased bulk of the low-pressure cylinder, frowning portly from above, emitted a faint wheeze at every thrust, and except for that low hiss the engines worked their steel limbs headlong or slow with a silent, determined smoothness. And all this, the white walls, the moving steel, the floor plates under Solomon Rout's feet, the floors of iron grating above his head, the dusk and the gleams, uprose and sank continuously, with one accord, upon the harsh wash of the waves against the ship's side. The whole loftiness of the place, booming hollow to the great voice of the wind, swayed at the top like a tree, would go over bodily, as if borne down this way and that by the tremendous blasts.

'You've got to hurry up,' shouted Mr Rout, as soon as he saw Jukes appear in the stokehold doorway.

Jukes' glance was wandering and tipsy; his red face was puffy, as though he had overslept himself. He had had an arduous road, and had travelled over it with immense vivacity, the agitation of his mind corresponding to the exertions of his body. He had rushed up out of the bunker, stumbling in the dark alleyway amongst a lot of bewildered men who, trod upon, asked, 'What's up, sir?' in awed mutters all round him; – down the stokehold ladder, missing many iron rungs in his hurry, down into a place deep as a well, black as Tophet, tipping over back and forth like a see-saw. The water in the bilges thundered at each roll, and lumps of coal skipped to and fro, from end to end, rattling like an avalanche of pebbles on a slope of iron.

Somebody in there moaned with pain, and somebody else could be seen crouching over what seemed the prone body of a dead man; a lusty voice blasphemed; and the glow under each fire-door was like a pool of flaming blood radiating quietly in a velvety blackness.

A gust of wind struck upon the nape of Jukes' neck, and next moment he felt it streaming about his wet ankles. The stokehold ventilators hummed: in front of the six fire-doors two wild figures, stripped to the waist, staggered and stooped, wrestling with two shovels.

'Hallo! Plenty of draught now,' yelled the second engineer at once, as though he had been all the time looking out for Jukes. The donkeyman, a dapper little chap with a dazzling fair skin and a tiny, gingery moustache, worked in a sort of mute transport. They were keeping a full head of steam, and a profound rumbling, as of an empty furniture van trotting over a bridge, made a sustained bass to all the other noises of the place.

'Blowing off all the time,' went on yelling the second. With a sound as of a hundred scoured saucepans, the orifice of a ventilator spat upon his shoulder a sudden gush of salt water, and he volleyed a stream of curses upon all things on earth including his own soul, ripping and raving, and all the time attending to his business. With a sharp clash of metal the ardent pale glare of the fire opened upon his bullet head, showing his spluttering lips, his insolent face, and with another clang closed like the white-hot wink of an iron eye.

'Where's the blooming ship? Can you tell me? Blast my eye! Under water – or what? It's coming down here in tons. Are the condemned cowls gone to Hades? Hey? Don't you know anything – you jolly sailor-man you ... ?'

Jukes, after a bewildered moment, had been helped by a roll to dart through; and as soon as his eyes took in the comparative vastness, peace and brilliance of the engine-room, the ship, setting her stern heavily in the water, sent him charging head down upon Mr Rout.

The chief's arm, long like a tentacle, and straightening as if worked by a spring, went out to meet him, and deflected his rush into a spin towards the speaking-tubes. At the same time Mr Rout repeated earnestly, 'You've got to hurry up, whatever it is.'

Jukes yelled, 'Are you there, sir?' and listened. Nothing. Suddenly the roar of the wind fell straight into his ear, but presently a small voice shoved aside the shouting hurricane quietly.

'You, Jukes? – Well?'

Jukes was ready to talk; it was only time that seemed to be wanting. It was easy enough to account for everything. He could perfectly imagine the coolies battened down in the reeking 'tween-deck lying sick and scared between the rows of chests. Then one of these chests – or perhaps several at once – breaking loose in a roll, knocking out others, sides splitting, lids flying open, and all these clumsy Chinamen rising up in a body to save their property. Afterwards every fling of the ship would hurl that tramping, yelling mob here and there, from side to side, in a whirl of smashed wood, torn clothing, rolling dollars. A struggle once started, they would be unable to stop themselves. Nothing could stop them now except main force. It was a disaster. He had seen it, and that was all he could say. Some of them must be dead, he believed. The rest would go on fighting . . .

He sent up his words, tripping over each other, crowding the narrow tube. They mounted as if into a silence of an enlightened comprehension dwelling alone up there with a storm. And Jukes wanted to be dismissed from the face of that odious trouble intruding on the great need of the ship.

5

He waited. Before his eyes the engines turned with slow labour, that in the moment of going off into a mad fling would stop dead at Mr Rout's shout, 'Look out, Beale!' They paused in an intelligent immobility, stilled in midstroke, a heavy crank arrested on the cant, as if conscious of danger and the passage of time. Then, with a 'Now, then!' from the chief, and the sound of a breath expelled through clenched teeth, they would accomplish the interrupted revolution and begin another.

There was the prudent sagacity of wisdom and the deliberation of enormous strength in their movements. This was their work – this patient coaxing of a distracted ship over the fury of the waves and into the very eye of the wind. At times Mr Rout's chin would sink on his breast, and he watched them with knitted eyebrows as if lost in thought.

The voice that kept the hurricane out of Jukes' ear began, 'Take the hands with you . . .' and left off unexpectedly.

'What could I do with them, sir?'

A harsh, abrupt, imperious clang exploded suddenly. The three pairs of eyes flew up to the telegraph dial to see the hand jump from FULL to STOP, as if snatched by a devil. And then these three men in the engine-room had the intimate sensation of a check upon the ship, of a strange shrinking, as if she had gathered herself for a desperate leap.

'Stop her!' bellowed Mr Rout.

Nobody – not even Captain MacWhirr, who alone on deck had caught sight of a white line of foam coming on at such a height that he couldn't believe his eyes – nobody was to know the steepness of that sea and the awful depth of the hollow the hurricane had scooped out behind the running wall of water.

It raced to meet the ship, and, with a pause, as of girding the loins, the *Nan-Shan* lifted her bows and leaped. The flames in all the lamps sank, darkening the engine-room. One went out. With a tearing crash and a swirling, raving tumult, tons of water fell upon the deck, as though the ship had darted under the foot of a cataract.

Down there they looked at each other, stunned.

'Swept from end to end, by God!' bawled Jukes.

She dipped into the hollow straight down, as if going over the edge of the world. The engine-room toppled forward menacingly, like the inside of a tower nodding in an earthquake. An awful racket, of iron things falling, came from the stokehold. She hung on this appalling slant long enough for Beale to drop on his hands and knees and begin to crawl as if he meant to fly on all fours out of the engine-room, and for Mr Rout to turn his head slowly, rigid, cavernous, with the lower jaw dropping. Jukes had shut his eyes, and his face in a moment

59

became hopelessly blank and gentle, like the face of a blind man.

At last she rose slowly, staggering, as if she had to lift a mountain with her bows.

Mr Rout shut his mouth; Jukes blinked; and little Beale stood up hastily.

'Another one like this, and that's the last of her,' cried the chief.

He and Jukes looked at each other, and the same thought came into their heads. The captain! Everything must have been swept away. Steering-gear gone – ship like a log. All over directly.

'Rush!' ejaculated Mr Rout thickly, glaring with enlarged, doubtful eyes at Jukes, who answered him by an irresolute glance.

The clang of the telegraph gong soothed them instantly. The black hand dropped in a flash from STOP to FULL.

'Now then, Beale!' cried Mr Rout.

The steam hissed low. The piston-rods slid in and out.

Jukes put his ear to the tube. The voice was ready for him. It said, 'Pick up all the money. Bear a hand now. I'll want you up here.' And that was all.

'Sir?' called up Jukes. There was no answer.

He staggered away like a defeated man from the field of battle. He had got, in some way or other, a cut above his left eyebrow – a cut to the bone. He was not aware of it in the least: quantities of the China Sea, large enough to break his neck for him, had gone over his head, had cleaned, washed, and salted that wound. It did not bleed, but only gaped red; and this gash over the eye, his dishevelled hair, the disorder of his clothes, gave him the aspect of a man worsted in a fight with fists.

'Got to pick up the dollars.' He appealed to Mr Rout, smiling pitifully at random.

'What's that?' asked Mr Rout wildly. 'Pick up . . . ? I don't care . . .' Then, quivering in every muscle, but with an exaggeration of paternal tone, 'Go away now, for God's sake. You deck people 'll drive me silly. There's that second mate been going for the old man. Don't you know? You fellows are going wrong for want of something to do ...'

At these words Jukes discovered in himself the beginnings of anger. Want of something to do – indeed .... Full of hot scorn against the chief, he turned to go the way he had come. In the stokehold the plump donkeyman toiled with his shovel mutely, as if his tongue had been cut out; but the second was carrying on like a noisy, undaunted maniac, who had preserved his skill in the art of stoking under a marine boiler.

'Hallo, you wandering officer! Hey! Can't you get some of your slush-slingers to wind up a few of them ashes? I am getting choked with them here. Curse it! Hallo! Hey! Remember the articles: *Sailors and firemen to assist each other*. Hey! D'ye hear?'

Jukes was climbing out frantically, and the other, lifting up his face after him, howled, 'Can't you speak? What are you poking about here for? What's your game, anyhow?'

A frenzy possessed Jukes. By the time he was back amongst the men in the darkness of the alleyway, he felt ready to wring all their necks at the slightest sign of hanging back. The very thought of it exasperated him. *He* couldn't hang back. They shouldn't.

The impetuosity with which he came amongst them carried them along. They had already been excited and startled at all his comings and goings – by the fierceness and rapidity of his movements; and more felt than seen in his rushes, he appeared formidable – busied with matters of life and death that brooked no delay. At his first word he heard them drop into the bunker one after another obediently, with heavy thumps.

They were not clear as to what would have to be done. 'What is it? What is it?' they were asking each other. The boatswain tried to explain; the sounds of a great scuffle surprised them: and the mighty shocks, reverberating awfully in the

61

black bunker, kept them in mind of their danger. When the boatswain threw open the door it seemed that an eddy of the hurricane, stealing through the iron sides of the ship, had set all these bodies whirling like dust. There came to them a confused uproar, a tempestuous tumult, at fierce mutter, gusts of screams dying away, and the tramping of feet mingling with the blows of the sea.

For a moment they glared amazed, blocking the doorway. Jukes pushed through them brutally. He said nothing, and simply darted in. Another lot of coolies on the ladder, struggling suicidally to break through the battened hatch to a swamped deck, fell off as before, and he disappeared under them like a man overtaken by a landslide.

The boatswain yelled excitedly, 'Come along. Get the mate out. He'll be trampled to death. Come on.'

They charged in, stamping on breasts, on fingers, on faces, catching their feet in heaps of clothing, kicking broken wood; but before they could get hold of him Jukes emerged waist deep in a multitude of clawing hands. In the instant he had been lost to view, all the buttons of his jacket had gone, its back had got split up to the collar, his waistcoat had been torn open. The central struggling mass of Chinamen went over to the roll, dark, indistinct, helpless, with a wild gleam of many eyes in the dim light of the lamps.

'Leave me alone – damn you. I am all right,' screeched Jukes. 'Drive them forward. Watch your chance when she pitches. Forward with 'em. Drive them against the bulkhead. Jam 'em up.'

The rush of the sailors into the seething 'tween-deck was like a splash of cold water into a boiling cauldron. The commotion sank for a moment.

The bulk of Chinamen were locked in such a compact scrimmage that, linking their arms and aided by an appalling dive of the ship, the seamen sent it forward in one great shove, like a solid block. Behind their backs small clusters and loose bodies tumbled from side to side.

The boatswain performed prodigious feats of strength. With his long arms open, and each great paw clutching at a stanchion, he stopped the rush of seven entwined Chinamen rolling like a boulder. His joints cracked; he said, 'Ha!' and they flew apart. But the carpenter showed the greater intelligence. Without saying a word to anybody he went back into the alleyway, to fetch several coils of cargo gear he had seen there – chain and rope. With these life-lines were rigged.

There was really no resistance. The struggle, however it began, had turned into a scramble of blind panic. If the coolies had started up after their scattered dollars they were by that time fighting only for their footing. They took each other by the throat merely to save themselves from being hurled about. Whoever got a hold anywhere would kick at the others who caught at his legs and hung on, till a roll sent them flying together across the deck.

The coming of the white devils was a terror. Had they come to kill? The individuals torn out of the ruck became very limp in the seamen's hands: some dragged aside by the heels, were passive, like dead bodies, with open, fixed eyes. Here and there a coolie would fall on his knees as if begging for mercy; several, whom the excess of fear made unruly, were hit with hard fists between the eyes, and cowered; while those who were hurt submitted to rough handling, blinking rapidly without a plaint. Faces streamed with blood; there were raw places on the shaven heads, scratches, bruises, torn wounds, gashes. The broken porcelain out of the chests was mostly responsible for the latter. Here and there a Chinaman, wild-eyed, with his tail unplaited, nursed a bleeding sole.

They had been ranged closely, after having been shaken into submission, cuffed a little to allay excitement, addressed in gruff words of encouragement that sounded like promises of evil. They sat on the deck in ghastly, drooping rows, and at the end the carpenter, with two hands to help him, moved busily from place to place, setting taut and hitching the life-lines. The boatswain, with one leg and one arm embracing a stanchion, struggled with a lamp pressed to his breast, trying to get a light, and growling all the time like an industrious gorilla. The figures of seamen stooped repeatedly, with the movements of gleaners, and everything was being flung into the bunker: clothing, smashed wood, broken china, and the dollars too, gathered up in men's jackets. Now and then a sailor would stagger towards the doorway with his arms full of rubbish; and dolorous, slanting eyes followed his movements.

With every roll of the ship the long rows of sitting Celestials would sway forward brokenly, and her headlong dives knocked together the line of shaven polls from end to end. When the wash of water rolling on the deck died away for a moment, it seemed to Jukes, yet quivering from his exertions, that in his mad struggle down there he had overcome the wind somehow: that a silence had fallen upon the ship, a silence in which the sea struck thunderously at her sides.

Everything had been cleared out of the 'tween-deck – all the wreckage, as the men said. They stood erect and tottering above the level of heads and drooping shoulders. Here and there a coolie sobbed for his breath. Where the high light fell, Jukes could see the salient ribs of one, the yellow, wistful face of another; bowed necks; or would meet a dull stare directed at his face. He was amazed that there had been no corpses; but the lot of them seemed at their last gasp, and they appeared to him more pitiful than if they had been all dead.

Suddenly one of the coolies began to speak. The light came and went on his lean, straining face: he threw his head up like a baying hound. From the bunker came the sounds of knocking and the tinkle of some dollars rolling loose; he stretched out his arm, his mouth yawned black, and the incomprehensible guttural hooting sounds, that did not seem to belong to a human language, penetrated Jukes with a strange emotion as if a brute had tried to be eloquent.

Two more started mouthing what seemed to Jukes fierce denunciations; the others stirred with grunts and growls. Jukes ordered the hands out of the 'tween-decks hurriedly. He left last himself, backing through the door, while the grunts rose to a loud murmur and hands were extended after him as after a malefactor. The boatswain shot the bolt, and remarked uneasily, 'Seems as if the wind had dropped, sir.'

The seamen were glad to get back into the alleyway. Secretly each of them thought that at the last moment he could rush out on deck – and that was a comfort. There is something horribly repugnant in the idea of being drowned under a deck. Now they had done with the Chinamen, they again became conscious of the ship's position.

Jukes on coming out of the alleyway found himself up to the neck in the noisy water. He gained the bridge, and discovered he could detect obscure shapes as if his sight had become preternaturally acute. He saw faint outlines. They recalled not the familiar aspect of the *Nan-Shan*, but something remembered – an old dismantled steamer he had seen years ago rotting on a mudbank. She recalled that wreck.

There was no wind, not a breath, except the faint currents created by the lurches of the ship. The smoke tossed out of the funnel was settling down upon her deck. He breathed it as he passed forward. He felt the deliberate throb of the engines, and heard small sounds that seemed to have survived the great uproar: the knocking of broken fittings, the rapid tumbling of some piece of wreckage on the bridge. He perceived dimly the squat shape of his captain holding on to a twisted bridge-rail, motionless and swaying as if rooted to the planks. The unexpected stillness of the air oppressed Jukes.

'We have done it, sir,' he gasped.

'Thought you would,' said Captain MacWhirr.

'Did you?' murmured Jukes to himself.

'Wind fell all at once,' went on the captain.

Jukes burst out, 'If you think it was an easy job—'

But his captain, clinging to the rail, paid no attention. 'According to the books the worst is not over yet.'

'If most of them hadn't been half dead with seasickness and fright, not one of us would have come out of that 'tween-deck alive,' said Jukes.

'Had to do what's fair by them,' mumbled MacWhirr stolidly. 'You don't find everything in books.'

'Why, I believe they would have risen on us if I hadn't ordered the hands out of that pretty quick,' continued Jukes with warmth.

After the whisper of their shouts, their ordinary tones, so distinct, rang out very loud to their ears in the amazing stillness of the air. It seemed to them they were talking in a dark and echoing vault.

Through a jagged aperture in the dome of clouds the light of a few stars fell upon the black sea, rising and falling confusedly. Sometimes the head of a watery cone would topple on board and mingle with the rolling flurry of foam on the swamped deck; and the *Nan-Shan* wallowed heavily at the bottom of a circular cistern of clouds. This ring of dense vapours, gyrating madly round the calm of the centre, encompassed the ship like a motionless and unbroken wall of an aspect inconceivably sinister. Within, the sea, as if agitated by an internal commotion, leaped in peaked mounds that jostled each other, slapping heavily against her sides; and a low moaning sound, the infinite plaint of the storm's fury, came from beyond the limits of the menacing calm. Captain MacWhirr remained silent, and Jukes' ready ear caught suddenly the faint, long-drawn roar of some immense wave rushing unseen under that thick blackness, which made the appalling boundary of his vision.

'Of course,' he started resentfully, 'they thought we had caught at the chance to plunder them. Of course! You said – pick up the money. Easier said than done. They couldn't tell what was in our heads. We came in, smash – right into the middle of them. Had to do it by a rush.'

'As long as it's done . . .' mumbled the captain, without attempting to look at Jukes. 'Had to do what's fair.'

'We shall find yet there's the devil to pay when this is over,' said Jukes, feeling very sore. 'Let them only recover a bit, and you'll see. They will fly at our throats, sir. Don't forget, sir, she isn't a British ship now. These brutes know it well, too. The damn'd Siamese flag.'

'We are on board, all the same,' remarked Captain Mac-Whirr.

'The trouble's not over yet,' insisted Jukes prophetically, reeling and catching on. 'She's a wreck,' he added faintly.

'The trouble's not over yet,' assented Captain MacWhirr, half aloud. . . . 'Look out for her a minute.'

'Are you going off the deck, sir?' asked Jukes hurriedly, as if the storm were sure to pounce upon him as soon as he had been left alone with the ship.

He watched her, battered and solitary, labouring heavily in a wild scene of mountainous black waters lit by the gleams of distant worlds. She moved slowly, breathing into the still core of the hurricane the excess of her strength in a white cloud of steam – and the deep-toned vibration of the escape was like the defiant trumpeting of a living creature of the sea impatient for the renewal of the contest. It ceased suddenly. The still air moaned. Above Jukes' head a few stars shone into the pit of black vapours. The inky edge of the cloud-disc frowned upon the ship under the patch of glittering sky. The stars too seemed to look at her intently, as if for the last time, and the cluster of their splendour sat like a diadem on a lowering brow.

Captain MacWhirr had gone into the chart-room. There was no light there; but he could feel the disorder of that place where he used to live tidily. His arm-chair was upset. The books had tumbled out on the floor: he scrunched a piece of glass under his boot. He groped for the matches and found a box on a shelf with a deep ledge. He struck one, and puckering the corners of his eyes, held out the little flame towards the barometer whose glittering top of glass and metals nodded at him continuously.

It stood very low – incredibly low, so low that Captain MacWhirr grunted. The match went out, and hurriedly he extracted another, with thick, stiff fingers.

Again a little flame flared up before the nodding glass and metal of the top. His eyes looked at it, narrowed with attention, as if expecting an imperceptible sign. With his grave face he resembled a booted and misshapen pagan burning incense before the oracle of a Joss. There was no mistake. It was the lowest reading he had ever seen in his life.

Captain MacWhirr emitted a low whistle. He forgot himself till the flame diminished to a blue spark, burnt his fingers and vanished. Perhaps something had gone wrong with the thing!

There was an aneroid glass screwed above the couch. He turned that way, struck another match, and discovered the white face of the other instrument looking at him from the bulkhead, meaningly, not to be gainsaid, as though the wisdom of men were made unerring by the indifference of matter. There was no room for doubt now. Captain MacWhirr pshawed at it, and threw the match down.

The worst was to come, then – and if the books were right this worst would be very bad. The experience of the last six hours had enlarged his conception of what heavy weather could be like. 'It'll be terrific,' he pronounced mentally. He had not consciously looked at anything by the light of the matches except at the barometer; and yet somehow he had seen that his water-bottle and the two tumblers had been flung out of their stand. It seemed to give a more intimate knowledge of the tossing the ship had gone through. 'I wouldn't have believed it,' he thought. And his table had been cleared too; his rulers, his pencils, the inkstand – all the things that had their safe appointed places – they were gone, as if a mischievous hand had plucked them out one by one and flung them on the wet floor. The hurricane had broken in upon the orderly arrangements of his privacy. This had never happened before, and the feeling of dismay reached the very seat of his composure. And the worst was to come yet! He was glad the trouble in the 'tween-deck had been discovered in time. If the ship had to go after all, then, at least, she wouldn't be going to the bottom with a lot of people in her fighting teeth and claw. That would have been odious. And in that feeling there was a humane intention and a vague sense of the fitness of things.

These instantaneous thoughts were yet in their essence heavy and slow, partaking of the nature of the man. He extended his hand to put back the matchbox in its corner of the shelf. There were always matches there – by his order. The steward had his instructions impressed upon him long before. 'A box . . . just there, see? Not so very full . . . where I can put my hand on it, steward. Might want a light in a hurry. Can't tell on board ship *what* you might want in a hurry. Mind, now.'

And of course on his side he would be careful to put it back in its place scrupulously. He did so now, but before he removed his hand it occurred to him that perhaps he would never have occasion to use that box any more. The vividness of the thought checked him, and for an infinitesimal fraction of a second his fingers closed again on the small object as though it had been the symbol of all these little habits that chain us to the weary round of life. He released it at last, and letting himself fall on the settee, listened for the first sounds of returning wind.

Not yet. He heard only the wash of water, the heavy splashes, the dull shocks of the confused seas boarding his ship from all sides. She would never have a chance to clear her decks.

But the quietude of the air was startlingly tense and unsafe, like a slender hair holding a sword suspended over his head. By this awful pause the storm penetrated the defences of the man and unsealed his lips. He spoke out in the solitude and the pitch darkness of the cabin, as if addressing another being awakened within his breast.

'I shouldn't like to lose her,' he said half aloud.

He sat unseen, apart from the sea, from his ship, isolated, as if withdrawn from the very current of his own existence, where such freaks as talking to himself surely had no place. His palms reposed on his knees, he bowed his short neck and puffed heavily, surrendering to a strange sensation of weariness he was not enlightened enough to recognize for the fatigue of mental stress.

From where he sat he could reach the door of a washstand locker. There should have been a towel there. There was. Good. . . . He took it out, wiped his face, and afterwards went on rubbing his wet head. He towelled himself with energy in the dark, and then remained motionless with the towel on his knees. A moment passed, of a stillness so profound that no one could have guessed there was a man sitting in that cabin. Then a murmur arose.

'She may come out of it yet.'

When Captain MacWhirr came out on deck, which he did brusquely, as though he had suddenly become conscious of having stayed away too long, the calm had lasted already more than fifteen minutes – long enough to make itself intolerable even to his imagination. Jukes, motionless on the forepart of the bridge, began to speak at once. His voice, blank and forced as though he were talking through hard-set teeth, seemed to flow away on all sides into the darkness, deepening again upon the sea.

'I had the wheel relieved. Hackett began to sing out that he was done. He's lying in there alongside the steering-gear with a face like death. At first I couldn't get anybody to crawl out and relieve the poor devil. That bos'n's worse than no good, I always said. Thought I would have had to go myself and haul out one of them by the neck.'

'Ah, well,' muttered the captain. He stood watchful by Jukes' side.

'The second mate's in there too, holding his head. Is he hurt, sir?'

'No – crazy,' said Captain MacWhirr, curtly.

'Looks as if he had a tumble, though.'

'I had to give him a push,' explained the captain.

Jukes gave an impatient sigh.

'It will come very sudden,' said Captain MacWhirr, 'and from over there, I fancy. God only knows, though. These books are only good to muddle your head and make you jumpy. It will be bad, and there's an end. If we only can steam her round in time to meet it . . .'

A minute passed. Some of the stars winked rapidly and vanished.

'You left them pretty safe?' began the captain abruptly, as though the silence were unbearable.

'Are you thinking of the coolies, sir? I rigged life-lines all ways across that 'tween deck.'

'Did you? Good idea, Mr Jukes.'

'I didn't . . . think you cared to . . . know,' said Jukes – the lurching of the ship cut his speech as though somebody had been jerking him around while he talked – 'how I got on with . . . that infernal job. We did it. And it may not matter in the end.'

'Had to do what's fair, for all – they are only Chinamen. Give them the same chance with ourselves – hang it all. She isn't lost yet. Bad enough to be shut up below in a gale——'

'That's what I thought when you gave me the job, sir,' interjected Jukes moodily.

'– without being battered to pieces,' pursued Captain Mac-Whirr with rising vehemence. 'Couldn't let that go on in my ship, if I knew she hadn't five minutes to live. Couldn't bear it, Mr Jukes.'

A hollow echoing noise, like that of a shout rolling in a rocky chasm, approached the ship and went away again. The last star, blurred, enlarged, as if returning to the fiery mist of its beginning, struggled with the colossal depth of blackness hanging over the ship – and went out.

'Now for it!' muttered Captain MacWhirr. 'Mr Jukes.'

'Here, sir.'

The two men were growing indistinct to each other.

'We must trust her to go through it and come out on the other side. That's plain and straight. There's no room for Captain Wilson's storm-strategy here.'

'No, sir.'

'She will be smothered and swept again for hours,' mumbled the captain. 'There's not much left by this time above deck for the sea to take away – unless you or me.'

'Both, sir,' whispered Jukes breathlessly.

'You are always meeting trouble half way, Jukes,' Captain MacWhirr remonstrated quaintly. 'Though it's a fact that the second mate is no good. D'ye hear, Mr Jukes? You would be left alone if . . .'

Captain MacWhirr interrupted himself, and Jukes glancing on all sides, remained silent.

'Don't you be put out by anything,' the captain continued, mumbling rather fast. 'Keep her facing it. They may say what they like, but the heaviest seas run with the wind. Facing it – always facing it – that's the way to get through. You are a young sailor. Face it. That's enough for any man. Keep a cool head.'

'Yes, sir,' said Jukes, with a flutter of the heart.

In the next few seconds the captain spoke to the engine-room and got an answer.

For some reason Jukes experienced an access of confidence, a sensation that came from outside like a warm breath, and made him feel equal to every demand. The distant muttering of the darkness stole into his ears. He noted it unmoved, out of that sudden belief in himself, as a man safe in a shirt of mail would watch a point.

The ship laboured without intermission amongst the black hills of water, paying with this hard tumbling the price of her life. She rumbled in her depths, shaking a white plummet of steam into the night, and Jukes' thought skimmed like a bird through the engine-room, where Mr Rout – good man – was ready. When the rumbling ceased it seemed to him that there was a pause of every sound, a dead pause in which Captain MacWhirr's voice rang out startlingly.

'What's that? A puff of wind?' – it spoke much louder than Jukes had ever heard it before – 'On the bow. That's right. She may come out of it yet.'

The mutter of the winds drew near apace. In the forefront could be distinguished a drowsy waking plaint passing on, and far off the growth of a multiple clamour, marching and expanding. There was the throb as of many drums in it, a vicious rushing note, and like the chant of a tramping multitude.

Jukes could no longer see his captain distinctly. The darkness was absolutely piling itself upon the ship. At most he made out movements, a hint of elbows spread out, of a head thrown up.

Captain MacWhirr was trying to do up the top button of his oilskin coat with unwonted haste. The hurricane, with its power to madden the seas, to sink ships, to uproot trees, to overturn strong walls and dash the very birds of the air to the ground, had found this taciturn man in its path, and, doing its utmost, had managed to wring out a few words. Before the renewed wrath of winds swooped on his ship, Captain Mac-Whirr was moved to declare, in a tone of vexation, as it were, 'I wouldn't like to lose her.'

He was spared that annoyance.

6

On a bright sunshiny day, with the breeze chasing her smoke far ahead, the *Nan-Shan* came into Fu-chau. Her arrival was at once noticed on shore, and the seamen in harbour said, 'Look! Look at that steamer. What's that? Siamese — isn't she? Just look at her!'

She seemed, indeed, to have been used as a running target for the secondary batteries of a cruiser. A hail of minor shells could not have given her upper works a more broken, torn, and devastated aspect: and she had about her the worn, weary air of ships coming from the far ends of the world – and indeed with truth, for in her short passage she had been very far; sighting, verily, even the coast of the Great Beyond, whence no ship ever returns to give up her crew to the dust of the earth. She was incrusted and grey with salt to the trucks of her masts and to the top of her funnel; as though (as some facetious seaman said) 'the crowd on board had fished her out somewhere from the bottom of the sea and brought her in here for salvage'. And further, excited by the felicity of his own wit, he offered to give five pounds for her – 'as she stands'.

Before she had been quite an hour at rest, a meagre little man, with a red-tipped nose and face cast in an angry mould, landed from a sampan on the quay of the Foreign Concession and incontinently turned to shake his fist at her.

A tall individual, with legs much too thin for a rotund stomach, and with watery eyes, strolled up and remarked, 'Just left her – eh? Quick work.'

He wore a soiled suit of blue flannel with a pair of dirty cricketing shoes; a dingy grey moustache drooped from his lip, and daylight could be seen in two places between the rim and the crown of his hat.

'Hallo! what are you doing here?' asked the ex-second-mate of the *Nan-Shan*, shaking hands hurriedly.

'Standing by for a job – chance worth taking – got a quiet hint,' explained the man with the broken hat, in jerky, apathetic wheezes.

The second shook his fist again at the *Nan-Shan*. 'There's a fellow there that ain't fit to have the command of a scow,' he declared, quivering with passion, while the other looked about listlessly.

'Is there?'

But he caught sight on the quay of a heavy seaman's chest, painted brown under a fringed sailcloth cover, and lashed with new manila line. He eyed it with awakened interest.

'I would talk and raise trouble if it wasn't for that damned Siamese flag. Nobody to go to – or I would make it hot for him. The fraud! Told his chief engineer – that's another fraud for you – I had lost my nerve. The greatest lot of ignorant fools that ever sailed the seas. No! You can't think...'

'Got your money all right?' inquired his seedy acquaintance suddenly.

'Yes. Paid me off on board,' raged the second mate. '"Get your breakfast on shore," says he.'

'Mean skunk!' commented the tall man vaguely, and passed his tongue on his lips. 'What about having a drink of some sort?'

'He struck me,' hissed the second mate.

'No! Struck! You don't say?' The man in blue began to bustle about sympathetically. 'Can't possibly talk here. I want to know all about it. Struck – eh? Let's get a fellow to carry your chest. I know a quiet place where they have some bottled beer . . . '

Mr Jukes, who had been scanning the shore through a pair of glasses, informed the chief engineer afterwards that 'our late second mate hasn't been long in finding a friend. A chap looking uncommonly like a bummer. I saw them walk away together from the quay.'

The hammering and banging of the needful repairs did not disturb Captain MacWhirr. The steward found in the letter he wrote, in a tidy chart-room, passages of such absorbing interest that twice he was nearly caught in the act. But Mrs MacWhirr, in the drawing-room of the forty-pound house, stifled a yawn – perhaps out of self-respect – for she was alone.

She reclined in a plush-bottomed and gilt hammock-chair near a tiled fireplace, with Japanese fans on the mantel and a glow of coals in the grate. Lifting her hands she glanced wearily here and there into the many pages. It was not her fault they were so prosy, so completely uninteresting – from 'My darling wife' at the beginning, to 'Your loving husband' at the end. She couldn't be really expected to understand all these ship affairs. She was glad, of course, to hear from him, but she had never asked herself why, precisely.

' . . . They are called typhoons. . . . The mate did not seem to like it. . . . Not in books . . . Couldn't think of letting it go on . . . '

The paper rustled sharply. ' . . . A calm that lasted over twenty minutes,' she read perfunctorily; and the next words her thoughtless eyes caught, on the top of another page, were, 'see you and the children again . . . ' She had a movement of impatience. He was always thinking of coming home. He had never had such a good salary before. What was the matter now?

It did not occur to her to turn back overleaf to look. She would have found it recorded there that between 4 and 6 a.m.

on December 25th, Captain MacWhirr did actually think that his ship could not possibly live another hour in such a sea, and that he would never see his wife and children again. Nobody was to know this (his letters got mislaid so quickly) – nobody whatever but the steward, who had been greatly impressed by that disclosure. So much so, that he tried to give the cook some idea of the 'narrow squeak we all had' by saying solemnly, 'The old man himself had a dam' poor opinion of our chance.'

'How do you know?' asked contemptuously the cook, an old soldier, 'He hasn't told you, maybe?'

'Well, he did give me a hint to that effect,' the steward brazened it out.

'Get along with you! He will be coming to tell *me* next,' jeered the old cook over his shoulder.

Mrs MacWhirr glanced farther, on the alert. '... Do what's fair.... Miserable objects.... Only three, with a broken leg each, and one.... Thought had better keep the matter quiet ... hope to have done the fair thing ...'

She let fall her hands. No: there was nothing more about coming home. Must have been merely expressing a pious wish. Mrs MacWhirr's mind was set at ease, and a black marble clock, priced by the local jeweller at £3 18s. 6d. had a discreet stealthy tick.

The door flew open, and a girl in the long-legged, short-frocked period of existence, flung into the room. A lot of colourless, rather lanky hair was scattered over her shoulders. Seeing her mother, she stood still, and directed her pale prying eyes upon the letter.

'From Father,' murmured Mrs MacWhirr. 'What have you done with your ribbon?'

The girl put her hands up to her head and pouted.

'He's well,' continued Mrs MacWhirr languidly. 'At least I think so. He never says.' She had a little laugh. The girl's face expressed a wandering indifference, and Mrs MacWhirr surveyed her with fond pride.

'Go and get your hat,' she said after a while. 'I am going

out to do some shopping. There is a sale at Linom's.'

'Oh, how jolly!' uttered the child impressively, in un-expectedly grave vibrating tones, and bounded out of the room.

It was a fine afternoon, with a grey sky and dry sidewalks. Outside the draper's Mrs MacWhirr smiled upon a woman in a black mantle of generous proportions, armoured in jet and crowned with flowers blooming falsely above a bilious matronly countenance. They broke into a swift little babble of greetings and exclamations both together, very hurried as if the street were ready to yawn open and swallow all that pleasure before it could be expressed.

Behind them the high glass doors were kept on the swing. People couldn't pass, men stood aside waiting patiently, and Lydia was absorbed in poking the end of her parasol between the stone flags. Mrs MacWhirr talked rapidly.

'Thank you very much. He's not coming home yet. Of course it's very sad to have him away, but it's such a comfort to know he keeps well.' Mrs MacWhirr drew breath. 'The climate there agrees with him,' she added beamingly, as if poor MacWhirr had been away touring in China for the sake of his health.

Neither was the chief engineer coming home yet. Mr Rout knew too well the value of a good billet.

'Solomon says wonders will never cease,' cried Mrs Rout joyously at the old lady in her arm-chair by the fire. Mr Rout's mother moved slightly, her withered hands lying in black half-mittens on her lap.

The eyes of the engineer's wife fairly danced on the paper. 'That captain of the ship he is in – a rather simple man, you remember, Mother? – has done something rather clever, Solomon says.'

'Yes, my dear,' said the old woman meekly, sitting with bowed silvery head, and that air of inward stillness charac-teristic of very old people who seem lost in watching the last flickers of life. 'I think I remember.'

Solomon Rout, Old Sol, Father Sol, The Chief, 'Rout, good man' – Mr Rout, the condescending and paternal friend of youth, had been the baby of her many children – all dead by this time. And she remembered him best as a boy of ten – long before he went away to serve his apprenticeship in some great engineering works in the North. She had seen so little of him since, she had gone through so many years, that she had now to retrace her steps very far back to recognize him plainly in the mist of time. Sometimes it seemed that her daughter-in-law was talking of some strange man.

Mrs Rout junior was disappointed. 'H'm. H'm.' She turned the page. 'How provoking! He doesn't say what it is. Says I couldn't understand how much there was in it. Fancy! What could it be so very clever? What a wretched man not to tell us!'

She read on without further remark soberly, and at last sat looking into the fire. The chief wrote just a word or two of the typhoon; but something had moved him to express an increased longing for the companionship of the jolly woman. 'If it hadn't been that Mother must be looked after, I would send you your passage-money today. You could set up a small house out here. I would have a chance to see you sometimes then. We are not growing younger . . .'

'He's well, Mother,' sighed Mrs Rout, rousing herself.

'He always was a strong healthy boy,' said the old woman placidly.

But Mr Jukes' account was really animated and very full. His friend in the Western Ocean trade imparted it freely to the other officers of his liner. 'A chap I know writes to me about an extraordinary affair that happened on board his ship in that typhoon – you know – that we read of in the papers two months ago. It's the funniest thing! Just see for yourself what he says. I'll show you his letter.'

There were phrases in it calculated to give the impression of light-hearted, indomitable resolution. Jukes had written them in good faith, for he felt thus when he wrote. He described with lurid effect the scenes in the 'tween-deck. '. . . It struck me in a flash that those confounded Chinamen couldn't tell we weren't a desperate kind of robbers. 'Tisn't good to part the Chinaman from his money if he is the stronger party. We need have been desperate indeed to go thieving in such weather, but what could these beggars know of us? So, without thinking of it twice, I got the hands away in a jiffy. Our work was done – that the old man had set his heart on. We cleared out without staying to inquire how they felt. I am convinced that if they had not been so unmercifully shaken, and afraid – each individual one of them – to stand up, we would have been torn to pieces. Oh! It was pretty complete, I can tell you; and you may run to and fro across the Pond to the end of time before you find yourself with such a job on your hands.'

After this he alluded professionally to the damage done to the ship, and went on thus:

'It was when the weather quieted down that the situation became confoundedly delicate. It wasn't made any better by us having been lately transferred to the Siamese flag; though the skipper can't see that it makes any difference – "as long as *we* are on board" – he says. There are feelings that this man simply hasn't got – and there's an end of it. You might just as well try to make a bedpost understand. But apart from this it is an infernally lonely state for a ship to be going about the China seas with no proper consuls, not even a gunboat of her own anywhere, nor a body to go to in case of some trouble.

'My notion was to keep these Johnnies under hatches for another fifteen hours or so; as we weren't much farther than that from Fu-chau. We would find there, most likely, some sort of a man-of-war, and once under her guns we were safe enough; for surely any skipper of a man-of-war – English, French or Dutch – would see white men through as far as row on board goes. We could get rid of them and their money afterwards by delivering them to their Mandarin or Taotai, or whatever they call these chaps in goggles you see being carried about in sedan-chairs through their stinking streets.

'The old man wouldn't see it somehow. He wanted to keep the matter quiet. He got that notion into his head, and a steam windlass couldn't drag it out of him. He wanted as little fuss made as possible, for the sake of the ship's name and for the sake of the owners – "for the sake of all concerned," says he, looking at me very hard. It made me angry hot. Of course you couldn't keep a thing like that quiet; but the chests had been secured in the usual manner and were safe enough for any earthly gale, while this had been an altogether fiendish business I couldn't give you even an idea of.

'Meantime, I could hardly keep on my feet. None of us had a spell of any sort for nearly thirty hours, and there the old man sat rubbing his chin, rubbing the top of his head, and so bothered he didn't even think of pulling his long boots off.

'"I hope, sir," says I, "you won't be letting them out on deck before we make ready for them in some shape or other." Not, mind you, that I felt very sanguine about controlling these beggars if they meant to take charge. A trouble with a cargo of Chinamen is no child's play. I was dam' tired too. "I wish," said I, "you would let us throw the whole lot of these dollars down to them and leave them to fight it out amongst themselves, while we get a rest."

'"Now you talk wild, Jukes," says he, looking up in his slow way that makes you ache all over, somehow. "We must plan out something that would be fair to all parties."

'I had no end of work on hand, as you may imagine, so I set the hands going, and then I thought I would turn in a bit. I hadn't been asleep in my bunk ten minutes when in rushes the steward and begins to pull at my leg.

'"For God's sake, Mr Jukes, come out! Come on deck quick, sir. Oh, do come out!"

'The fellow scared all the sense out of me. I didn't know what had happened: another hurricane – or what. Could hear no wind.

'"The captain's letting them out. Oh, he is letting them out! Jump on deck, sir, and save us. The chief engineer has just run below for his revolver."

'That's what I understood the fool to say. However, Father Rout swears he went in there only to get a clean pocket-handkerchief. Anyhow, I made one jump into my trousers and flew on deck aft. There was certainly a good deal of noise going on forward of the bridge. Four of the hands with the bos'n were at work abaft. I passed up to them some of the rifles all the ships on the China coast carry in the cabin, and led them on the bridge. On the way I ran against Old Sol, looking startled and sucking at an unlighted cigar.

'"Come along," I shouted to him.

'We charged, the seven of us, up to the chart-room. All was over. There stood the old man with his seaboots still drawn up to the hips and in shirt-sleeves – got warm thinking it out, I suppose. Bun Hin's dandy clerk at his elbow, as dirty as a sweep, was still green in the face. I could see directly I was in for something.

'"What the devil are these monkey tricks, Mr Jukes?" asks the old man, as angry as ever he could be. I tell you frankly it made me lose my tongue. "For God's sake, Mr Jukes," says he, "do take away these rifles from the men. Somebody's sure to get hurt before long if you don't. Damme, if this ship isn't worse than Bedlam! Look sharp now. I want you up here to help me and Bun Hin's Chinamen to count that money. You wouldn't mind lending a hand too, Mr Rout, now you are here. The more of us the better."

'He had settled it all in his mind while I was having a snooze. Had we been an English ship, or only going to land our cargo of coolies in an English port, like Hong Kong, for instance, there would have been no end of inquiries and bother, claims for damages and so on. But these Chinamen know their officials better than we do.

'The hatches had been taken off already, and they were all on deck after a night and a day down below.

'It made you feel queer to see so many gaunt, wild faces together. The beggars stared about at the sky, at the sea, at the ship, as though they had expected the whole thing to have been blown to pieces. And no wonder! They had had a doing that would have shaken the soul out of a white man. But then they say a Chinaman has no soul. He has, though, something about him that is deuced tough. There was a fellow (amongst others of the badly hurt) who had had his eye all but knocked out. It stood out of his head the size of half a hen's egg. This would have laid out a white man on his back for a month: and yet there was that chap elbowing here and there in the crowd and talking to the others as if nothing had been the matter. They made a great hubbub amongst themselves, and whenever the old man showed his bald head on the foreside of the bridge, they would all leave off jawing and look at him from below.

'It seems that after he had done his thinking he made that Bun Hin's fellow go down and explain to them the only way they could get their money back. He told me afterwards that, all the coolies having worked in the same place and for the same length of time, he reckoned he would be doing the fair thing by them as near as possible if he shared all the cash we had picked up equally among the lot. You couldn't tell one man's dollars from another's, he said, and if you asked each man how much money he brought on board he was afraid they would lie, and he would find himself a long way short. I think he was right there. As to giving up the money to any Chinese official he could scare up in Fu-chau, he said he might just as well put the lot in his own pocket at once for all the good it would be to them. I suppose they thought so too.

'We finished the distribution before dark. It was rather a sight: the sea running high, the ship, a wreck to look at, these Chinamen staggering up on the bridge one by one for their share, and the old man still booted, and in his shirt-sleeves, busy paying out at the chart-room door, perspiring like anything, and now and then coming down sharp on myself or Father Rout about one thing or another not quite to his mind. He took the share of those who were disabled himself to them on the No. 2 hatch. There were three dollars left over, and these went to the three most damaged coolies, one to each. We turned-to afterwards, and shovelled out on deck heaps of wet rags, all sorts of fragments of things without shape, and that you couldn't give a name to, and let them settle the ownership themselves.

'This certainly is coming as near as can be to keeping the thing quiet for the benefit of all concerned. What's your opinion, you pampered mail-boat swell? The old chief says that this was plainly the only thing that could be done. The skipper remarked to me the other day, "There are things you find nothing about in books." I think that he got out of it very well for such a stupid man.'

COMMENTARY

Sometime in September 1900. Conrad started work on the earliest, longest and finest of the three stories included in this collection. *Typhoon* – which is strictly speaking a novella, or short novel – was completed in January 1901 and published a year later both in instalments (in the *Pall Mall Magazine*) and in book form. The description of the storm which occupies the central part of the tale is by any standards a *tour de force*, yet it is not to this that our attention is lastingly drawn so much as to Conrad's account of the behaviour of the crew and passengers of the *Nan-Shan* during her life and death struggle with the elements. Indeed, Conrad makes it clear in the introduction he wrote for the story when it first appeared in its entirety that it is a positive mistake to regard *Typhoon*, as some critics had done, merely as a virtuoso 'storm-piece'; its chief interest lies, he maintains, not in the 'bad weather' but in the 'extraordinary complication brought into a ship's life at a moment of exceptional stress by the human element below her deck'. His purpose, thus, is as much psychological as narrative; his aim as much an examination of human nature as an account of exciting adventure. That is not to say that excitement and adventure are not present in the story; merely that to fix our eyes on them and ignore the deeper human implications is to miss much of what the author himself was trying to make clear, and to savour only part of the feast with which he regales us.

We have already seen, in the introduction, that the storm sequence in *Typhoon* and at least one of its characters were in part derived from Conrad's experiences in 1887, while he was serving in the *Highland Forest* – a sailing ship bound for Java, under the command of a certain Captain John McWhirr. It was McWhirr's laconic manner which seems more than anything else to have found its way into the makeup of the master of the *Nan-Shan*, the dour understatement evident in the conversation which the author recalls having had with him at their first encounter. Conrad, as first mate of the *Highland Forest*, had been overseeing the loading of her cargo the day before Mc-Whirr arrived:

> The sudden, spontaneous agility with which he bounded aboard right off the rail afforded me the first glimpse of his real character. Without further preliminaries than a friendly nod, he addressed me: 'You have got her pretty well in her fore and aft trim. Now, what about your weights?' I told him I had managed to keep the weight sufficiently well up, as I thought, one third of the whole being in the upper part 'above the beams', as the technical expression has it. He whistled 'Phew!' scrutinising me from head to foot. A sort of smiling vexation was visible on his ruddy face.
>
> 'Well, we shall have a lively time of it this passage, I bet,' he said.

And so, as we know, they did. It may come as something of a surprise, however, to discover Conrad also putting it on record that, rather like the events which inspired *The Secret Sharer*, this story of a ship carrying a large number of coolies being caught in a typhoon was part of the sea lore of the eastern shipping routes in the closing years of the nineteenth century; or to read his assertion that Mac Whirr of the *Nan-Shan* 'is not an acquaintance of a few hours, or a few weeks, or a few months. He is the product of twenty years of life. My own life. Conscious invention had little to do with him.' All of which evidence, conflicting as it may appear at first sight, adds up to the fact that although the story of *Typhoon* may be based on hints and observations from a variety of sources, it is essentially a work of imaginative fiction in which real events and characters have been fused and reformed by the creative instinct of a writer of genius. MacWhirr clearly owes something to his namesake of the *Highland Forest* as well as to Conrad's own

experience of command. But what is more important is that
he emerges from the story as a fascinating and magnificently
credible individual. He is 'Captain MacWhirr, of the steamer
Nan-Shan' and none other.

I

Typhoon falls into six sections or chapters of which only the
central four deal directly with the storm itself. The first presents
a necessary background, introducing us both to the ship and
also to the men who are about to undertake in her the fateful
journey to Fu-chau. Who are they? What are they like? How
will they respond to crisis and stress? It also introduces us to
some of Conrad's favourite narrative techniques – a certain dry
humour, a love of sudden contrasts, the observation of one
character through the eyes of others, the pointing of significant
details and, above all, the stern irony which seems to tinge
so much of his view of men and events. It is the purpose of this
commentary (as it is of those on *The Black Mate* and *The Secret
Sharer*) to remark on these as well as other aspects of the narrative
as it progresses, and to assist the reader in forming an appreciation both of the work's structural unity and its thematic
richness. So let us begin at the beginning.

The opening paragraphs magnificently demonstrate Conrad's artistic authority, his control over his readers' reactions.
He has us securely in his grasp. His description of Captain
MacWhirr, simple and unambiguous as it seems at first sight,
is in fact cleverly deceptive: here is a man who, on superficial
acquaintance, is as 'ordinary, irresponsive, and unruffled' as
his own appearance. He is an everyday man, his looks and
manner signalling nothing in the least bit remarkable or worthy
of admiration. But before our interest has a chance to flag or
to be diverted elsewhere, Conrad catches at it with his quietly
ironical consideration of the impossibility of understanding
'what under heaven could have induced that perfectly satisfactory son of a petty grocer in Belfast to run away to sea'. Is there,

perhaps, a gentle mockery in his suggestion that anything as grand or awesome as a *destiny* should govern the career of so ordinary a character? Irony or mockery apart, however, this talk of 'inconceivable goals and ... undreamt-of directions' is enough to keep our attention on MacWhirr. Perhaps there is more to him after all.

So far as external appearances are concerned, the information with which we are provided comes both through Conrad's own direct objective description of MacWhirr and also through the subjective reactions of other characters to the man and his ways. It is worth noticing that whereas the one is generally straightforward and unequivocal even if occasionally touched, as we have seen, with discreet humour, the other (be it the response of Jukes or Rout, or of MacWhirr's own parents) has a tendency towards ambiguity. How are we meant to interpret, for instance, the chief mate's exaggerated deference in rolling his captain's umbrella, how the chief engineer's furtive smile at the ritual, how the parental pronouncement that 'Tom's an ass'? Are we to take such reactions at face value or are we to detect in them the thinly veiled condescension of those who consider themselves innately superior to this 'ordinary, irresponsive, and unruffled' man? It is surely part of the author's intention both here and later in the story to lead us by means of the cynical and indifferent attitudes of his crew and family into misjudging and undervaluing MacWhirr. As we shall see in due course, it does not matter that he dresses quaintly or that he is awkward and cannot roll his own umbrella; it does not matter that he appears absurd, even incompetent, to some of the *Nan-Shan*'s crew, that he does indeed make mistakes; it does not matter that his running away to sea may appear heartless or that his view of the world is dull and unimaginative, that he is a worthy butt for his father's teasing or the junior partner's contempt, what matters is that, in the end, he will be the right man to cope with the terrifying situation that lies in store for him.

Whatever else emerges at this stage in the story, one thing is abundantly clear: MacWhirr's preoccupation with the sea is paramount; and not just the sea, but all aspects of sea-going – the ship, the ports, the owners. He is, moreover, an eminently practical man. There is little room in his life for sentiment or fancy. He is dour, unromantic; to him, marriage and commanding a ship are of equal importance. The names, we are told, of ships and skippers, of shipowners, 'of seas, oceans, straits, promontories', of ports and islands, used to crowd the pages of the letters he sent home to his parents during his voyages. Almost incidentally, the name of his 'young woman' appeared among them. 'She was called Lucy. It did not suggest itself to him to mention whether he thought the name pretty.' Such is MacWhirr's perspective on life. His may, indeed, be qualities at which we join others in smiling or being impatient. Now, yes – but not later. For Conrad is deliberately allowing us to assume the same air of superiority over MacWhirr that Jukes and even Rout display in their own private ways, so that our admiration for him later will be the more profound. We watch him apparently obliviously hanging his coat on the end of a steam windlass 'embodying all the latest improvements'; we remark his offering no further comment on the *Nan-Shan*'s 'perfections' than a complaint about the faulty lock on his cabin door; we note no sign of 'pride in his ship, gratitude for his appointment, or satisfaction at his prospects'; and we are mystified at his obtuseness over the matter of the Siamese flag (does he *really* not see what Jukes is getting at, that his concern is not for the flag itself but for what it represents?) Mystified certainly, but also amused. Because we begin to realize that, consciously or unconsciously, MacWhirr's reaction to pretentiousness or excitability in others is a stolidness, a down-to-earth realism which, though it seems a trifle absurd at times, is the quality which will carry him through in the crisis. And our amusement turns from being simply at *his* expense to focusing on the people who fail to appreciate his true qualities. We sense increasingly that Conrad has something important to say in the contrast he makes between MacWhirr and the other characters.

The business of the Siamese flag highlights this contrast. Jukes is scornful of the idea of sailing under an ensign whose central motif is 'a ridiculous Noah's Ark elephant'. He is suspicious of and, as we see from his treatment of Bun Hin's clerk, feels himself superior to orientals in general. To be obliged to serve in a ship registered in Siam and sailing under Siamese protection constitutes a severe blow to his professional pride. To him, appearances are of first importance. To Mac-Whirr, on the other hand, they do not matter a jot. The important thing, for him, is that the *Nan-Shan* is under the control of men who know their business. There is perhaps more than a hint of teasing in the way, by his apparent incomprehension, he staunchly refuses to allow Jukes' agitation to ruffle his calm. The flag episode is important, however, not only because it points the contrast between these two characters but also because it reminds us of the increased vulnerability of the ship in the light of what happens in the forward 'tween-decks during and after the storm – at least as far as some of her crew are concerned. As Jukes later writes to his friend in the Western Ocean trade: 'it is an infernally lonely state for a ship to be going about the China seas with no proper consuls, not even a gunboat of her own anywhere, nor a body to go to in case of some trouble.'

MacWhirr, significantly, contains the trouble among the coolies without the help of a consul and, ironically, it is the very fact that the *Nan-Shan* is *not* British registered that prevents the dismissed and disgruntled second mate stirring up difficulties for his skipper at the end of the story. Clearly MacWhirr was right not to share Jukes' scepticism about the flag.

Conrad makes a second important point of contrast between MacWhirr and his fellows in his references to their letters to respective families and friends. The captain, on the one hand, is quite unselfconscious about what he writes home. He records events faithfully, setting them down 'with painstaking care upon many pages' when time and his duties allow. It does not concern him that these pages might be – and indeed are –

scrutinized by his steward or any other members of the *Nan-Shan*'s crew. Because, to him, his letters are essentially a vehicle for the accurate recording of his day-to-day experiences. Their format, tone and contents are so predictable that they have long ceased to be of any interest to Mrs MacWhirr and her two children. Indeed, communication between husband and wife seems to have broken down in more ways than one. The prettily named Lucy of long ago has become 'a pretentious person with a scraggy neck and a disdainful manner'; her ladylike demeanour and superior attitudes are in stark contrast to MacWhirr's quiet undemonstrativeness. We are told that 'the only secret of her life was her abject terror of the time when her husband would come home to stay for good'. Her outlook is shared by her children: Lydia, who is rather ashamed of her father and his calling, and Tom, who is 'frankly and utterly indifferent' to him. This failure on MacWhirr's part to make adequate contact with other people – either through the written word (as here) or through the spoken (as in his failure to respond with suitable appreciation to being offered the command of the *Nan-Shan*, in his dullness with Jukes over the Siamese flag, in his half-embarrassed references to his 'gamp' or his just audible, almost apologetic remark about the necessity for the ship to call at Fu-chau on the current trip) – is put into perspective when we read of his close understanding of and communication with the China seas. He may lisp and stutter in the language of society but he speaks eloquently and can interpret surely those daily encountered facts of life on board ship, 'facts, such as islands, sandbanks, reefs, swift and change-able currents – tangled facts that nevertheless speak to a seaman' like himself 'in a clear and definite language'. Mac-Whirr may have his inadequacies as a man of the world, but as a man of the sea he is worthily endowed.

But back to the matter of the letters. Look, by way of contrast, at Rout's chatty, jocular manner, his recording not of facts only but of opinions too, and the effect these have on his 'high-bosomed, jolly' wife. And notice how his articulate utterances reside under lock and key between instalments. There are clearly views in them which it would not do for his colleagues to peruse; but this is not the only reason for his secrecy. He is also aware of the wit and stylishness of what he writes and like so many people who share his gifts he prefers not to make too obvious a display of them. He is, indeed, rather a private man in a number of ways: perhaps we begin to understand his smile at the umbrella ritual and see its relation to his not imperceptive observation about MacWhirr's honesty being of the lumpish variety and his being a skipper of the 'dull ass' rather than the 'slippery rogue' sort.

For a further contrast, look at Jukes' letters, always striving to demonstrate his awareness of his surroundings and his fellows but seldom really hitting the mark with accuracy. He regards Rout as a good friend but does not perceive the engineer's pensively amused attitude towards him. He sees the *Nan-Shan* as a ship of brothers – a view which he will be tempted to re-examine before the storm is over. And, needless to say, in keeping with Conrad's intentions at this point in the tale, he misinterprets MacWhirr's character, feeling distinctly superior to his commander – 'sometimes you would think he hadn't sense enough to see anything wrong' – but he cannot fully fathom him and will not go out of his way to impress him. Jukes is a young man with much to learn.

So much for the ship, the setting and some of the characters. This first chapter concerns itself pretty well exclusively with establishing the background to the events to come. Pretty well – but not entirely. For there are one or two narrative clues left in the path of the watchful reader: the fall of the barometer, the likelihood of 'uncommonly dirty weather', the heaving of the 'oily sea . . . without a sparkle' and the 'queer white misty patch in the sky like a halo of the sun'. And, perhaps most important of all, the fact the MacWhirr has never experienced a really bad storm:

Captain MacWhirr had sailed over the surface of the oceans

as some men go skimming over the years of existence to sink gently into a placid grave, ignorant of life to the last, without ever having been made to see all it may contain of perfidy, of violence, and of terror.

With this ominous statement and its suggestion that the story we are about to read may be interpreted on more than the simple narrative level, we are led on into the action.

2

Chapter 2 depicts the rising of the storm and its effect on the men aboard the *Nan-Shan*. It falls roughly into four sections in which passages of striking and evocative description of the sea and weather are made to alternate with an account of the reactions of the crew both to the conditions they are experiencing and to each other. But we begin with an elaboration of the theme of MacWhirr's inexperience of typhoons that was stated briefly at the end of the first chapter:

The wisdom of his country had pronounced by means of an Act of Parliament that before he could be considered as fit to take charge of a ship he should be able to answer certain simple questions on the subject of circular storms such as hurricanes, cyclones, typhoons; and apparently he had answered them, since he was now in command of the *Nan-Shan* in the China Seas during the season of typhoons. But if he had answered he remembered nothing of it.

It is typical of MacWhirr that he should apply the understatement 'dirty weather' to something as cataclysmic as a typhoon, but he knows what a typhoon means for all that.

Some hours have passed since the 'fine morning' and the setting in at about ten o'clock of the cross-swell which we are told did little to disturb the ship's passengers. Things are different now. There is a distinct unpleasantness and unnaturalness about the afternoon which disturbs everyone from the captain downwards. A languor pervades the entire vessel.

Even the smoke 'struggled with difficulty out of the funnel, and instead of streaming away spread itself out like an infernal sort of cloud, smelling of sulphur and raining soot all over the deck'. We are reminded of nothing so strongly as of a scene in hell. It is theme to which the author returns on more than one occasion later in the story.

As the swell builds up from the north-east we encounter increasing references to the ship's lurching and rolling, to the 'floundering' of men and vessel. Irritation rising to positive anger affects the whole crew. Down in the overheated engine-room and stokehold even inanimate objects seem to be endowed with the capacity for rage: we hear the 'angry clangs and scrapes of metal, as if men with limbs of iron and throats of bronze had been quarrelling down there'. The stokers turn on the second engineer in reckless fashion, slamming their furnace doors 'with the fury of despair'. The second engineer, in his turn, takes things out on Jukes, who has already suffered an 'unprovoked attack' from his captain. So much for the 'brotherly' nature of relations between the crew, as Conrad remarks with some irony.

For all this growing discord on the *Nan-Shan*, MacWhirr manages to retain something of his generally phlegmatic outlook on things. While Jukes and Harry, the second engineer, indulge in brooding conjecture about the source of the weather, as if it had some supernatural origin, their literal captain turns his slow, impassive thinking to the possibility of dismissing the engineer because of his violent nature, to quibbling with Jukes over his expression about having his head 'tied up in a woollen blanket', to questioning the logicality of his mate's assertion that the weather is enough to make a saint swear or, later on, to misunderstanding his reference to the coolies as 'passengers'. Even so, there is clearly more irritability than usual in his manner; Jukes is moved to remark that 'somebody's put a new inside to my old man. Here's temper if you like.'

This section of character reaction and interaction is followed by another piece of illuminating description. From watching

93

the antics of our fellow men on the steamer, we look out at the portentous sunset: we observe nothing more than 'an expiring brown, rayless glow'. There is a dense bank of cloud to the north, olive-tinted, sinister; it lies 'low and motionless on the sea, resembling a solid obstacle in the path of the ship'. The *Nan-Shan* goes floundering towards it 'like an exhausted creature driven to its death'. This sense of overwhelming and inevitable menace even invades Jukes' compiling of the log – 'heat very oppressive', he writes, and 'sunset threatening'. He rounds off his entry with a conclusion which has the air of having been reluctantly arrived at: 'every appearance of a typhoon coming on.' From this point forward, the description of the seas and the night which gathers rapidly about the ship seems calculated to emphasize the smallness and vulnerability of the vessel. We are reminded of the insignificance of man, of the immense courage needed for him to face his destiny and responsibilities, of the fact that *Typhoon* is not just a thrilling story of the sea but a metaphor about life and how we should approach its catastrophes.

The closing pages of this chapter bring us back to the men on board the *Nan-Shan* and their differing responses to the crisis with which they are faced. Our admiration for MacWhirr is heightened by the introduction of a new character: the unsympathetic, unpleasant, gloating second mate. He is a man who has neither love nor loyalty for the *Nan-Shan* and who will not commit himself to an open opinion about what lies in store for the ship, but enjoys the prospect of Jukes getting into hot water for voicing his views too freely. 'I've known some real good men get into trouble with their skippers,' he declares, for saying less than Jukes has. This second mate is a skulking, solitary man, bitter and untrustworthy. We would do well to watch out for mischief from him in the future.

As to MacWhirr himself, we are reminded particularly now of his qualities of facing facts squarely, of not giving way to fantasy, of not being shaken from his purpose by mere conjecture about something of which he has had no hard experience. Jukes is all for altering the course of the ship, going head-on into the waves in order to reduce her rolling motion, and steaming round the storm. His commander, however, has no time for such tactics, which he likens to the ideas he has been reading in one of the seafaring manuals he keeps in the chart-room or to Captain Wilson's 'storm-strategy'. To Mac-Whirr's simple understanding 'a gale is a gale' – that's a fact. And a full-powered steamship ought to be able to cope with it – that's another fact. He is more concerned about the realities of the extra fuel consumption that would be entailed by his changing course than about the speculation of what he might find in the eye of a typhoon.

This attitude provokes not only vexation in Jukes, but, we may note, 'astonished respect' as well. We are also aware at this stage of the atmosphere of isolation which is being developed about MacWhirr (we have already seen something of this in the poor relations he has with his family and colleagues). If he opts to sail round the storm he will need to explain a delay of two days in arriving at Fu-chau to people who will know nothing of the storm's existence. He is beginning to see the matter as a personal one. 'There's just so much dirty weather knocking about the world, and the proper thing is to go through it.' This is his 'belief matured in the course of meditative years', this is his 'confession of faith' and it has as much to do with life as with seamanship. It is worth noting that in the discussion with Jukes from which these sentiments are drawn we hear more from MacWhirr than at any other time in the story. It is a fact which the mate regards as verging on the miraculous. As far as Conrad is concerned, it is the captain of the *Nan-Shan* defining his role in life.

Conrad demonstrates a fine artistry in his organization of this part of *Typhoon*. Instead, after that baleful sunset, of describing the gradual build-up of this particular storm in detail, as a lesser writer might have done, he diverts us with Mac-Whirr's discussion of how to deal with storms in general. We thus experience an emotional lull before the ferocious onslaught of the wind and seas and the terrifying pitching and rolling of the ship that rouse her captain from his sleep. When he wakes he finds all hell let loose. The sense of his confrontation with the storm being a personal one is re-emphasized: once outside, he finds himself 'engaged with the wind in a sort of personal scuffle'. Conversation, in the teeth of the gale, is possible only in snatches. Yet he is undaunted. It is his destiny, after all, to face up to his storm, 'to confront whatever it might mean'.

3

After our first introduction to the tumult of the storm at the end of the last chapter, it comes as something of a relief to discover that while MacWhirr was resting, Jukes – in spite of the fact that he was not officially on duty – was using his initiative, taking necessary precautions to protect the *Nan-Shan* from the ravages of wind and waves. We are led to believe that perhaps the captain is not indispensable after all: 'Jukes was as ready a man as any half-dozen young mates that may be caught by casting a net upon the waters.' He has acted sensibly, organizing the putting up of the wheelhouse shutters, the positioning of the ventilator covers and the battening down of any hatches that are still unsecured. There is a heroic quality about him, 'he had pulled himself together on the instant', his voice is 'fresh, stentorian' and full of assumed authority. He looks good – perhaps he can save the situation by himself. There is no doubt that Conrad uses this moment to tempt his readers into making false assumptions about the first mate. But he soon puts us right. Look at how 'uncritically glad' he is when MacWhirr emerges from below. Jukes may be promising in some respects but he lacks the necessary stature and doggedness of his captain. He may act and speak intelligently, but in his heart he knows that he is not really up to coping with this sort of crisis alone. He is relieved at MacWhirr's appearance 'as though that man had, by simply coming on deck, taken most of the gale's weight upon his shoulders'. And the next words are crucial: 'such is the prestige, the privilege, and the burden of command.' MacWhirr's isolation, his responsibility for taking on the typhoon virtually singlehanded is as much professional as it is personal. From now on if we are watchful we will see his gradual emergence as the true hero of the story. 'Captain MacWhirr could expect no relief . . . from anyone on earth. Such is the loneliness of command.'

And now we begin to have a few doubts about Jukes. There seems, for all his awareness of the danger they are in, to be a forced optimism, an unjustified hopefulness about his assessment of the situation. He lacks MacWhirr's capacity for facing facts. Conrad underlines this quite simply by setting his misplaced confidence beside the actual horror of the storm. As he explains to MacWhirr the preparations he has made to secure the ship, we are told of 'a sudden lowering of darkness . . . falling before their vision like something palpable. It was as if the masked lights of the world had been turned down.' Again, he yells 'cheerily' to his silent skipper the opinion that they must have got the worst of it all at once. As if in mocking reply 'a faint burst of lightning quivered all round, as if flashed into a cavern – into a black and secret chamber of the sea, with a floor of foaming crests'. When, some time later, we find him trying to 'compose his mind and judge things coolly' against a background of the steamer's tumbling 'as if dropped back into a boiling cauldron', we know that he is far from capable of doing so. For it becomes increasingly apparent that Jukes cannot survive without MacWhirr's aid.

This dependence is brought home most forcibly in the moment when, driven away from MacWhirr by the motion of the ship and the fury of the gale and sheeting rain, Jukes grabs one of the rail-stanchions and hangs on to it for dear life, until an immense and towering wave snatches it from him. He is 'tossed, flung, and rolled in great volumes of water' and all the while he is threshing about he repeats in his mind the words 'My God! My God! My God! My God!' Significantly, the assistance which comes to him at this very moment is human, not divine – it comes in the form of MacWhirr, in the firm clasp of whose stout arms he finds safety. As if to emphasize the mate's growing reliance on and respect for his superior officer, Conrad refers to MacWhirr on several occasions here not by his name but as Jukes' 'captain', 'his commander'.

The reminders of Jukes' inadequacy come thick and fast now. He experiences distress; though he has 'seen some bad weather' this is 'so much beyond his powers of fancy' that he does not think any ship ever built could withstand it. He thinks of the typhoon as a personal enemy – he 'came out of it rather horrified, as though he had escaped some unparalleled outrage directed at his feelings'. He begins to lose faith in himself, this young man whose letters to his friend showed so much confidence in his own opinions. As he observes that two of the *Nan-Shan*'s lifeboats have been ripped from their davits and he peers through the pressing and impenetrable gloom of the night at the signs of desolation about him, he gives way to a sudden despair: 'a dull conviction seized upon Jukes that there was nothing to be done.' 'She's done for,' he tells himself, and there is a callousness in his added reflection that 'the men on board . . . no longer matter'; the ship cannot possibly survive. So long as MacWhirr keeps a hold on his mate, Jukes keeps his fears to himself and tries to check them; but once the two men become separated, his sense of utter loneliness (a loneliness for which, unlike his captain, he is untrained and unprepared) becomes all-consuming. He begins to give up; 'after a tense stiffening of every muscle' he lets himself go limp all over and succumbs to a feeling of great drowsiness. There is a vivid contrast between his offended and impatient reaction to the boatswain's physical contact with him on the bridge and his own utter dependence on the security afforded him by Mac-Whirr's 'firm clasp'. There is something mildly comic about the boatswain's arrival 'crawling on all fours against the wind' so that he finds the chief mate's legs with the top of his head. 'Immediately he crouched and began to explore Jukes' person upwards, with prudent, apologetic touches, as became an inferior.' But Jukes responds without either warmth or sympathy: 'what could that fraud of a bos'n want on the bridge?' His sentiment denies that very spirit of brotherhood of which he was so anxious to boast to his friend.

But if Jukes changes under the stress of the storm, MacWhirr remains very much himself. He speaks little, but the sound of his voice has a remarkable effect: though it is necessarily 'forced and ringing feebly' it has 'a penetrating effect of quietness in the enormous discord of noises'. The words it speaks are typical of its owner's unshakeable realism. There's no point in giving way to hysteria at the discovery of the loss of the boats – it serves no purpose, it 'can't be helped'. It 'stands to reason' that something must give under such an enormous hammering. The ship may nonetheless survive – she was built by reliable builders and her engine room is manned by a 'good man'. This is the calm to which Jukes must cling. They must take their chances . . .

4

Many of the ideas Conrad brings forward in Chapter 3 are developed further in its successor. We continue, for instance, to witness Jukes's uselessness and to admire MacWhirr's stoicism. There is no question but that 'the spell of the storm' has fallen on the chief mate. He remains indifferent to the information the boatswain has brought his captain 'as if rendered irresponsible by the force of the hurricane'. He is too engrossed in his own relationship with the storm to be in the least concerned about the fate of the coolies in the fore 'tween-deck. 'He was penetrated by it, absorbed by it.' He is benumbed more than he is aware; visions of his past life preoccupy him so that he does not, cannot act. Even when MacWhirr calls to him in a tone of deep concern he fails to respond. His heart has become 'corrupted by the storm' and rebels against the sense of discipline and duty which should have been bred into it by his training.

There is a deliberate irony in the fact that he is made to

appear, at this point in the story, much less admirable than the man he finds it so easy to criticize – the boatswain. We recall his opinion that the man is a fraud. We are left with his assertion to MacWhirr that he is 'a confounded fool' ringing in our ears. And yet the picture we are given of the boatswain's response to the crisis on board the *Nan-Shan* bears out the more readily his captain's estimation of him as a first-rate petty officer. There is courage and concern in his attitude to the huddle of sailors in the blackness of the port alleyway. He may not like their mutterings and near-indiscipline, but he does his best for them and sets out on the dangerous mission of procuring the light for which they ask, almost breaking his neck as he drops, unaided, into the coal bunker. There he is pitched wildly hither and thither by the motion of the ship, with the imminent likelihood of being struck down in the darkness by the coal-trimmer's slice that is 'sliding and clattering' about him at random. He knocks his head twice and is a little dazed. But for all that we are told that he thinks 'quickly, clearly, competently, like a seaman'. Unlike Jukes.

Unlike the second mate, as well. We have already been alerted to this man's shortcomings in the second chapter. Now the boatswain comes upon him in the lee of the wheelhouse, 'lying low, like a malignant little animal under a hedge'. Unlike Jukes, who is immobilized by the storm and *cannot* do his duty for the moment, the second simply *will* not do his. A little later MacWhirr finds him inside the wheelhouse, and when he questions his being there instead of lending a hand like the other officers, the mate's reply is that it is his watch below. In his cynicism, he blames MacWhirr for the crisis through which they are passing. He is convinced that they will not see another daybreak. MacWhirr, however, knows how to deal with him. There is a gritty humour in the way in which he tells the helmsman, Hackett, who is sticking heroically to his post ('as if forgotten by all his shipmates'), not to be discouraged by the second's profound pessimism: 'don't pay any attention to what that man says . . . he isn't on duty.'

For MacWhirr, there is still hope. He notes with satisfaction the arrival of a new day. He is determined that a proper discipline and order be maintained on the *Nan-Shan*, for only by these means can they hope to win through. His commands to Jukes and the boatswain are firm, not to be questioned. He will not permit the fighting to continue among the coolies. They must be sorted out, settled. MacWhirr has a deep 'sense of the fitness of things'. And we are still reminded of the authority and inspiration that others find in the sound of his voice. Below, in the engine room, Jukes listens as that 'small voice shoved aside the shouting hurricane quietly'. For a moment, it seems to him almost as if MacWhirr has acquired a kind of divinity: he speaks back up the tube 'as if into a silence of enlightened comprehension dwelling alone up there with the storm'. There is still, too, the captain's marvellous understatement and directness of action. He tells Rout, again through the speaking-tube, that 'the second mate's lost . . . lost his nerve . . . damned awkward circumstance'. There is no fuss or hysteria in his reaction to the second's attack on him; 'rushed at me . . . Just now. Had to knock him down.' That's all there is to it.

Conrad's detailed examination of the different reactions of these men to the conditions they are encountering serves to highlight an important fact. Though Jukes, the men in the port alleyway and the second mate have their shortcomings, Mac-Whirr is not alone in the stand he makes against the storm. The boatswain, the helmsman, Rout and his engineers are all sticking to their posts, doing their respective duties in the face of hideous difficulties. The survival of the *Nan-Shan* is seen to depend at least as much on their responsiveness and teamwork as on MacWhirr's inspired command.

In the second chapter, we noticed how Conrad described the progress of the *Nan-Shan* towards the storm as being 'like an exhausted creature driven to its death', while her captain's struggle against the typhoon was likened to a scuffle between two people rather than between man and nature. The present chapter sees a continuation of this idea of both ship and storm as living beings. Our attention is drawn, for example, to the vulnerability of the 'slender body of the ship' and to her engine room as having 'the functions of a living organism'. The pulsation of her engines themselves is likened to 'the beat of the ship's heart'. Meanwhile, the storm's 'howls and shrieks seemed to take on . . . something of the human character, of human rage and pain'. By this means Conrad conditions our minds, enabling us to appreciate the more readily the very striking parallel which he wishes to draw between the external conflict of ship and storm and the vicious riot among the coolies in the 'tween-decks.

It is in his description of the tumult down below, as witnessed both by the boatswain and by Jukes, that Conrad creates most vividly an impression of dangerous anarchy. In their struggle to retain possession of their dollars, the coolies lose all semblance of humanity. 'A great howl came from that mass that had the slant of fallen earth.' All is contorted: 'a man went sliding over, open-eyed, on his back, straining with uplifted arms for nothing: and another came bounding like a detached stone with his head between his legs and his hands clenched.' Or fragmented: the boatswain witnesses 'an inextricable confusion of heads and shoulders, naked soles kicking upwards, fists raised, tumbling backs, legs, pigtails, faces', while 'Jukes saw a head bang the deck violently, two thick calves waving on high, muscular arms twined round a naked body, a yellow face, open-mouthed and with a set wild stare, look up and slide away'. Or heaped together: here, a 'mound of writhing bodies', on the hatchway ladder a swarm of coolies 'like bees on a branch', 'a crawling, stirring cluster'. The noise they make, too, has little to do with humanity or reason (utterly unlike the voice of MacWhirr): we hear 'rancorous, guttural cries' and a 'strange panting'. In the next chapter we are told quite explicitly that such sounds – incomprehensible, hooting – do not seem to belong to any human language.

No wonder the boatswain refers to the scene as 'a regular

little hell'. And it is precisely because MacWhirr sees it as a
human extension of the typhoon raging about his head that
he decides it must be confronted, coped with and set in order.
The identification of storm with riot, the hell outside with that
within, is carried through into the next chapter. 'It seemed,'
we are told, 'that an eddy of the hurricane . . . had set all these
bodies whirling like dust'. The uproar when the boatswain
opens the door so that the sailors can enter the 'tween-decks
area is likened to 'a tempestuous tumult' with 'gusts of screaming
dying away'. Moreover, it seems to Jukes, once he has organized
the pacification of the coolies, the clearing of the debris and
the rigging up of lifelines, that 'in his mad struggle down there
he had overcome the wind somehow'. We are not, therefore,
surprised, when the wind starts to rise again after the lull at
the centre of the typhoon, that its doing so is conveyed in human
terms – 'the growth of a multiple clamour, marching and
expanding . . . the chant of a tramping multitude'.

5

Chapter 5 opens with the moment of greatest danger to the
Nan-Shan in her entire battle with the elements:

> Nobody – not even Captain MacWhirr, who alone on deck
> caught sight of a white line of foam coming on at such a
> height that he couldn't believe his eyes – nobody was to
> know the steepness of that sea and the awful depth of the
> hollow the hurricane had scooped out behind the running
> wall of water.

Jukes, below in the engine room, cannot believe that any human
being could survive the 'tearing crash and . . . swirling, raving
tumult . . . as though the ship had darted under the foot of a
cataract'. And yet, to his amazement, all it does is to occasion
a pause in MacWhirr's conversation with him about what he
wants done with the coolies. Jukes, Beale, Rout – who do not
even see the wave – are stunned by its effect. Their captain,

on the other hand, remains as passionless as the telegraph by means of which he controls the advance of the ship. To the occupants of the engine room, he is a kind of godlike, omnipotent disposer; he is the voice that keeps the hurricane out of Jukes' ear. He maintains his customary unruffled attitude to the conduct of the ship. The coolies, who are very much his responsibility, must be given the same chance as the crew. He must do 'what's fair by them'. If the *Nan-Shan* has to go down, he would not like to think of her doing so with a riot aboard. Everything must be put systematically in order. When he comes to tell Jukes of how he dealt with the second mate, again it is with his usual understatement: 'I had to give him a push.'

As they prepare to enter the second phase of the storm, knowing that the worst is yet to come, he reiterates his 'confession of faith':

> 'Don't be put out by anything . . . Keep her facing it. They may say what they like, but the heaviest seas run with the wind. Facing it – always facing it – that's the way to get through. You are a young sailor. Face it. That's enough for any man. Keep a cool head.'

The immediate consequence of this advice is that Jukes 'experienced an access of confidence, a sensation that came from outside like a warm breath, and made him feel equal to every demand'. Indeed, Chapter 5 shows the mate's steady return from the doldrums of despair which gripped him soon after the first attack of the storm. The change begins with his being utterly bowled over, 'defeated' by MacWhirr's doggedness and implacability. Then he is roused to hot scorn by Rout's suggestion that the deck officers are underemployed. Finally, he is stung to a frenzy at the second engineer's jibe that sailors and firemen are supposed to assist each other. He goes back to the port alleyway to organize the hands into a party to deal with the coolies. His impetuosity is infectious and carries along with him the very men whose insolence worried the boatswain. He is determined to fulfil his duties and to ensure that they fulfil theirs. '*He* couldn't hang back. They shouldn't.'

It is interesting that shortly after this restoration of the old, more buoyant Jukes through the example of his captain and the taunting of his fellow officers, MacWhirr himself experiences the only moment of real self-doubt that is to arrest him during the entire adventure. Returned to the chart-room to consult the barometer, he is deeply disturbed at the disorder that he discovers in 'that place where he used to live tidily'. The true magnitude of the storm comes home to him not through even that huge wave which swept the *Nan-Shan* from end to end, but through the chaos which has been inflicted on his own domestic arrangements. He is chilled by the realization. A feeling of dismay 'reached the very seat of his composure.' As he replaces the box of matches it occurs to him that perhaps he may never have occasion to use it again. Sobered by the thought, he sits 'unseen . . . isolated' . . . weary. But the moment and the awareness also bring a new – if underplayed – resolution: 'I shouldn't like to lose her.' Having towelled himself down, he emerges on deck briskly. 'She may come out of it yet.' His heroism though undemonstrative is unquestionable. As Conrad reminds us at the end of the chapter:

> The hurricane, with its power to madden the seas, to sink ships, to uproot trees, to overturn strong walls and dash the very birds of the air to the ground, had found this taciturn man in its path, and, doing its utmost, had managed to wring out a few words . . . 'I wouldn't like to lose her.'

6

Calm is restored. The *Nan-Shan* reaches Fu-chau intact and there is a return to relaxed normality. It is interesting to see how Conrad takes up again certain aspects of the narrative technique he introduced in the first chapter – in particular, the revelation and contrasting of characters through their letters to family or friends. Some commentators have criticized Conrad for not giving a full account of the second, apparently worse, phase of the storm. They feel it a weakness that he should be content merely to record that the *Nan-Shan* came through it safely. What they seem to miss is the fact that by describing in detail the further horrors that the ship had to face, the author might well have reduced considerably the force of what he had already achieved in his account of the typhoon's impact on men who had no previous experience of tackling such extreme conditions. In any case, as we have seen, descriptive writing, however powerful and evocative, was not his first consideration in writing the story. As it stands, it possesses a satisfying structural balance, the chapters of calm framing those of turmoil in a way which enables them to make their point clearly, without being overshadowed by the more obvious attractions of the storm-writing. For it is surely Conrad's intention that, by comparing the two outermost chapters, we see exactly what sort of lasting impression their experiences have made on the men of the *Nan-Shan*. In other words, when we speak of 'relaxed normality' what, in human terms, do we think of as truly 'normal'?

One or two of the reactions are almost certainly what we would expect. The second mate, for instance, shows nothing but resentment. Ignoring the fact that he has been brought through so apocalyptic a catastrophe unscathed, this 'meagre little man', shaking his fist at the ship, declares 'quivering with passion' at his dismissal that 'there's a fellow there that ain't fit to have the command of a scow'. He is only prevented from stirring up trouble for MacWhirr because the vessel is Siamese registered, not British, and he cannot be sure that the authorities will take any notice of him. Set beside his captain's heroism, the second's smallminded conduct only serves to heighten the sense of solitary unpleasantness in his character to which Conrad drew our attention earlier. Solomon Rout, on the other hand, demonstrates his proverbial wisdom in appreciating that MacWhirr has in fact 'done something rather clever', something so clever that his wife could not possibly understand its full implications. The typhoon may have prompted him to reflect more closely on the shortness of life, that he and his wife are 'not growing younger' and that he ought perhaps to start considering settling down at home, but, for the present, he will stay with his ship and skipper. He knows 'too well the value of a good billet'.

The surprise comes when we turn to Jukes. Here is a man whose very survival, spiritual as well as physical, has depended entirely on the solid reliability of his captain's example. We have watched his collapse under the stress of the storm and we have watched his revival, inspired by the unshakeable determination of the storm's enemy. But what has he learned during his ordeal? Precious little, it would seem. Returning to normality for him means returning to misdirected self-confidence, a marked hysteria in his approach to crises and a patent lack of insight when it comes to evaluating his fellow men. He still fails to get his priorities right, continuing to resent the Siamese flag and refusing to allow the wisdom of MacWhirr's opinion that it is the quality of a ship's crew that matters, not the colours under which she sails. He remains fearful and suspicious of the Chinese and wants to shuffle them off the *Nan-Shan* as opportunely as possible without bothering to sort out the problem of their lost dollars. He cannot, at first, trust Mac-Whirr's judgment over the matter of the coolies' money, but allows himself to be whipped into a frenzy at the thought of trouble and reacts with foolish impulsiveness in leading an armed charge on the chart-room. In this action, as at the beginning of the typhoon, he lives up to his captain's criticism that he never waits to see how trouble will develop but rushes out to meet it half-way. It is perhaps worth noting in passing just how accurate is MacWhirr's reading of men and situations in contrast to that of some others of the *Nan-Shan*'s crew. It is possible that Jukes grudgingly accepts MacWhirr's solution of the coolie problem in the end, encouraged to do so by Rout's assertion that it 'was plainly the only thing that could be done'. But the most disturbing aspect of his attitude is the deep ingratitude of his final comment on the man to whom he owes so much: 'I think that he got out of it very well for such a stupid man.' Such, Conrad is saying, is human nature once the pressures are past.

A similar profound irony is to be found in the reception of MacWhirr's letter to his wife 'in the drawing-room of the forty-pound house'. Compared, as at the beginning of the story, with the steward's absorbed interest in what the captain has to say, all she can do is glance wearily here and there into the many pages. She does not give him a chance – 'she couldn't be really expected to understand all these ship affairs'. Her reading is perfunctory, thoughtless. Heedless of the difficulties and discomforts he has undergone, the only moment at which her interest is at all stimulated is when she mistakenly understands him to be intending a visit home. She is irritated and vexed: 'he had never had such a good salary before.' Her only concern in leafing through the remainder of the letter is to ensure that her routine is *not* to be disturbed. She knows nothing of MacWhirr's adventures, nor does she wish to know. She little realizes in her selfishness how close that good salary came to being terminated. Conrad underlines the cruel complacency of her attitude by mentioning the comforts of her home – the 'plush-bottomed and gilt hammock-chair near a tiled fireplace, with Japanese fans on the mantel and a glow of coals in the grate'. A far cry from the devastated chart-room. Such, we hear Conrad saying, is the way the world treats its great men, its heroes. With misunderstanding and indifference. Not that MacWhirr, this 'ordinary, irresponsive, and unruffled' man, would have known how to deal with recognition or adulation. What really matters is that *we* should be able to see just how misguided the second mate, Jukes and Mrs MacWhirr are; that theirs are the false values, MacWhirr's the sound ones. It is typical of Conrad's genius that he should leave us not with a neatly obvious ending to his tale, but one that invites us to consider further its wider, its universal implications.

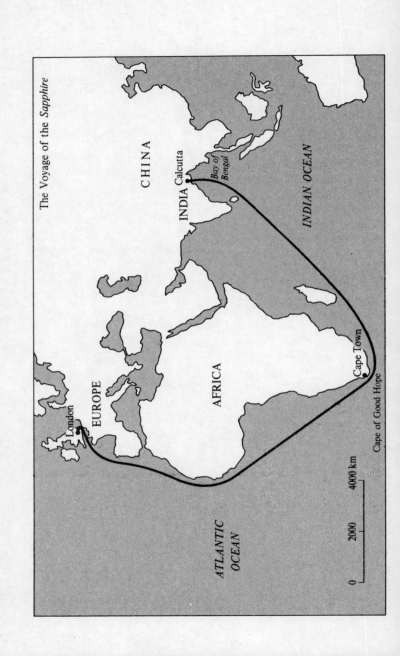

The Voyage of the *Sapphire*

THE BLACK MATE

A good many years ago there were several ships loading at the Jetty, London Dock. I am speaking here of the 'eighties of the last century, of the time when London had plenty of fine ships in the docks, though not so many fine buildings in its streets.

The ships at the Jetty were fine enough; they lay one behind the other; and the *Sapphire*, third from the end, was as good as the rest of them, and nothing more. Each ship at the Jetty had, of course, her chief officer on board. So had every other ship in dock.

The policeman at the gates knew them all by sight, without being able to say at once, without thinking, to what ship any particular man belonged. As a matter of fact, the mates of the ships then lying in the London Dock were like the majority of officers in the Merchant Service – a steady, hard-working, staunch, unromantic-looking set of men, belonging to various classes of society, but with the professional stamp obliterating the personal characteristics, which were not very marked anyhow.

This last was true of them all, with the exception of the mate of the *Sapphire*. Of him the policemen could not be in doubt. This one had a presence.

He was noticeable to them in the street from a great distance; and when in the morning he strode down the Jetty to his ship, the lumpers and the dock labourers rolling the bales and trundling the cases of cargo on their hand-trucks would remark to each other:

'Here's the black mate coming along.'

That was the name they gave him, being a gross lot, who could have no appreciation of the man's dignified bearing. And to call him black was the superficial impressionism of the ignorant.

Of course, Mr Bunter, the mate of the *Sapphire*, was not black. He was no more black then you or I, and certainly as white as any chief mate of a ship in the whole of the Port of London. His complexion was of the sort that did not take the tan easily; and I happen to know that the poor fellow had had a month's illness just before he joined the *Sapphire*.

From this you will perceive that I knew Bunter. Of course I knew him. And, what's more, I knew his secret at the time, this secret which – never mind just now. Returning to Bunter's personal appearance, it was nothing but ignorant prejudice on the part of the foreman stevedore to say, as he did in my hearing: 'I bet he's a furriner of some sort.' A man may have black hair without being set down for a Dago. I have known a West-country sailor, boatswain of a fine ship, who looked more Spanish than any Spaniard afloat I've ever met. He looked like a Spaniard in a picture.

Competent authorities tell us that this earth is to be finally the inheritance of men with dark hair and brown eyes. It seems that already the great majority of mankind is dark-haired in various shades. But it is only when you meet one that you notice how men with really black hair, black as ebony, are rare. Bunter's hair was absolutely black, black as a raven's wing. He wore, too, all his beard (clipped, but a good length all the same), and his eyebrows were thick and bushy. Add to this steely blue eyes, which in a fair-haired man would have been nothing so extraordinary, but in that sombre framing made a startling contrast, and you will easily understand that Bunter was noticeable enough. If it had not been for the quietness of his movements, for the general soberness of his demeanour, one would have given him credit for a fiercely passionate nature.

Of course, he was not in his first youth; but if the expression 'in the force of his age' has any meaning, he realized it completely. He was a tall man, too, though rather spare. Seeing him from his poop indefatigably busy with his duties, Captain Ashton, of the clipper ship *Elsinore*, lying just ahead of the

Sapphire, remarked once to a friend that 'Johns has got somebody there to hustle his ship along for him'.

Captain Johns, master of the *Sapphire*, having commanded ships for many years, was well known without being much respected or liked. In the company of his fellows he was either neglected or chaffed. The chaffing was generally undertaken by Captain Ashton, a cynical and teasing sort of man. It was Captain Ashton who permitted himself the unpleasant joke of proclaiming once in company that 'Johns is of the opinion that every sailor above forty years of age ought to be poisoned – shipmasters in actual command excepted'.

It was in a City restaurant, where several well-known shipmasters were having lunch together. There was Captain Ashton, florid and jovial, in a large white waistcoat and with a yellow rose in his buttonhole; Captain Sellers in a sack-coat, thin and pale-faced, with his iron-gray hair tucked behind his ears, and, but for the absence of spectacles, looking like an ascetical mild man of books; Captain Bell, a bluff sea-dog with hairy fingers, in blue serge and a black felt hat pushed far back off his crimson forehead. There was also a very young shipmaster, with a little fair moustache and serious eyes, who said nothing, and only smiled faintly from time to time.

Captain Johns, very much startled, raised his perplexed and credulous glance, which, together with a low and horizontally wrinkled brow, did not make a very intellectual *ensemble*. This impression was by no means mended by the slightly pointed form of his bald head.

Everybody laughed outright, and, thus guided, Captain Johns ended by smiling rather sourly, and attempted to defend himself. It was all very well to joke, but nowadays, when ships, to pay anything at all, had to be driven hard on the passage and in harbour, the sea was no place for elderly men. Only young men and men in their prime were equal to modern conditions of push and hurry. Look at the great firms: almost every single one of them was getting rid of men showing any signs of age. He, for one, didn't want any oldsters on board his ship.

And, indeed, in this opinion Captain Johns was not singular. There was at that time a lot of seamen, with nothing against them but that they were grizzled, wearing out the soles of their last pair of boots on the pavements of the City in the heart-breaking search for a berth.

Captain Johns added with a sort of ill-humoured innocence that from holding that opinion to thinking of poisoning people was a very long step.

This seemed final but Captain Ashton would not let go his joke.

'Oh, yes. I am sure you would. You said distinctly "of no use". What's to be done with men who are "of no use"? You are a kind-hearted fellow, Johns. I am sure that if only you thought it over carefully you would consent to have them poisoned in some painless manner.'

Captain Sellers twitched his thin, sinuous lips.

'Make ghosts of them,' he suggested, pointedly.

At the mention of ghosts Captain Johns became shy, in his perplexed, sly, and unlovely manner.

Captain Ashton winked.

'Yes. And then perhaps you would get a chance to have a communication with the world of spirits. Surely the ghosts of seamen should haunt ships. Some of them would be sure to call on an old shipmate.'

Captain Sellers remarked drily:

'Don't raise his hopes like this. It's cruel. He won't see anything. You know, Johns, that nobody has ever seen a ghost.'

At this intolerable provocation Captain Johns came out of his reserve. With no perplexity whatever, but with a positive passion of credulity giving momentary lustre to his dull little eyes, he brought up a lot of authenticated instances. There were books and books full of instances. It was merest ignorance to deny supernatural apparitions. Cases were published every month in a special newspaper. Professor Cranks saw ghosts daily. And Professor Cranks was no small potatoes either. One of the biggest scientific men living. And there was that newspaper fellow – what's his name? – who had a girl-ghost visitor. He printed in his paper things she said to him. And to say there were no ghosts after that!

'Why, they have been photographed! What more proof do you want?'

Captain Johns was indignant. Captain Bell's lips twitched, but Captain Ashton protested now.

'For goodness' sake don't keep him going with that. And by the by, Johns, who's that hairy pirate you've got for your new mate? Nobody in the Dock seems to have seen him before.'

Captain Johns, pacified by the change of subjects answered simply that Willy, the tobacconist at the corner of Fenchurch Street, had sent him along.

Willy, his shop, and the very house in Fenchurch Street, I believe, are gone now. In his time, wearing a careworn, absent-minded look on his pasty face, Willy served with tobacco many southern-going ships out of the Port of London. At certain times of the day the shop would be full of shipmasters. They sat on casks, they lounged against the counter.

Many a youngster found his first lift in life there; many a man got a sorely needed berth by simply dropping in for four pennyworth of birds'-eye at an auspicious moment. Even Willy's assistant, a red-headed, uninterested, delicate-looking young fellow, would hand you across the counter sometimes a bit of valuable intelligence with your box of cigarettes, in a whisper, lips hardly moving, thus: 'The *Bellona*, South Dock. Second officer wanted. You may be in time for it if you hurry up.'

And didn't one just fly!

'Oh, Willy sent him,' said Captain Ashton. 'He's a very striking man. If you were to put a red sash round his waist and a red handkerchief round his head he would look exactly like one of them buccaneering chaps that made men walk the plank and carried women off into captivity. Look out, Johns, he don't cut your throat for you and run off with the *Sapphire*. What ship has he come out of last?'

Captain Johns, after looking up credulously as usual, wrinkled his brow, and said placidly that the man had seen better days. His name was Bunter.

'He's had command of a Liverpool ship, the *Samaria*, some years ago. He lost her in the Indian Ocean, and had his certificate suspended for a year. Ever since then he has not been able to get another command. He's been knocking about in the Western Ocean trade lately.'

'That accounts for him being a stranger to everybody about the Docks,' Captain Ashton concluded as they rose from table.

Captain Johns walked down to the Dock after lunch. He was short of stature and slightly bandy. His appearance did not inspire the generality of mankind with esteem; but it must have been otherwise with his employers. He had the reputation of being an uncomfortable commander, meticulous in trifles, always nursing a grievance of some sort and incessantly nagging. He was not a man to kick up a row with you and be done with it, but to say nasty things in a whining voice; a man capable of making one's life a perfect misery if he took a dislike to an officer.

That very evening I went to see Bunter on board, and sympathized with him on his prospects for the voyage. He was subdued. I suppose a man with a secret locked up in his breast loses his buoyancy. And there was another reason why I could not expect Bunter to show a great elasticity of spirits. For one thing he had been very seedy lately, and besides – but of that later.

Captain Johns had been on board that afternoon and had loitered and dodged about his chief mate in a manner which had annoyed Bunter exceedingly.

'What could he mean?' he asked with calm exasperation. 'One would think he suspected I had stolen something and tried to see in what pocket I had stowed it away; or that somebody told him I had a tail and he wanted to find out how I managed to conceal it. I don't like to be approached from behind several times in one afternoon in that creepy way and then to be looked up at suddenly in front from under my elbow. Is it a new sort of peep-bo game? It doesn't amuse me. I am no longer a baby.'

I assured him that if anyone were to tell Captain Johns that he – Bunter – had a tail, Johns would manage to get himself to believe the story in some mysterious manner. He would. He was suspicious and credulous to an inconceivable degree. He would believe any silly tale, suspect any man of anything, and crawl about with it and ruminate the stuff, and turn it over and over in his mind in the most miserable, inwardly whining perplexity. He would take the meanest possible view in the end, and discover the meanest possible course of action by a sort of natural genius for that sort of thing.

Bunter also told me that the mean creature had crept all over the ship on his little, bandy legs, taking him along to grumble and whine to about a lot of trifles. Crept about the decks like a wretched insect – like a cockroach, only not so lively.

Thus did the self-possessed Bunter express himself with great disgust. Then, going on with his usual stately deliberation, made sinister by the frown of his jet-black eyebrows:

'And the fellow is mad, too. He tried to be sociable for a bit, and could find nothing else but to make big eyes at me, and ask me if I believed "in communication beyond the grave". Communication beyond – I didn't know what he meant at first. I didn't know what to say. "A very solemn subject, Mr Bunter," says he. "I've given a great deal of study to it".'

Had Johns lived on shore he would have been the predestined prey of fraudulent mediums; or even if he had had any decent opportunities between the voyages. Luckily for him, when in England, he lived somewhere far away in Leytonstone, with a maiden sister ten years older than himself, a fearsome virago twice his size, before whom he trembled. It was said she bullied him terribly in general; and in the particular instance of his spiritualistic leanings she had her own views.

These leanings were to her simply satanic. She was reported as having declared that, 'With God's help, she would prevent that fool from giving himself up to the Devil.' It was beyond doubt that Johns' secret ambition was to get into personal communication with the spirits of the dead – if only his sister would let him. But she was adamant. I was told that while in London he had to account to her for every penny of the money he took with him in the morning, and for every hour of his time. And she kept the bankbook, too.

Bunter (he had been a wild youngster, but he was well connected; had ancestors; there was a family tomb somewhere in the home counties) – Bunter was indignant, perhaps on account of his own dead. Those steely-blue eyes of his flashed with positive ferocity out of that black-bearded face. He impressed me – there was so much dark passion in his leisurely contempt.

'The cheek of the fellow! Enter into relations with . . . A mean little cad like this! It would be an impudent intrusion. He wants to enter! . . . What is it? A new sort of snobbishness or what?'

I laughed outright at this original view of spiritism – or whatever the ghost craze is called. Even Bunter himself condescended to smile. But it was an austere, quickly vanished smile. A man in his almost, I may say, tragic position couldn't be expected – you understand. He was really worried. He was ready eventually to put up with any dirty trick in the course of the voyage. A man could not expect much consideration should he find himself at the mercy of a fellow like Johns. A misfortune is a misfortune, and there's an end of it. But to be bored by mean, low-spirited, inane ghost stories in the Johns style, all the way out to Calcutta and back again, was an intolerable apprehension to be under. Spiritism was indeed a solemn subject to think about in that light. Dreadful, even!

Poor fellow! Little we both thought that before very long he himself . . . However, I could give him no comfort. I was rather appalled myself.

Bunter had also another annoyance that day. A confounded berthing master came on board on some pretence or other, but in reality, Bunter thought, simply impelled by an incon-venient curiosity – inconvenient to Bunter, that is. After some beating about the bush, that man suddenly said:

'I can't help thinking. I've seen you before somewhere, Mr Mate. If I heard your name, perhaps——'

Bunter – that's the worst of a life with a mystery in it – was much alarmed. It was very likely that the man had seen him before – worse luck to his excellent memory. Bunter himself could not be expected to remember every casual dock walloper he might have had to do with. Bunter brazened it out by turning upon the man, making use of that impressive, black-as-night sternness of expression his unusual hair furnished him with:

'My name's Bunter, sir. Does that enlighten your inquisitive intellect? And I don't ask what your name may be. I don't want to know. I've no use for it, sir. An individual who calmly tells me to my face that he is *not sure* if he has seen me before, either means to be impudent or is no better than a worm, sir. Yes, I said a worm – a blind worm!'

Brave Bunter. That was the line to take. He fairly drove the beggar out of the ship, as if every word had been a blow. But the pertinacity of that brass-bound Paul Pry was astonishing. He cleared out of the ship, of course, before Bunter's ire, not saying anything, and only trying to cover up his retreat by a sickly smile. But once on the Jetty he turned deliberately round, and set himself to stare in dead earnest at the ship. He remained planted there like a mooring-post, absolutely motionless, and with his stupid eyes winking no more than a pair of cabin portholes.

What could Bunter do? It was awkward for him, you know. He could not go and put his head into the bread-locker. What he did was to take up a position abaft the mizzen-rigging, and stare back as unwinking as the other. So they remained, and I don't know which of them grew giddy first; but the man on the Jetty, not having the advantage of something to hold on to, got tired the soonest, flung his arm, giving the contest up, as it were, and went away at last.

Bunter told me he was glad the *Sapphire*, 'that gem amongst ships' as he alluded to her sarcastically, was going to sea next day. He had had enough of the Dock. I understood his impatience. He had steeled himself against any possible worry the voyage might bring, though it is clear enough now that he was not prepared for the extraordinary experience that was awaiting him already, and in no other part of the world than the Indian Ocean itself; the very part of the world where the poor fellow had lost his ship and had broken his luck, as it seemed for good and all, at the same time.

As to his remorse in regard to a certain secret action of his life, well, I understand that a man of Bunter's fine character would suffer not a little. Still, between ourselves, and without the slightest wish to be cynical, it cannot be denied that with the noblest of us the fear of being found out enters for some considerable part into the composition of remorse. I didn't say this in so many words to Bunter, but, as the poor fellow harped a bit on it, I told him that there were skeletons in a good many honest cupboards, and that, as to his own particular guilt, it wasn't writ large on his face for everybody to see – so he needn't worry as to that. And besides, he would be gone to sea in about twelve hours from now.

He said there was some comfort in that thought, and went off then to spend his last evening for many months with his wife. For all his wildness, Bunter had made no mistake in his marrying. He had married a lady. A perfect lady. She was a dear little woman, too. As to her pluck, I, who know what times they had to go through, I cannot admire her enough for it. Real, hard-wearing every day and day after day pluck that only a woman is capable of when she is of the right sort – the undismayed sort I would call it.

The black mate felt this parting with his wife more than any of the previous ones in all the years of bad luck. But she was of the undismayed kind, and showed less trouble in her gentle face than the black-haired, buccaneer-like, but dignified mate of the *Sapphire*. It may be that her conscience was less disturbed than her husband's. Of course, his life had no secret places for her; but a woman's conscience is somewhat more resourceful in finding good and valid excuses. It depends greatly on the person that needs them, too.

They had agreed that she should not come down to the Dock to see him off. 'I wonder you care to look at me at all,' said the sensitive man. And she did not laugh.

Bunter was very sensitive; he left her rather brusquely at the last. He got on board in good time, and produced the usual impression on the mud-pilot in the broken-down straw hat who took the *Sapphire* out of dock. The river-man was very polite to the dignified, striking-looking chief mate. 'The five-inch manila for the check-rope, Mr – Bunter, thank you – Mr Bunter, please.' The sea-pilot who left the 'gem of ships' heading comfortably down Channel off Dover told some of his friends that, this voyage, the *Sapphire* had for chief mate a man who seemed a jolly sight too good for old Johns. 'Bunter's his name. I wonder where he's sprung from? Never seen him before in any ship I piloted in or out all these years. He's the sort of man you don't forget. You couldn't. A thorough good sailor, too. And won't old Johns just worry his head off! Unless the old fool should take fright at him – for he does not seem the sort of man that would let himself be put upon without letting you know what he thinks of you. And that's exactly what old Johns would be more afraid of than of anything else.'

As this is really meant to be the record of a spiritualistic experience which came, if not precisely to Captain Johns himself, at any rate to his ship, there is no use in recording the other events of the passage out. It was an ordinary passage, the crew was an ordinary crew, the weather was of the usual kind. The black mate's quiet, sedate method of going to work had given a sober tone to the life of the ship. Even in gales of wind everything went on quietly somehow.

There was only one severe blow which made things fairly lively for all hands for full four-and-twenty hours. That was off the coast of Africa, after passing the Cape of Good Hope. At the very height of it several heavy seas were shipped with no serious results, but there was a considerable smashing of breakable objects in the pantry and in the staterooms. Mr Bunter, who was so greatly respected on board, found himself treated scurvily by the Southern Ocean, which, bursting open the door of his room like a ruffianly burglar, carried off several useful things, and made all the others extremely wet.

Later, on the same day, the Southern Ocean caused the *Sapphire* to lurch over in such an unrestrained fashion that the two drawers fitted under Mr Bunter's sleeping-berth flew out altogether, spilling all their contents. They ought, of course, to have been locked, and Mr Bunter had only to thank himself for what had happened. He ought to have turned the key on each before going out on deck.

His consternation was very great. The steward, who was paddling about all the time with swabs, trying to dry out the flooded cuddy, heard him exclaim 'Hallo!' in a startled and dismayed tone. In the midst of his work the steward felt a sympathetic concern for the mate's distress.

Captain Johns was secretly glad when he heard of the damage. He was indeed afraid of his chief mate, as the sea-pilot had ventured to foretell, and afraid of him for the very reason the sea-pilot had put forward as likely.

Captain Johns, therefore, would have liked very much to hold that black mate of his at his mercy in some way or other. But the man was irreproachable, as near absolute perfection as could be. And Captain Johns was much annoyed, and at the same time congratulated himself on his chief officer's efficiency.

He made a great show of living sociably with him, on the principle that the more friendly you are with a man the more easily you may catch him tripping; and also for the reason that he wanted to have somebody who would listen to his stories of manifestations, apparitions, ghosts, and all the rest of the imbecile spook-lore. He had it all at his fingers' ends; and he spun those ghostly yarns in a persistent, colourless voice, giving them a futile turn peculiarly his own.

'I like to converse with my officers,' he used to say. 'There are masters that hardly ever open their mouths from beginning to end of a passage for fear of losing their dignity. What's that, after all – this bit of position a man holds!'

His sociability was most to be dreaded in the second dog-watch, because he was one of those men who grow lively towards the evening, and the officer on duty was unable then to find excuses for leaving the poop. Captain Johns would pop up the companion suddenly, and, sidling up in his creeping way to poor Bunter, as he walked up and down, would fire into him some spiritualistic proposition, such as:

'Spirits, male and female, show a good deal of refinement in a general way, don't they?'

To which Bunter, holding his black-whiskered head high, would mutter:

'I don't know.'

'Ah! that's because you don't want to. You are the most obstinate, prejudiced man I've ever met, Mr Bunter. I told you you may have any book out of my bookcase. You may just go into my stateroom and help yourself to any volume.'

And if Bunter protested that he was too tired in his watches below to spare any time for reading, Captain Johns would smile nastily behind his back, and remark that of course some people needed more sleep than others to keep themselves fit for their work. If Mr Bunter was afraid of not keeping properly awake when on duty at night, that was another matter.

'But I think you borrowed a novel to read from the second mate the other day – a trashy pack of lies,' Captain Johns sighed. 'I am afraid you are not a spiritually minded man, Mr Bunter. That's what's the matter.'

Sometimes he would appear on deck in the middle of the night, looking very grotesque and bandy-legged in his sleeping-suit. At that sight the persecuted Bunter would wring his hands stealthily, and break out into moisture all over his forehead. After standing sleepily by the binnacle, scratching himself in an unpleasant manner, Captain Johns was sure to start on some aspect or other of his only topic.

He would, for instance, discourse on the improvement of morality to be expected from the establishment of general and close intercourse with the spirits of the departed. The spirits, Captain Johns thought, would consent to associate familiarly with the living if it were not for the unbelief of the great mass of mankind. He himself would not care to have anything to do with a crowd that would not believe in his – Captain Johns' – existence. Then why should a spirit? This was asking too much.

He went on breathing hard by the binnacle and trying to reach round his shoulder-blades; then, with a thick, drowsy severity, declared:

'Incredulity, sir, is the evil of the age!'

It rejected the evidence of Professor Cranks and of the journalist chap. It resisted the production of photographs.

For Captain Johns believed firmly that certain spirits had been photographed. He had read something of it in the papers. And the idea of it having been done had got a tremendous hold on him, because his mind was not critical. Bunter said afterwards that nothing could be more weird than this little man, swathed in a sleeping-suit three sizes too large for him, shuffling with excitement in the moonlight near the wheel, and shaking his fist at the serene sea.

'Photographs! photographs!' he would repeat, in a voice as creaky as a rusty hinge.

The very helmsman just behind him got uneasy at that performance, not being capable of understanding exactly what the 'old man was kicking up a row with the mate about'.

Then Johns, after calming down a bit, would begin again.

'The sensitized plate can't lie. No, sir.'

Nothing could be more funny than this ridiculous little man's conviction – his dogmatic tone. Bunter would go on swinging up and down the poop like a deliberate, dignified pendulum. He said not a word. But the poor fellow had not a trifle on his conscience, as you know; and to have imbecile ghosts rammed down his throat like this on top of his own worry nearly drove him crazy. He knew that on many occasions he was on the verge of lunacy, because he could not help indulging in half-delirious visions of Captain Johns being picked up by the scruff of the neck and dropped over the taffrail into the ship's wake – the sort of thing no sane sailorman would think of doing to a cat or any other animal, anyhow. He imagined him bobbing up – a tiny black speck left far astern on the moonlit ocean.

I don't think that even at the worst moments Bunter really desired to drown Captain Johns. I fancy that all his disordered imagination longed for was merely to stop the ghostly inanity of the skipper's talk.

But, all the same, it was a dangerous form of self-indulgence. Just picture to yourself that ship in the Indian Ocean, on a clear, tropical night, with her sails full and still, the watch on deck stowed away out of sight; and on her poop, flooded with moonlight, the stately black mate walking up and down with measured, dignified steps, preserving an awful silence, and that grotesquely mean little figure in striped flannelette alternately creaking and droning of 'personal intercourse beyond the grave'.

It makes me creepy all over to think of. And sometimes the folly of Captain Johns would appear clothed in a sort of weird utilitarianism. How useful it would be if the spirits of the departed could be induced to take a practical interest in the affairs of the living! What a help, say, to the police, for instance, in the detection of crime! The number of murders, at any rate, would be considerably reduced, he guessed with an air of great sagacity. Then he would give way to grotesque discouragement.

Where was the use of trying to communicate with people that had no faith, and more likely than not would scorn the offered information? Spirits had their feelings. They were *all* feelings in a way. But he was surprised at the forbearance shown towards murderers by their victims. That was the sort of apparition that no guilty man would dare to pooh-pooh. And perhaps the undiscovered murderers – whether believing or not – were haunted. They wouldn't be likely to boast about it, would they?

'For myself,' he pursued, in a sort of vindictive, malevolent whine, 'if anybody murdered me I would not let him forget it. I would wither him up – I would terrify him to death.'

The idea of his skipper's ghost terrifying anyone was so ludicrous that the black mate, little disposed to mirth as he was, could not help giving vent to a weary laugh. And this laugh, the only acknowledgment of a long and earnest discourse, offended Captain Johns.

'What's there to laugh at in this conceited manner, Mr Bunter?' he snarled. 'Supernatural visitations have terrified better men than you. Don't you allow me enough soul to make a ghost of?'

I think it was the nasty tone that caused Bunter to stop short and turn about.

'I shouldn't wonder,' went on the angry fanatic of spiritism, 'if you weren't one of them people that take no more account of a man than if he were a beast. You would be capable, I don't doubt, to deny the possession of an immortal soul to your own father.'

And then Bunter, being bored beyond endurance, and also exasperated by the private worry, lost his self-possession.

He walked up suddenly to Captain Johns, and, stooping a little to look close into his face, said, in a low, even tone:

'You don't know what a man like me is capable of.'

Captain Johns threw his head back, but was too astonished to budge. Bunter resumed his walk; and for a long time his measured footsteps and the low wash of the water alongside were the only sounds which troubled the silence brooding over the great waters. Then Captain Johns cleared his throat uneasily, and, after sidling away towards the companion for greater safety, plucked up enough courage to retreat under an act of authority:

'Raise the starboard clew of the mainsail, and lay the yards dead square, Mr Bunter. Don't you see the wind is nearly right aft?'

Bunter at once answered 'Ay, ay, sir,' though there was not the slightest necessity to touch the yards, and the wind was well out on the quarter. While he was executing the order Captain Johns hung on the companion-steps, growling to himself : 'Walk this poop like an admiral and don't even notice when the yards want trimming!' – loud enough for the helmsman to overhear. Then he sank slowly backwards out of the man's sight; and when he reached the bottom of the stairs he stood still and thought.

'He's an awful ruffian, with all his gentlemanly airs. No more gentleman mates for me.'

Two nights afterwards he was slumbering peacefully in his berth, when a heavy thumping just above his head (a well-understood signal that he was wanted on deck) made him leap out of bed, broad awake in a moment.

'What's up?' he muttered, running out barefooted. On passing through the cabin he glanced at the clock. It was the middle watch. 'What on earth can the mate want me for?' he thought.

Bolting out of the companion, he found a clear, dewy moonlit night and a strong, steady breeze. He looked around wildly. There was no one on the poop except the helmsman, who addressed him at once.

'It was me, sir. I let go the wheel for a second to stamp over your head. I am afraid there's something wrong with the mate.'

'Where's he got to?' asked the captain sharply.

The man, who was obviously nervous, said :

'The last I saw of him was as he fell down the port poop-ladder.'

'Fell down the poop-ladder! What did he do that for? What made him?'

'I don't know, sir. He was walking the port side. Then just as he turned towards me to come aft . . .'

'You saw him?' interrupted the captain.

'I did. I was looking at him. And I heard the crash, too – something awful. Like the mainmast going overboard. It was as if something had struck him.'

Captain Johns became very uneasy and alarmed.

'Come,' he said sharply. 'Did anybody strike him? What did you see?'

'Nothing, sir, so help me! There was nothing to see. He just gave a little sort of hallo! threw his hands before him, and over he went – crash. I couldn't hear anything more, so I just let go the wheel for a second to call you up.'

'You're scared!' said Captain Johns.

'I am, sir, straight!'

Captain Johns stared at him. The silence of his ship driving on her way seemed to contain a danger – a mystery. He was reluctant to go and look for his mate himself, in the shadows of the main-deck, so quiet, so still.

All he did was to advance to the break of the poop, and call for the watch. As the sleepy men came trooping aft, he shouted to them fiercely:

'Look at the foot of the port poop-ladder, some of you! See the mate lying there?'

Their startled exclamations told him immediately that they did see him. Somebody even screeched out emotionally:

'He's dead!'

Mr Bunter was laid in his bunk and when the lamp in his room was lit he looked indeed as if he were dead, but it was obvious also that he was breathing yet. The steward had been roused out, the second mate called and sent on deck to look after the ship, and for an hour or so Captain Johns devoted himself silently to the restoring of consciousness. Mr Bunter at last opened his eyes, but he could not speak. He was dazed and inert. The steward bandaged a nasty scalp-wound while Captain Johns held an additional light. They had to cut away a lot of Mr Bunter's jet-black hair to make a good dressing. This done, and after gazing for a while at their patient, the two left the cabin.

'A rum go, this, steward,' said Captain Johns in the passage.

'Yessir.'

'A sober man that's right in his head does not fall down a poop-ladder like a sack of potatoes. The ship's as steady as a church.'

'Yessir. Fit of some kind, I shouldn't wonder.'

'Well, I should. He doesn't look as if he were subject to fits and giddiness. Why, the man's in the prime of life. I wouldn't have another kind of mate – not if I knew it. You don't think he has a private store of liquor, do you, eh? He seemed to me a bit strange in his manner several times lately. Off his feed, too, a bit, I noticed.'

'Well, sir, if he ever had a bottle or two of grog in his cabin, that must have gone a long time ago. I saw him throw some broken glass overboard after the last gale we had; but that didn't amount to anything. Anyway, sir, you couldn't call Mr Bunter a drinking man.'

'No,' conceded the captain, reflectively. And the steward, locking the pantry door, tried to escape out of the passage, thinking he could manage to snatch another hour of sleep before it was time for him to turn out for the day.

Captain Johns shook his head.

'There's some mystery there.'

'There's special Providence that he didn't crack his head like an eggshell on the quarter-deck mooring-bits, sir. The men tell me he couldn't have missed them by more than an inch.'

And the steward vanished skilfully.

Captain Johns spent the rest of the night and the whole of the ensuing day between his own room and that of the mate.

In his own room he sat with his open hands reposing on his knees, his lips pursed up, and the horizontal furrows on his forehead marked very heavily. Now and then raising his arm by a slow, as if cautious movement, he scratched lightly the top of his bald head. In the mate's room he stood for long periods of time with his hand to his lips, gazing at the half-conscious man.

For three days Mr Bunter did not say a single word. He looked at people sensibly enough but did not seem to be able to hear any questions put to him. They cut off some more of his hair and swathed his head in wet cloths. He took some nourishment, and was made as comfortable as possible. At dinner on the third day the second mate remarked to the captain, in connection with the affair:

'These half-round brass plates on the steps of the poop-ladders are beastly dangerous things!'

'Are they?' retorted Captain Johns, sourly. 'It takes more than a brass plate to account for an ablebodied man crashing down in this fashion like a felled ox.'

The second mate was impressed by that view. There was something in that, he thought.

'And the weather fine, everything dry, and the ship going along as steady as a church!' pursued Captain Johns, gruffly.

As Captain Johns continued to look extremely sour, the second mate did not open his lips any more during the dinner. Captain Johns was annoyed and hurt by an innocent remark, because the fitting of the aforesaid brass plates had been done at his suggestion only the voyage before, in order to smarten up the appearance of the poop-ladders.

On the fourth day Mr Bunter looked decidedly better; very languid yet, of course, but he heard and understood what was said to him, and even could say a few words in a feeble voice.

Captain Johns, coming in, contemplated him attentively, without much visible sympathy.

'Well, can you give us your account of this accident, Mr Bunter?'

Bunter moved slightly his bandaged head, and fixed his cold blue stare on Captain Johns' face, as if taking stock and appraising the value of every feature; the perplexed forehead, the credulous eyes, the inane droop of the mouth. And he gazed so long that Captain Johns grew restive, and looked over his shoulder at the door.

'No accident,' breathed out Bunter, in a peculiar tone.

'You don't mean to say you've got the falling sickness,' said Captain Johns. 'How would you call it signing as chief mate of a clipper ship with a thing like that on you?'

Bunter answered him only by a sinister look. The skipper shuffled his feet a little.

'Well, what made you have that tumble, then?'

Bunter raised himself a little, and, looking straight into Captain Johns' eyes said, in a very distinct whisper:

'You – were – right!'

He fell back and closed his eyes. Not a word more could Captain Johns get out of him; and, the steward coming into the cabin, the skipper withdrew.

But that very night, unobserved, Captain Johns, opening the door cautiously, entered again the mate's cabin. He could wait no longer. The suppressed eagerness, the excitement expressed in all his mean, creeping little person, did not escape the chief mate, who was lying awake, looking frightfully pulled down and perfectly impassive.

'You are coming to gloat over me, I suppose,' said Bunter without moving, and yet making a palpable hit.

'Bless my soul!' exclaimed Captain Johns with a start, and assuming a sobered demeanour. 'There's a thing to say!'

'Well, gloat, then! You and your ghosts, you've managed to get over a live man.'

This was said by Bunter without stirring, in a low voice, and with not much expression.

'Do you mean to say,' inquired Captain Johns, in awe-struck whisper, 'that you had a supernatural experience that night? You saw an apparition, then, on board my ship?'

Reluctance, shame, disgust, would have been visible on poor Bunter's countenance if the great part of it had not been swathed up in cotton-wool and bandages. His ebony eyebrows, more sinister than ever amongst all that lot of white linen, came together in a frown as he made a mighty effort to say:

'Yes, I have seen.'

The wretchedness in his eyes would have awakened the compassion of any other man than Captain Johns. But Captain Johns was all agog with triumphant excitement. He was just a little bit frightened, too. He looked at that unbelieving scoffer laid low, and did not even dimly guess at his profound, humiliating distress. He was not generally capable of taking much part in the anguish of his fellow-creatures. This time, moreover, he was excessively anxious to know what had happened. Fixing his credulous eyes on the bandaged head, he asked, trembling slightly:

'And did it – did it knock you down?'

'Come! am I the sort of man to be knocked down by a ghost?' protested Bunter in a little stronger tone. 'Don't you remember what you said yourself the other night? Better men than me – Ha! you'll have to look a long time before you find a better man for a mate of your ship.'

Captain Johns pointed a solemn finger at Bunter's bedplace.

'You've been terrified,' he said. 'That's what's the matter. You've been terrified. Why, even the man at the wheel was scared, though he couldn't see anything. He *felt* the supernatural. You are punished for your incredulity, Mr Bunter. You were terrified.'

'And suppose I was,' said Bunter. 'Do you know what I had seen? Can you conceive the sort of ghost that would haunt a man like me? Do you think it was a ladyish, afternoon call, another-cup-of-tea-please apparition that visits your Professor Cranks and that journalist chap you are always talking about? No; I can't tell you what it was like. Every man has his own ghosts. You couldn't conceive . . .'

Bunter stopped, out of breath; and Captain Johns remarked, with the glow of inward satisfaction reflected in his tone:

'I've always thought you were the sort of man that was ready for anything; from pitch-and-toss to wilful murder, as the saying goes. Well, well! So you were terrified.'

'I stepped back,' said Bunter, curtly. 'I don't remember anything else.'

'The man at the wheel told me you went backwards as if something had hit you.'

'It was a sort of inward blow,' explained Bunter. 'Something

132

too deep for you, Captain Johns, to understand. Your life and mine haven't been the same. Aren't you satisfied to see me converted?'

'And you can't tell me any more?' asked Captain Johns, anxiously.

'No, I can't. I wouldn't. It would be no use if I did. That sort of experience must be gone through. Say I am being punished. Well, I take my punishment, but talk of it I won't.'

'Very well,' said Captain Johns; 'you won't. But, mind, I can draw my own conclusions from that.'

'Draw what you like; but be careful what you say, sir. You don't terrify me. *You* aren't a ghost.'

'One word. Has it any connection with what you said to me on that last night, when we had a talk together on spiritualism?'

Bunter looked weary and puzzled.

'What did I say?'

'You told me that I couldn't know what a man like you was capable of.'

'Yes, yes. Enough!'

'Very good. I am fixed, then,' remarked Captain Johns. 'All I say is that I am jolly glad not to be you, though I would have given almost anything for the privilege of personal communication with the world of spirits. Yes, sir, but not in that way.'

Poor Bunter moaned pitifully.

'It has made me feel twenty years older.'

Captain Johns retired quietly. He was delighted to observe this overbearing ruffian humbled to the dust by the moralizing agency of the spirits. The whole occurrence was a source of pride and gratification; and he began to feel a sort of regard for his chief mate. It is true that in further interviews Bunter showed himself very mild and deferential. He seemed to cling to his captain for spiritual protection. He used to send for him, and say, 'I feel so nervous,' and Captain Johns would stay patiently for hours in the hot little cabin, and feel proud of the call.

For Mr Bunter was ill, and could not leave his berth for a

good many days. He became a convinced spiritualist, not enthusiastically – that could hardly have been expected from him – but in a grim, unshakeable way. He could not be called exactly friendly to the disembodied inhabitants of our globe, as Captain Johns was. But he was now a firm, if gloomy, recruit of spiritualism.

One afternoon, as the ship was already well to the north in the Gulf of Bengal, the steward knocked at the door of the captain's cabin, and said, without opening it

'The mate asks if you could spare him a moment, sir. He seems to be in a state in there.'

Captain Johns jumped up from the couch at once.

'Yes. Tell him I am coming.'

He thought: Could it be possible there had been another spiritual manifestation – in the daytime, too!

He revelled in the hope. It was not exactly that, however. Still, Bunter, whom he saw sitting collapsed in a chair – he had been up for several days, but not on deck as yet – poor Bunter had something startling enough to communicate. His hands covered his face. His legs were stretched straight out, dismally.

'What's the news now?' croaked Captain Johns, not unkindly, because in truth it always pleased him to see Bunter – as he expressed it – tamed.

'News!' exclaimed the crushed sceptic through his hands. 'Ay, news enough, Captain Johns. Who will be able to deny the awfulness, the genuineness? Another man would have dropped dead. You want to know what I had seen. All I can tell you is that since I've seen it my hair is turning white.'

Bunter detached his hands from his face, and they hung on each side of his chair as if dead. He looked broken in the dusky cabin.

'You don't say!' stammered out Captain Johns. 'Turned white! Hold on a bit! I'll light the lamp!'

When the lamp was lit, the startling phenomenon could be seen plainly enough. As if the dread, the horror, the anguish of the supernatural were being exhaled through the pores of his skin, a sort of silvery mist seemed to cling to the cheeks and the head of the mate. His short beard, his cropped hair, were growing, not black, but gray – almost white.

When Mr Bunter, thin-faced and shaky, came on deck for duty, he was clean-shaven, and his head was white. The hands were awe-struck. 'Another man,' they whispered to each other. It was generally and mysteriously agreed that the mate had 'seen something', with the exception of the man at the wheel at the time, who maintained that the mate was 'struck by something'.

This distinction hardly amounted to a difference. On the other hand, everybody admitted that, after he picked up his strength a bit, he seemed even smarter in his movements than before.

One day in Calcutta, Captain Johns, pointing out to a visitor his white-headed chief mate standing by the main-hatch, was heard to say oracularly:

'That man's in the prime of life.'

Of course, while Bunter was away, I called regularly on Mrs Bunter every Saturday, just to see whether she had any use for my services. It was understood I would do that. She had just his half-pay to live on – it amounted to about a pound a week. She had taken one room in a quiet little square in the East End.

And this was affluence to what I had heard that the couple were reduced to for a time after Bunter had to give up the Western Ocean trade – he used to go as mate of all sorts of hard packets after he lost his ship and his luck together – it was affluence to that time when Bunter would start at seven o'clock in the morning with but a glass of hot water and a crust of dry bread. It won't stand thinking about, especially for those who know Mrs Bunter. I had seen something of them, too, at that time; and it just makes me shudder to remember what that born lady had to put up with. Enough!

Dear Mrs Bunter used to worry a good deal after the *Sapphire* left for Calcutta. She would say to me: 'It must be so awful for poor Winston' – Winston is Bunter's name – and I tried to comfort her the best I could. Afterwards, she got some small children to teach in a family, and was half the day with them, and the occupation was good for her.

In the very first letter she had from Calcutta, Bunter told her he had had a fall down the poop-ladder, and cut his head, but no bones broken, thank God. That was all. Of course, she had other letters from him, but that vagabond Bunter never gave me a scratch of the pen the solid eleven months. I supposed, naturally, that everything was going on all right. Who could imagine what was happening?

Then one day dear Mrs Bunter got a letter from a legal firm in the City, advising her that her uncle was dead – her old curmudgeon of an uncle – a retired stockbroker, a heartless, petrified antiquity that had lasted on and on. He was nearly ninety, I believe; and if I were to meet his venerable ghost this minute, I would try to take him by the throat and strangle him.

The old beast would never forgive his niece for marrying Bunter; and years afterwards, when people made a point of letting him know that she was in London, pretty nearly starving at forty years of age, he only said: 'Serve the little fool right!' I believe he meant her to starve. And, lo and behold, the old cannibal died intestate, with no other relatives but that very identical little fool. The Bunters were wealthy people now.

Of course, Mrs Bunter wept as if her heart would break. In any other woman it would have been mere hypocrisy. Naturally, too, she wanted to cable the news to her Winston in Calcutta, but I showed her, *Gazette* in hand, that the ship was on the homeward-bound list for more than a week already. So we sat down to wait, and talked meantime of dear old Winston every day. There were just one hundred such days before the *Sapphire* got reported 'All well' in the chops of the Channel by an incoming mailboat.

'I am going to Dunkirk to meet him,' says she. The *Sapphire* had a cargo of jute for Dunkirk. Of course, I had to escort the

dear lady in the quality of her 'ingenious friend'. She calls me
'our ingenious friend' to this day; and I've observed some
people – strangers – looking hard at me, for the signs of the
ingenuity, I suppose.

After settling Mrs Bunter in a good hotel in Dunkirk, I
walked down to the docks – late afternoon it was – and what
was my surprise to see the ship actually fast alongside. Either
Johns or Bunter, or both, must have been driving her hard up
Channel. Anyway, she had been in since the day before last,
and her crew was already paid off. I met two of her apprenticed
boys going off home on leave with their dunnage on a Frenchman's barrow, as happy as larks, and I asked them if the mate
was on board.

'There he is, on the quay, looking at the moorings,' says one
of the youngsters as he skipped past me.

You may imagine the shock to my feelings when I beheld
his white head. I could only manage to tell him that his wife
was at an hotel in town. He left me at once, to go and get his
hat on board. I was mightily surprised by the smartness of his
movements as he hurried up the gangway.

Whereas the black mate struck people as deliberate, and
strangely stately in his gait for a man in the prime of life, this
white-headed chap seemed the most wonderfully alert of old
men. I don't suppose Bunter was any quicker on his pins than
before. It was the colour of the hair that made all the difference
in one's judgment.

The same with his eyes. Those eyes, that looked at you so
steely, so fierce, and so fascinating out of a bush of a buccaneer's
black hair, now had an innocent, almost boyish expression in
their good-humoured brightness under those white eyebrows.

I led him without any delay into Mrs Bunter's private sitting-
room. After she had dropped a tear over the late cannibal, given
a hug to her Winston, and told him that he must grow his
moustache again, the dear lady tucked her feet upon the sofa,
and I got out of Bunter's way.

He started at once to pace the room, waving his long arms.

He worked himself into a regular frenzy, and tore Johns limb from limb many times over that evening.

'Fell down? Of course I fell down, by slipping backwards on that fool's patent brass plates. 'Pon my word, I had been walking that poop in charge of the ship, and I didn't know whether I was in the Indian Ocean or in the moon. I was crazy. My head spun round and round with sheer worry. I had made my last application of your chemist's wonderful stuff.' (This to me.) 'All the store of bottles you gave me got smashed when those drawers fell out in the last gale. I had been getting some dry things to change, when I heard the cry: "All hands on deck!" and made one jump of it, without even pushing them in properly. Ass! When I came back and saw the broken glass and the mess, I felt ready to faint.

'No; look here – deception is bad; but not to be able to keep it up after one has been forced into it. You know that since I've been squeezed out of the Western Ocean packets by younger men, just on account of my grizzled muzzle – you know how much chance I had to ever get a ship. And not a soul to turn to. We have been a lonely couple, we two – she threw away everything for me – and to see her want a piece of dry bread——'

He banged with his fist fit to split the Frenchman's table in two.

'I would have turned a sanguinary pirate for her, let alone cheating my way into a berth by dyeing my hair. So when you came to me with your chemist's wonderful stuff——'

He checked himself.

'By the way, that fellow's got a fortune when he likes to pick it up. It is a wonderful stuff – you tell him salt water can do nothing to it. It stays on as long as your hair will.'

'All right,' I said. 'Go on.'

Thereupon he went for Johns again with a fury that frightened his wife, and made me laugh till I cried.

'Just you try to think what it would have meant to be at the mercy of the meanest creature that ever commanded a ship! Just fancy what a life that crawling Johns would have led me!

And I knew that in a week or so the white hair would begin to show. And the crew. Did you ever think of that? To be shown up as a low fraud before all hands. What a life for me till we got to Calcutta! And once there – kicked out, of course. Half-pay stopped. Annie here alone without a penny – starving; and I on the other side of the earth, ditto. You see?

'I thought of shaving twice a day. But could I shave my head, too? No way – no way at all. Unless I dropped Johns over-board; and even then——Do you wonder now that with all these things boiling in my head I didn't know where I was putting down my foot that night? I just felt myself falling – then crash, and all dark.

'When I came to myself that bang on the head seemed to have steadied my wits somehow. I was so sick of everything that for two days I wouldn't speak to anyone. They thought it was a slight concussion of the brain. Then the idea dawned upon me as I was looking at that ghost-ridden, wretched fool. "Ah, you love ghosts," I thought. "Well, you shall have something from beyond the grave."

'I didn't even trouble to invent a story. I couldn't imagine a ghost if I wanted to. I wasn't fit to lie connectedly if I had tried. I just bulled him on to it. Do you know, he got, quite by himself, a notion that at some time or other I had done some-body to death in some way, and that——'

'Oh, the horrible man!' cried Mrs Bunter from the sofa. There was a silence.

'And didn't he bore my head off on the home passage!' began Bunter again in a weary voice. 'He loved me. He was proud of me. I was converted. I had had a manifestation. Do you know what he was after? He wanted me and him "to make a *seance*", in his own words, and to try to call up that ghost (the one that had turned my hair white – the ghost of my supposed victim), and, as he said, talk it over with him – the ghost – in a friendly way.

'"Or else, Bunter," he says, "you may get another manifesta-tion when you least expect it, and tumble overboard perhaps, or something. You ain't really safe till we pacify the spirit-world in some way."

'Can you conceive a lunatic like that? No – say?'

I said nothing. But Mrs Bunter did, in a very decided tone.

'Winston, I don't want you to go on board that ship again any more.'

'My dear,' says he, 'I have all my things on board yet.'

'You don't want the things. Don't go near that ship at all.'

He stood still; then, dropping his eyes with a faint smile, said slowly, in a dreamy voice:

'The haunted ship.'

'And your last,' I added.

We carried him off, as he stood, by the night train. He was very quiet; but crossing the Channel, as we two had a smoke on deck, he turned to me suddenly, and, grinding his teeth, whispered:

'He'll never know how near he was being dropped overboard!'

He meant Captain Johns. I said nothing.

But Captain Johns, I understand, made a great to-do about the disappearance of his chief mate. He set the French police scouring the country for the body. In the end, I fancy he got word from his owners' office to drop all this fuss – that it was all right. I don't suppose he ever understood anything of that mysterious occurrence.

To this day he tries at times (he's retired now, and his conversation is not very coherent) – he tries to tell the story of a black mate he once had, 'a murderous, gentlemanly ruffian', with raven-black hair which turned white all at once in consequence of a manifestation from beyond the grave'. An avenging apparition. What with reference to black and white hair, to poop-ladders, and to his own feelings and views, it is difficult to make head or tail of it. If his sister (she's very vigorous still) should be present she cuts all this short – peremptorily:

'Don't you mind what he says. He's got devils on the brain.'

COMMENTARY

A certain mystery surrounds the writing of *The Black Mate*, the author giving one account of its origins, his wife Jessie another. If Conrad is correct in maintaining that he produced a first version as early as 1886 while his sea-going career was at its height, as his unsuccessful entry for a competition in the magazine *Tit-Bits*, it would make the story his first completed work in English. What we have today is seemingly a revised version, prepared for the *London Magazine* in 1908 and published in book form seventeen years later.

In one respect it is rather a deceptive work on first acquaintance. Compared with *Typhoon* or *The Secret Sharer* it seems lightweight, lacking either the vigorous intensity of their narrative or their concern with wide philosophical issues. Its easy tone owes more to the rambling sea yarn or pub story than to any carefully wrought literary form. But if, in the course of its relatively few pages, we hear Conrad's voice in more relaxed mood than that to which we are perhaps accustomed, we are left in no doubt that it is indeed to *his* voice we are listening. We remark and appreciate the flashes of dry humour, the unexpected twists, the illuminating contrasts. We recognize his authentic insight into the sea-going character in its various manifestations and the grand, often grim, irony with which he invests so much of his observation of life. We notice, too, on closer inspection, that beneath the apparent informality of his narrative there lies an organization of material that is at once precise and resourceful.

Perhaps our most immediate impression of *The Black Mate* is the intimacy of its tone. We experience the sensation not of being part of some vast impersonal audience, but of being drawn into the easy fellowship of a group of sea-going friends enjoying together an evening round the fire or an after-dinner drink. Personalities have been discussed, reminiscences exchanged. One of the company begins to tell us a tale – a true one, of course – of the old days. About Bunter. He enjoys the advantage of having known his subject well at the time the events took place and of having obtained the details from him at first hand. He was even involved in a minor way himself, being the 'ingenious friend' who first introduced Bunter to a way round his problems. So he can speak with authority. What is more, he also knows us well, so that his manner can afford to be at once chatty and confiding. He puts in remarks 'between ourselves' that he might not perhaps venture to include were he addressing a public at large. He knows he can count on our sympathy and discretion, so that it is not always needful for him to complete what he is saying or to be absolutely literal. We can supply the appropriate response, the missing words, for ourselves: 'a man in his almost, I may say, tragic position couldn't be expected – you understand.' We find ourselves nodding in agreement, glancing perhaps at our immediate neighbours in the listening circle: 'poor fellow! Little we both thought that before very long he himself . . .' Some things are, indeed, better left unsaid. Instinct is enough.

This leaving of things unsaid is, however, part of a wider purpose on the narrator's part. As we listen to him speaking we are made increasingly aware that he is a born storyteller, one who not only knows his audience but is also expert in judging the pace and progress of his shaggy-dog narrative. Compared with *Typhoon* or *The Secret Sharer* there is little in this tale in the way of gripping incident or spectacular description – no riot, no murder, no towering catastrophe overshadowing vessel and crew alike, just a man slipping down a ladder on a calm night in the Indian Ocean. There is little brooding tension or sense of impending danger, the tale's chief interest deriving from the conflicting personalities of its central characters. Indeed, it might with some justification be said to concern itself with attitudes rather than with action. The rare moments when the pace does quicken for a paragraph or so of more highly charged writing – an outburst from Johns, for instance, or some colourful expression of Bunter's frustration – are soon forgotten as we return to the narrator's undemonstrative account of events and his apparent determination not so much to act them out with vivid gesture as to confide them with even-toned impassivity. Yet, for all his avoidance of ear-catching histrionics, there can be no doubt that the speaker exercises a powerful control over his audience. Nor does it take much for us to appreciate just how shamelessly we are being manipulated. The key lies, of course, in the strange mystery about Bunter. It is the subject of several allusions in the early part of the story, with the result that, by the time the *Sapphire* sets sail, it has been so firmly imprinted in our consciousness that we would have to be dense indeed not to be eaten up with curiosity as to its nature. We are told quite simply at the outset that the lack of 'buoyancy' in the black mate's manner is due to his having some 'secret locked up in his breast', but we also note his touchiness with both his captain and the berthing master, when the one takes to watching him closely and the other to prying into his past. We learn a little more about its nature when the narrator refers to Bunter's almost 'tragic position' and the fact that he is 'really worried' about the situation in which he finds himself. The nearest we get to an explanation comes on the eve of the ship's departure

As to his remorse in regard to a certain secret action of his life, well, I understand that a man of Bunter's fine character would suffer not a little. Still, between ourselves, and without the slightest wish to be cynical, it cannot be denied that with the noblest of us the fear of being found out enters for some considerable part into the composition of remorse. I didn't say this in so many words to Bunter, but, as the poor fellow harped a bit on it, I told him that there were skeletons in a good many honest cupboards, and that, as to his own particular guilt, it wasn't writ large on his face for everybody to see.

What is this? Honesty and yet guilt? Secret action – worry – tragic position – remorse – skeletons in cupboards? The possibilities flash through our minds is it drink? something to do with his marriage? with the loss of the *Samaria*? has he been the buccaneer his appearance suggests? or has he – like Leggatt in *The Secret Sharer* – killed a man? The firmness of the speaker's control over us is demonstrated beautifully in the fact that we react to these melodramatic suggestions in exactly the way he intends 'the mystery must surely be rooted in one of them – the whole thing's so obvious – the story's weakness lies in Conrad's giving the game away far too soon'. And this may indeed appear to be the case until we come to the very end of the story and discover the true nature of Bunter's guilty secret. It is then that we see that the joke has, after all, been on us: that Conrad's irony and his sense of the absurd have triumphed yet again. It is then, too, that – looking back – we begin to realize that he has been placing silent clues for us all along, but that we have ignored them in our preoccupation with more sinister possibilities. The loss of the *Samaria* and Bunter's inability to get another command; the poverty which has overtaken him and his wife as a consequence; his almost unnaturally black hair; his captain's unshakeable opinion that 'the sea was no place for elderly men'; his own dismay at the breakage of certain of his belongings during the spell of rough weather off the coast of Africa; the fact that he was seen by the steward to throw some broken glass overboard shortly afterwards; the extraordinary way in which his hair and beard turned white later in the voyage – all these apparently inconsequential and isolated details, as we look back, are now seen to have been subtly related. A rambling sea yarn, a shaggy-dog story, maybe, but how cunningly, how masterfully contrived!

What then of these two central characters on whose relationship the whole story turns? Winston Bunter is clearly the type of man for whom Conrad intends us to have sympathy and admiration. On a somewhat lower plane he has the tenacity of a MacWhirr or a Leggatt. His appearance, significantly, encourages confidence. The sea-pilot responsible for taking the *Sapphire* out into the Channel acknowledges that he is 'the sort of man you don't forget . . . a thorough good sailor, too' and even goes so far as to opine that the ship has for chief mate someone who seems 'a jolly sight too good' for her captain. Like his storm-conquering counterparts in *Typhoon* and *The Secret Sharer*, Bunter manages to ensure that even in gale-force winds everything somehow goes on as it should. He is a man, for the most part, of few words, and even they tend to be understated. When his precious bottles are smashed during the 'severe blow' to which the *Sapphire* is subjected after rounding the Cape, all he is heard to exclaim is 'Hallo', albeit in a 'startled and dismayed tone'. That he should once have had his own command comes as little surprise. It must, however, take all of his considerable self-control to endure Johns' continued ranting and dogmatism about 'spiritism', especially since, beneath his unruffled exterior, there lurks that terrible secret of his. Even so, he maintains his silence, pacing back and forth on the poop deck 'like a deliberate, dignified pendulum'. The narrator underlines his self-possession for us in the fact that throughout that part of the story where Johns is subjecting him to the miseries and frustrations of his 'sociability', only three of Bunter's replies are recorded. Two of these are distinctly non-committal, moreover, while the menace of 'you don't know what a man like me is capable of' pales into insignificance beside the thoughts he leaves unuttered – the 'half-delirious visions' of picking his captain up by the scruff of the neck and dropping him overboard. The contrast between Bunter's enforced exterior impassivity and his inner turmoil is brought home most vividly when in his wife's hotel room in Dunkirk he is at last able to give a true account of his feelings. The effect is volcanic. 'He started at once to pace the room, waving his long arms. He worked himself into a regular frenzy, and tore Johns limb from limb many times over that evening.' It is a clear demonstration of his strength of character that he should have concealed such emotions so successfully while at sea. But then he belongs to a breed of men whom – as we have seen – Conrad much respects those who can face up to problems – undertake them, even, with open eyes – and see them through without fuss or hysteria. Bunter knows from the start that he may have to put up 'with any dirty trick in the course of the voyage'. He also knows that for his wife's sake he dare not put a foot wrong: the very notion of his being stranded on the other side of the earth as a result of some error or mishap, and her at home 'alone without a penny – starving' is sufficient to ensure his utmost care in his relations with the 'ghost-ridden' Captain Johns. This need to conceal his true feelings and also his 'disabilities' from an unscrupulous superior in order to complete the voyage and thus be in a position to support his family is reminiscent of the situation of Captain Whalley in Conrad's fine story *The End of the Tether*.

Captain Johns has absolutely nothing in common with his chief mate – least of all the narrator's sympathy. He has been a captain for many years 'without being much respected or liked'. In appearance, he is as unlike Bunter as can be imagined – look at his 'low and horizontally wrinkled brow', 'the slightly pointed form of his bald head', his 'dull little eyes'. He is 'short of stature and slightly bandy'. His voice comes across to us as 'whining', 'persistent, colourless'. He has a creeping manner, a way of sidling up to people when he is not expected. No wonder he is suspicious and jealous of his new mate, that he would like very much to have so fine a fellow at his mercy, that he makes a great show of sociability purely and simply 'on the principle that the more friendly you are with a man the more easily you may catch him tripping'. We are not surprised to hear of his secret pleasure at the damage sustained by Bunter's belongings during the rough weather. He is humourless to the point of sourness, except when enjoying a smile at someone else's expense. He cannot take a joke, as is evident from his reaction to the implication that he would like to see every sailor over forty years of age poisoned. However

COMMENTARY ON *The Black Mate*

justified his objection to such a suggestion might be, the fact
remains that he is 'not generally capable of taking much part
in the anguish of his fellow-creatures' – a plainly unhelpful
state of affairs when we consider the depths of anguish to which
Bunter is being subjected while sharing a deck with him. He
is a great finder of fault in other people, perhaps as a result of
his sister's browbeating ways – 'always nursing a grievance of
some sort and incessantly nagging'.

We notice, furthermore, a particularly unsavoury quality
in the language and imagery the narrator employs in describing
him: he creeps about the decks 'like a wretched insect – like
a cockroach, only not so lively'; he stands sleepily by the binnacle 'scratching himself in an unpleasant manner'; his voice is
'creaky as a rusty hinge'. It is illuminating to compare Johns
with a captain Conrad plainly respects, MacWhirr of the *Nan-
Shan*. Both men, it is true, share certain characteristics which
the author seems to associate with command: they are 'meticulous in trifles' and they appear to have earned with the years
the confidence of their employers. But look at the different ways
in which they react in similar circumstances: when MacWhirr
wakes out of his sleep to the fearful noises of the storm and the
alarm of his chief mate in the second chapter of *Typhoon*, he acts
with calm and deliberation; but when Johns is roused and called
on deck after Bunter's accident, his liability to panic is reflected
in his running out of his cabin barefoot, his looking round
'wildly' and the unease and alarm which prompt him to call out
the watch instead of making investigations in the silent shadows
of the main deck for himself. His apprehensiveness on this
occasion is, of course, closely related to his preoccupation with
the world of ghosts and spirits, the very subject over which his
fellow captains like to taunt him and his sister to exercise her
bullying repression. It is the subject, too, for the airing of which
Johns's boasted sociability with his officers is little more than an
excuse. He makes a big thing of this sociability. Not for him the
aloofness of command, the detachment which enables Mac-
Whirr or the narrator of *The Secret Sharer* to assess clearly and

come safely through the perils that confront them, but a forced familiarity, always harping on the same fixation, which in the end breeds nothing but boredom and resentment. There is little doubt that most of us would trust our lives and safety the more readily to a solid, taciturn commander like MacWhirr than to 'this little man, swathed in a sleeping suit three sizes too large for him, shuffling with excitement in the moonlight near the wheel, and shaking his fist at the serene sea'. It is significant that, for all his years as a leader of men, Johns' preoccupation with things supernatural makes him incapable of judging Bunter's character and worth or of appreciating just what, for all his prying, is going on under his very nose. As so often in Conrad, this character's views on others tell us as much (if not more) about *him* as they do about *them*. There is a considerable irony in his delighted observation that his 'overbearing ruffian' of a chief mate has been 'humbled to the dust by the moralizing agency of the spirits'.

A thread of good-humoured subtle irony thus seems to be woven throughout the entire fabric of *The Black Mate*. Irony not only at Johns' expense, but also, as we have seen, at ours. The humour, much more pervasive here than in the other stories in this collection, is typically quietly stated, never raucous. The continuing image of Bunter's smouldering frustration at being forced to listen to 'that grotesquely mean little figure in striped flanelette' as he rants excitedly against the calmly perfect backdrop of the moonlit ocean is presented with the barely smiling directness that we also find in episodes like that of the Siamese flag in *Typhoon*. In this, as in the other respects with which we have been concerned here, *The Black Mate* is characteristic Conrad. That this story has not achieved the wide popularity of its companions is perhaps due, as I remarked earlier, to its lack of narrative intensity or interest in philosophical ideas. If this is the case, it is a pity. For *The Black Mate* is a beautifully controlled piece of storytelling, with much to enjoy as well as to admire. It certainly deserves a wider audience than it has had to date.

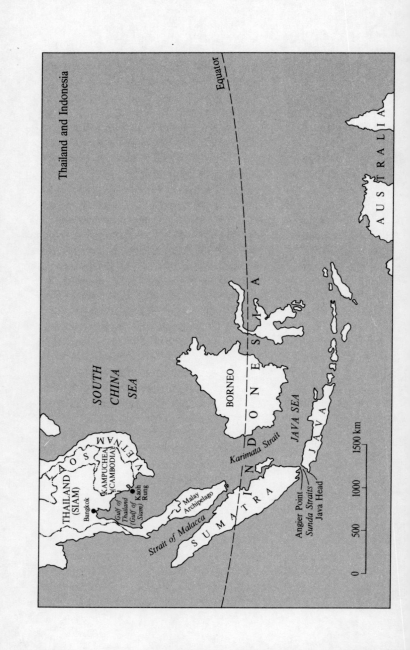

Thailand and Indonesia

THE SECRET SHARER

I

On my right hand there were lines of fishing-stakes resembling a mysterious system of half-submerged bamboo fences, incomprehensible in its division of the domain of tropical fishes, and crazy of aspect as if abandoned for ever by some nomad tribe of fishermen now gone to the other end of the ocean; for there was no sign of human habitation as far as the eye could reach. To the left a group of barren islets, suggesting ruins of stone walls, towers, and blockhouses, had its foundations set in a blue sea that itself looked solid, so still and stable did it lie below my feet; even the track of light from the westering sun shone smoothly, without that animated glitter which tells of an imperceptible ripple. And when I turned my head to take a parting glance at the tug which had just left us anchored outside the bar, I saw the straight line of the flat shore joined to the stable sea, edge to edge, with a perfect and unmarked closeness, in one levelled floor half brown, half blue under the enormous dome of the sky. Corresponding in their insignificance to the islets of the sea, two small clumps of trees, one on each side of the only fault in the impeccable joint, marked the mouth of the river Meinam we had just left on the first preparatory stage of our homeward journey; and, far back on the inland level, a larger and loftier mass, the grove surrounding the great Paknam pagoda, was the only thing on which the eye could rest from the vain task of exploring the monotonous sweep of the horizon. Here and there gleams as of a few scattered pieces of silver marked the windings of the great river; and on the nearest of them, just within the bar, the tug steaming right into the land became lost to my sight, hull and funnel and masts, as though the impassive earth had swallowed her up without an effort, without a tremor. My eye followed the light cloud of her smoke, now here, now there, above the plain, according to the devious curves of the stream, but always fainter and farther away, till I lost it at last behind the mitre-shaped hill of the great pagoda. And then I was left alone with my ship, anchored at the head of the Gulf of Siam.

She floated at the starting-point of a long journey, very still in an immense stillness, the shadows of her spars flung far to the eastward by the setting sun. At that moment I was alone on her decks. There was not a sound in her – and around us nothing moved, nothing lived, not a canoe on the water, not a bird in the air, not a cloud in the sky. In this breathless pause at the threshold of a long passage we seemed to be measuring our fitness for a long and arduous enterprise, the appointed task of both our existences to be carried out, far from all human eyes, with only sky and sea for spectators and for judges.

There must have been some glare in the air to interfere with one's sight, because it was only just before the sun left us that my roaming eyes made out beyond the highest ridge of the principal islet of the group something which did away with the solemnity of perfect solitude. The tide of darkness flowed on swiftly; and with tropical suddenness a swarm of stars came out above the shadowy earth, while I lingered yet, my hand resting lightly on my ship's rail as if on the shoulder of a trusted friend. But, with all that multitude of celestial bodies staring down at one, the comfort of quiet communion with her was gone for good. And there were also disturbing sounds by this time – voices, footsteps forward; the steward flitted along the main-deck, a busily ministering spirit; a hand-bell tinkled urgently under the poop-deck . . .

I found my two officers waiting for me near the supper table, in the lighted cuddy. We sat down at once, and as I helped the chief mate, I said:

'Are you aware that there is a ship anchored inside the islands? I saw her mastheads above the ridge as the sun went down.'

He raised sharply his simple face, overcharged by a terrible growth of whisker, and emitted his usual ejaculations: 'Bless my soul, sir! You don't say so!'

My second mate was a round-cheeked, silent young man, grave beyond his years, I thought; but as our eyes happened to meet I detected a slight quiver on his lips. I looked down at once. It was not my part to encourage sneering on board my ship. It must be said, too, that I knew very little of my officers. In consequence of certain events of no particular significance, except to myself, I had been appointed to the command only a fortnight before. Neither did I know much of the hands forward. All these people had been together for eighteen months or so, and my position was that of the only stranger on board. I mention this because it has some bearing on what is to follow. But what I felt most was my being a stranger to the ship; and if all the truth must be told, I was somewhat of a stranger to myself. The youngest man on board (barring the second mate), and untried as yet by a position of the fullest responsibility, I was willing to take the adequacy of the others for granted. They had simply to be equal to their tasks; but I wondered how far I should turn out faithful to that ideal conception of one's own personality every man sets up for himself secretly.

Meantime the chief mate, with an almost visible effect of collaboration on the part of his round eyes and frightful whiskers, was trying to evolve a theory of the anchored ship. His dominant trait was to take all things into earnest consideration. He was of a painstaking turn of mind. As he used to say, he 'liked to account to himself' for practically everything that came in his way, down to a miserable scorpion he had found in his cabin a week before. The why and the wherefore of that scorpion – how it got on board and came to select his room rather than the pantry (which was a dark place and more what a scorpion would be partial to), and how on earth it managed to drown itself in the inkwell of his writing-desk – had exercised him infinitely. The ship within the islands was

153

much more easily accounted for; and just as we were about to
rise from table he made his pronouncement. She was, he
doubted not, a ship from home lately arrived. Probably she
drew too much water to cross the bar except at the top of
spring tides. Therefore she went into that natural harbour to
wait for a few days in preference to remaining in an open
roadstead.

'That's so,' confirmed the second mate, suddenly, in his
slightly hoarse voice. 'She draws over twenty feet. She's the
Liverpool ship *Sephora* with a cargo of coal. Hundred and
twenty-three days from Cardiff.'

We looked at him in surprise.

'The tugboat skipper told me when he came on board for
your letters, sir,' explained the young man. 'He expects to take
her up the river the day after tomorrow.'

After thus overwhelming us with the extent of his information
he slipped out of the cabin. The mate observed regretfully that
he 'could not account for that young fellow's whims'. What
prevented him telling us all about it at once, he wanted to
know.

I detained him as he was making a move. For the last two
days the crew had had plenty of hard work, and the night before
they had very little sleep. I felt painfully that I – a stranger – was
doing something unusual when I directed him to let all hands
turn in without setting an anchor-watch. I proposed to keep
on deck myself till one o'clock or thereabouts. I would get the
second mate to relieve me at that hour.

'He will turn out the cook and the steward at four,' I concluded, 'and then give you a call. Of course at the slightest
sign of any sort of wind we'll have the hands up and make a
start at once.'

He concealed his astonishment. 'Very well, sir.' Outside the
cuddy he put his head in the second mate's door to inform him
of my unheard-of caprice to take a five hours' anchor-watch
on myself. I heard the other raise his voice incredulously –
'What? The Captain himself?' Then a few more murmurs, a

door closed, then another. A few moments later I went on deck.

My strangeness, which had made me sleepless, had prompted that unconventional arrangement, as if I had expected in those solitary hours of the night to get on terms with the ship of which I knew nothing, manned by men of whom I knew very little more. Fast alongside a wharf, littered like any ship in port with a tangle of unrelated things, invaded by unrelated shore people, I had hardly seen her yet properly. Now, as she lay cleared for sea, the stretch of her main-deck seemed to me very fine under the stars. Very fine, very roomy for her size, and very inviting. I descended the poop and paced the waist, my mind picturing to myself the coming passage through the Malay Archipelago, down the Indian Ocean, and up the Atlantic. All its phases were familiar enough to me, every characteristic, all the alternatives which were likely to face me on the high seas – everything! . . . except the novel responsibility of command. But I took heart from the reasonable thought that the ship was like other ships, the men like other men, and that the sea was not likely to keep any special surprises expressly for my discomfiture.

Arrived at that comforting conclusion, I bethought myself of a cigar and went below to get it. All was still down there. Everybody at the after end of the ship was sleeping profoundly. I came out again on the quarter-deck, agreeably at ease in my sleeping-suit on that warm breathless night, barefooted, a glowing cigar in my teeth, and, going forward, I was met by the profound silence of the fore end of the ship. Only as I passed the door of the forecastle I heard a deep, quiet, trustful sigh of some sleeper inside. And suddenly I rejoiced in the great security of the sea as compared with the unrest of the land, in my choice of that untempted life presenting no disquieting problems, invested with an elementary moral beauty by the absolute straightforwardness of its appeal and by the singleness of its purpose.

The riding-light in the fore-rigging burned with a clear, untroubled, as if symbolic, flame, confident and bright in the mysterious shades of the night. Passing on my way aft along the other side of the ship, I observed that the rope side-ladder, put over, no doubt, for the master of the tug when he came to fetch away our letters, had not been hauled in as it should have been. I became annoyed at this, for exactitude in small matters is the very soul of discipline. Then I reflected that I had myself peremptorily dismissed my officers from duty, and by my own act had prevented the anchor-watch being formally set and things properly attended to. I asked myself whether it was wise ever to interfere with the established routine of duties even from the kindest of motives. My action might have made me appear eccentric. Goodness only knew how that absurdly whiskered mate would 'account' for my conduct, and what the whole ship thought of that informality of their new captain. I was vexed with myself.

Not from compunction certainly, but, as it were mechanically, I proceeded to get the ladder in myself. Now a side-ladder of that sort is a light affair and comes in easily, yet my vigorous tug, which should have brought it flying on board, merely recoiled upon my body in a totally unexpected jerk. What the devil! . . . I was so astounded by the immovableness of that ladder that I remained stock-still, trying to account for it to myself like that imbecile mate of mine. In the end, of course, I put my head over the rail.

The side of the ship made an opaque belt of shadow on the darkling glassy shimmer of the sea. But I saw at once something elongated and pale floating very close to the ladder. Before I could form a guess a faint flash of phosphorescent light, which seemed to issue suddenly from the naked body of a man, flickered in the sleeping water with the elusive, silent play of summer lightning in a night sky. With a gasp I saw revealed to my stare a pair of feet, the long legs, a broad livid back immersed right up to the neck in a greenish cadaverous glow. One hand, awash, clutched the bottom rung of the ladder. He was complete but for the head. A headless corpse! The cigar dropped out of my gaping mouth with a tiny plop and a short hiss quite audible in the absolute stillness of all things under heaven. At that I suppose he raised up his face, a dimly pale oval in the shadow of the ship's side. But even then I could only barely make out down there the shape of his black-haired head. However, it was enough for the horrid, frost-bound sensation which had gripped me about the chest to pass off. The moment of vain exclamations was past, too. I only climbed on the spare spar and leaned over the rail as far as I could, to bring my eyes nearer to that mystery floating alongside.

As he hung by the ladder, like a resting swimmer, the sea-lightning played about his limbs at every stir; and he appeared in it ghastly, silvery, fish-like. He remained as mute as a fish, too. He made no motion to get out of the water, either. It was inconceivable that he should not attempt to come on board, and strangely troubling to suspect that perhaps he did not want to. And my first words were prompted by just that troubled incertitude.

'What's the matter?' I asked in my ordinary tone, speaking down to the face upturned exactly under mine.

'Cramp,' it answered, no louder. Then slightly anxious, 'I say, no need to call any one.'

'I was not going to,' I said.

'Are you alone on deck?'

'Yes.'

I had somehow the impression that he was on the point of letting go the ladder to swim away beyond my ken – mysterious as he came. But, for the moment, this being appearing as if he had risen from the bottom of the sea (it was certainly the nearest land to the ship) wanted only to know the time. I told him. And he, down there, tentatively:

'I suppose your captain's turned in?'

'I am sure he isn't,' I said.

He seemed to struggle with himself, for I heard something like the low, bitter murmur of doubt. 'What's the good?' His next words came out with a hesitating effort.

'Look here, my man. Could you call him out quietly?'

I thought the time had come to declare myself.

'*I* am the captain.'

I heard a 'By Jove!' whispered at the level of the water. The phosphorescence flashed in the swirl of the water all about his limbs, his other hand seized the ladder.

'My name's Leggatt.'

The voice was calm and resolute. A good voice. The self-possession of that man had somehow induced a corresponding state in myself. It was very quietly that I remarked:

'You must be a good swimmer.'

'Yes. I've been in the water practically since nine o'clock. The question for me now is whether I am to let go this ladder and go on swimming till I sink from exhaustion, or – to come on board here.'

I felt this was no mere formula of desperate speech, but a real alternative in the view of a strong soul. I should have gathered from this that he was young; indeed, it is only the young who are ever confronted by such clear issues. But at the time it was pure intuition on my part. A mysterious communication was established already between us two – in the face of that silent, darkened tropical sea. I was young, too; young enough to make no comment. The man in the water began suddenly to climb up the ladder, and I hastened away from the rail to fetch some clothes.

Before entering the cabin I stood still, listening in the lobby at the foot of the stairs. A faint snore came through the closed door of the chief mate's room. The second mate's door was on the hook, but the darkness in there was absolutely soundless. He, too, was young and could sleep like a stone. Remained the steward, but he was not likely to wake up before he was called. I got a sleeping-suit out of my room and, coming back on deck, saw the naked man from the sea sitting on the main-hatch, glimmering white in the darkness, his elbows on his knees and his head in his hands. In a moment he had concealed his damp body in a sleeping-suit of the same grey-stripe pattern as the one I was wearing and followed me like my double on the poop. Together we moved right aft, barefooted, silent.

'What is it?' I asked in a deadened voice, taking the lighted lamp out of the binnacle, and raising it to his face.

'An ugly business.'

He had rather regular features; a good mouth; light eyes under somewhat heavy, dark eyebrows; a smooth, square forehead; no growth on his cheeks; a small, brown moustache, and a well-shaped, round chin. His expression was concentrated, meditative, under the inspecting light of the lamp I held up to his face; such as a man thinking hard in solitude night wear. My sleeping-suit was just right for his size. A well-knit young fellow of twenty-five at most. He caught his lower lip with the edge of white, even teeth.

'Yes,' I said, replacing the lamp in the binnacle. The warm, heavy tropical night closed upon his head again.

'There's a ship over there,' he murmured.

'Yes, I know. The *Sephora*. Did you know of us?'

'Hadn't the slightest idea. I am the mate of her—' He paused and corrected himself. 'I should say I *was*.'

'Aha! Something wrong?'

'Yes. Very wrong indeed. I've killed a man.'

'What do you mean? Just now?'

'No, on the passage. Weeks ago. Thirty-nine south. When I say a man—'

'Fit of temper,' I suggested, confidently.

The shadowy, dark head, like mine, seemed to nod imperceptibly above the ghostly grey of my sleeping-suit. It was, in the night, as though I had been faced by my own reflection in the depths of a sombre and immense mirror.

'A pretty thing to have to own up to for a Conway boy.' murmured my double, distinctly.

'You're a Conway boy?'

'I am,' he said, as if startled. Then, slowly . . . 'Perhaps you too—'

It was so; but being a couple of years older I had left before he joined. After a quick interchange of dates a silence fell; and

I thought suddenly of my absurd mate with his terrific whiskers and the 'Bless my soul – you don't say so' type of intellect. My double gave me an inkling of his thoughts by saying: 'My father's a parson in Norfolk. Do you see me before a judge and jury on that charge? For myself I can't see the necessity. There are fellows that an angel from heaven – And I am not that. He was one of those creatures that are just simmering all the time with a silly sort of wickedness. Miserable devils that have no business to live at all. He wouldn't do his duty and wouldn't let anybody else do theirs. But what's the good of talking! You know well enough the sort of ill-conditioned snarling cur—'

He appealed to me as if our experiences had been as identical as our clothes. And I knew well enough the pestiferous danger of such a character where there are no means of legal repression. And I knew well enough also that my double there was no homicidal ruffian. I did not think of asking him for details, and he told me the story roughly in brusque, disconnected sentences. I needed no more. I saw it all going on as though I were myself inside that other sleeping-suit.

'It happened while we were setting a reefed foresail, at dusk. Reefed foresail! You understand the sort of weather. The only sail we had left to keep the ship running; so you may guess what it had been like for days. Anxious sort of job, that. He gave me some of his cursed insolence at the sheet. I tell you I was overdone with this terrific weather that seemed to have no end to it. Terrific, I tell you—and a deep ship. I believe the fellow himself was half crazed with funk. It was no time for gentlemanly reproof, so I turned round and felled him like an ox. He up and at me. We closed just as an awful sea made for the ship. All hands saw it coming and took to the rigging, but I had him by the throat, and went on shaking him like a rat, the men above us yelling, "Look out! look out!" Then a crash as if the sky had fallen on my head. They say that for over ten minutes hardly anything was to be seen of the ship – just the three masts and a bit of the forecastle head and of the poop all awash driving along in a smother of foam. It was a miracle that they found us, jammed together behind the forebits. It's clear that I meant business, because I was holding him by the throat still when they picked us up. He was black in the face. It was too much for them. It seems they rushed us aft together, gripped as we were, screaming "Murder!" like a lot of lunatics, and broke into the cuddy. And the ship running for her life, touch and go all the time, any minute her last in a sea fit to turn your hair grey only a-looking at it. I understand that the skipper, too, started raving like the rest of them. The man had been deprived of sleep for more than a week, and to have this sprung on him at the height of a furious gale nearly drove him out of his mind. I wonder they didn't fling me overboard after getting the carcass of their precious ship-mate out of my fingers. They had rather a job to separate us, I've been told. A sufficiently fierce story to make an old judge and a respectable jury sit up a bit. The first thing I heard when I came to myself was the maddening howling of that endless gale, and on that the voice of the old man. He was hanging on to my bunk, staring into my face out of his sou'wester.

' "Mr Leggatt, you have killed a man. You can act no longer as chief mate of this ship." '

His care to subdue his voice made it sound monotonous. He rested a hand on the end of the skylight to steady himself with, and all that time did not stir a limb, so far as I could see. 'Nice little tale for a quiet tea-party,' he concluded in the same tone.

One of my hands, too, rested on the end of the skylight; neither did I stir a limb, so far as I knew. We stood less than a foot from each other. It occurred to me that if old 'Bless my soul – you don't say so' were to put his head up the companion and catch sight of us, he would think he was seeing double, or imagine himself come upon a scene of weird witchcraft; the strange captain having a quiet confabulation by the wheel with his own grey ghost. I became very much concerned to prevent anything of the sort. I heard the other's soothing undertone.

'My father's a parson in Norfolk,' it said. Evidently he had forgotten he had told me this important fact before. Truly a nice little tale.

'You had better slip down into my stateroom now,' I said, moving off stealthily. My double followed my movements; our bare feet made no sound; I let him in, closed the door with care, and, after giving a call to the second mate, returned on deck for my relief.

'Not much sign of any wind yet,' I remarked when he approached.

'No, sir. Not much,' he assented, sleepily, in his hoarse voice, with just enough deference, no more, and barely suppressing a yawn.

'Well, that's all you have to look out for. You have got your orders.'

'Yes, sir.'

I paced a turn or two on the poop and saw him take up his position face forward with his elbow in the ratlines of the mizzen-rigging before I went below. The mate's faint snoring was still going on peacefully. The cuddy lamp was burning over the table on which stood a vase with flowers, a polite attention from the ship's provision merchant – the last flowers we should see for the next three months at the very least. Two bunches of bananas hung from the beam symmetrically, one on each side of the rudder-casing. Everything was as before in the ship – except that two of her captain's sleeping-suits were simultaneously in use, one motionless in the cuddy, the other keeping very still in the captain's stateroom.

It must be explained here that my cabin had the form of the capital letter L the door being within the angle and opening into the short part of the letter. A couch was to the left, the bed-place to the right; my writing-desk and the chronometers' table faced the door. But any one opening it, unless he stepped right inside, had no view of what I call the long (or vertical) part of the letter. It contained some lockers surmounted by a bookcase; and a few clothes, a thick jacket or two, caps, oilskin coat, and such like, hung on hooks. There was at the bottom of that part a door opening into my bath-room, which could be entered also directly from the saloon. But that way was never used.

The mysterious arrival had discovered the advantage of this particular shape. Entering my room, lighted strongly by a big bulkhead lamp swung on gimbals above my writing-desk, I did not see him anywhere till he stepped out quietly from behind the coats hung in the recessed part.

'I heard somebody moving about, and went in there at once,' he whispered.

I, too, spoke under my breath.

'Nobody is likely to come in here without knocking and getting permission.'

He nodded. His face was thin and the sunburn faded, as though he had been ill. And no wonder, He had been, I heard presently, kept under arrest in his cabin for nearly seven weeks. But there was nothing sickly in his eyes or in his expression. He was not a bit like me, really; yet, as we stood leaning over my bed-place, whispering side by side, with our dark heads together and our backs to the door, anybody bold enough to open it stealthily would have been treated to the uncanny sight of a double captain busy talking in whispers with his other self.

'But all this doesn't tell me how you came to hang on to our side-ladder,' I inquired, in the hardly audible murmurs we used, after he had told me something more of the proceedings on board the *Sephora* once the bad weather was over.

'When we sighted Java Head I had had time to think all those matters out several times over. I had six weeks of doing nothing else, and with only an hour or so every evening for a tramp on the quarter-deck.'

He whispered, his arms folded on the side of my bed-place, staring through the open port. And I could imagine perfectly the manner of this thinking out – a stubborn if not a steadfast operation; something of which I should have been perfectly incapable.

'I reckoned it would be dark before we closed with the land,' he continued, so low that I had to strain my hearing, near as we were to each other, shoulder touching shoulder almost. 'So I asked to speak to the old man. He always seemed very sick when he came to see me – as if he could not look me in the face. You know, that foresail saved the ship. She was too deep to have run long under bare poles. And it was I that managed to set it for him. Anyway, he came. When I had him in my cabin – he stood by the door looking at me as if I had the halter round my neck already – I asked him right away to leave my cabin door unlocked at night while the ship was going through Sunda Straits. There would be the Java coast within two or three miles, off Angier Point. I wanted nothing more. I've had a prize for swimming my second year in the Conway.'

'I can believe it,' I breathed out.

'God only knows why they locked me in every night. To see some of their faces you'd have thought they were afraid I'd go about at night strangling people. Am I a murdering brute? Do I look it? By Jove! if I had been he wouldn't have trusted himself like that into my room. You'll say I might have chucked him aside and bolted out, there and then – it was dark already. Well, no. And for the same reason I wouldn't think of trying to smash the door. There would have been a rush to stop me at the noise, and I did not mean to get into a confounded scrimmage. Somebody else might have got killed – for I would not have broken out only to get chucked back, and I did not want any more of that work. He refused, looking more sick than ever. He was afraid of the men, and also of that old second mate of his who had been sailing with him for years – a grey-headed old humbug; and his steward, too, had been with him devil knows how long – seventeen years or more – a dogmatic sort of loafer who hated me like poison, just because I was the chief mate. No chief mate ever made more than one voyage in the *Sephora*, you know. Those two old chaps ran the ship. Devil only knows what the skipper wasn't afraid of (all his nerve went to pieces altogether in that hellish spell of bad weather we had) – of what the law would do to him – of his wife, perhaps. Oh, yes!

she's on board. Though I don't think she would have meddled. She would have been only too glad to have me out of the ship in any way. The "brand of Cain" business, don't you see. That's all right. I was ready enough to go off wandering on the face of the earth – and that was price enough to pay for an Abel of that sort. Anyhow, he wouldn't listen to me. "This thing must take its course. I represent the law here." He was shaking like a leaf. "So you won't?" "No!" "Then I hope you will be able to sleep on that," I said, and turned my back on him. "I wonder that *you* can," cries he, and locks the door.

'Well, after that, I couldn't. Not very well. That was three weeks ago. We have had a slow passage through the Java Sea; drifted about Carimata for ten days. When we anchored here they thought, I suppose, it was all right. The nearest land (and that's five miles) is the ship's destination; the consul would soon set about catching me; and there would have been no object in bolting to these islets there. I don't suppose there's a drop of water on them. I don't know how it was, but tonight that steward, after bringing me my supper, went out to let me eat it, and left the door unlocked. And I ate it – all there was, too. After I had finished I strolled out on the quarter-deck. I don't know that I meant to do anything. A breath of fresh air was all I wanted, I believe. Then a sudden temptation came over me. I kicked off my slippers and was in the water before I had made up my mind fairly. Somebody heard the splash and they raised an awful hullabaloo. "He's gone! Lower the boats! He's committed suicide! No, he's swimming." Certainly I was swimming. It's not so easy for a swimmer like me to commit suicide by drowning. I landed on the nearest islet before the boat left the ship's side. I heard them pulling about in the dark, hailing, and so on, but after a bit they gave up. Everything quieted down and the anchorage became as still as death. I sat down on a stone and began to think. I felt certain they would start searching for me at daylight. There was no place to hide on those stony things – and if there had been, what would have been the good? But now I was clear of that ship,

I was not going back. So after a while I took off all my clothes, tied them up in a bundle with a stone inside, and dropped them in the deep water on the outer side of that islet. That was suicide enough for me. Let them think what they liked, but I didn't mean to drown myself. I meant to swim till I sank – but that's not the same thing. I struck out for another of these little islands, and it was from that one that I first saw your riding-light. Something to swim for. I went on easily, and on the way I came upon a flat rock a foot or two above water. In the daytime, I dare say, you might make it out with a glass from your poop. I scrambled up on it and rested myself for a bit. Then I made another start. That last spell must have been over a mile.'

His whisper was getting fainter and fainter, and all the time he stared straight out through the port-hole, in which there was not even a star to be seen. I had not interrupted him. There was something that made comment impossible in his narrative, or perhaps in himself; a sort of feeling, a quality, which I can't find a name for. And when he ceased, all I found was a futile whisper: 'So you swam for our light?'

'Yes – straight for it. It was something to swim for. I couldn't see any stars low down because the coast was in the way, and I couldn't see the land, either. The water was like glass. One might have been swimming in a confounded thousand-feet deep cistern with no place for scrambling out anywhere; but what I didn't like was the notion of swimming round and round like a crazed bullock before I gave out; and as I didn't mean to go back . . . No. Do you see me being hauled back, stark naked, off one of these little islands by the scruff of the neck and fighting like a wild beast? Somebody would have got killed for certain, and I did not want any of that. So I went on. Then your ladder——'

'Why didn't you hail the ship?' I asked, a little louder.

He touched my shoulder lightly. Lazy footsteps came right over our heads and stopped. The second mate had crossed from the other side of the poop and might have been hanging over the rail, for all we knew.

'He couldn't hear us talking – could he?' My double breathed into my very ear, anxiously.

His anxiety was an answer, a sufficient answer, to the question I had put to him. An answer containing all the difficulty of that situation. I closed the port-hole quietly, to make sure. A louder word might have been overheard.

'Who's that?' he whispered then.

'My second mate. But I don't know much more of the fellow than you do.'

And I told him a little about myself. I had been appointed to take charge while I least expected anything of the sort, not quite a fortnight ago. I didn't know either the ship or the people. Hadn't had the time in port to look about me or size anybody up. And as to the crew, all they knew was that I was appointed to take the ship home. For the rest, I was almost as much of a stranger on board as himself, I said. And at the moment I felt it most acutely. I felt that it would take very little to make me a suspect person in the eyes of the ship's company.

He had turned about meantime; and we, the two strangers in the ship, faced each other in identical attitudes.

'Your ladder——' he murmured, after a silence. 'Who'd have thought of finding a ladder hanging over at night in a ship anchored out here! I felt just then a very unpleasant faintness. After the life I've been leading for nine weeks, anybody would have got out of condition. I wasn't capable of swimming round as far as your rudder-chains. And, lo and behold! there was a ladder to get hold of. After I gripped it I said to myself, 'What's the good?' When I saw a man's head looking over I thought I would swim away presently and leave him shouting – in whatever language it was. I didn't mind being looked at. I – I liked it. And then you speaking to me so quietly – as if you had expected me – made me hold on a little longer. It had been a confounded lonely time – I don't mean while swimming. I was glad to talk a little to somebody that didn't belong to the *Sephora*. As to asking for the captain, that was a mere impulse. It could have been no use, with all the ship knowing about me and the other people pretty certain to be round here in the morning. I don't know – I wanted to be seen, to talk with somebody, before I went on. I don't know what I would have said. . . . "Fine night, isn't it?" or something of the sort.'

'Do you think they will be round here presently?' I asked with some incredulity.

'Quite likely,' he said, faintly.

He looked extremely haggard all of a sudden. His head rolled on his shoulders.

'H'm. We shall see then. Meantime get into that bed,' I whispered. 'Want help? There.'

It was a rather high bed-place with a set of drawers underneath. This amazing swimmer really needed the lift I gave him by seizing his leg. He tumbled in, rolled over on his back, and flung one arm across his eyes. And then, with his face nearly hidden, he must have looked exactly as I used to look in that bed. I gazed upon my other self for a while before drawing across carefully the two green serge curtains which ran on a brass rod. I thought for a moment of pinning them together for greater safety, but I sat down on the couch, and once there I felt unwilling to rise and hunt for a pin. I would do it in a moment. I was extremely tired, in a peculiarly intimate way, by the strain of stealthiness, by the effort of whispering and the general secrecy of this excitement. It was three o'clock by now and I had been on my feet since nine, but I was not sleepy; I could not have gone to sleep. I sat there, fagged out, looking at the curtains, trying to clear my mind of the confused sensation of being in two places at once, and greatly bothered by an exasperating knocking in my head. It was a relief to discover suddenly that it was not in my head at all, but on the outside of the door. Before I could collect myself the words 'Come in' were out of my mouth, and the steward entered with a tray, bringing in my morning coffee. I had slept, after all, and I was so frightened that I shouted, 'This way! I am here, steward,' as though he had been miles away. He put down the tray on the table next the couch and only then said, very quietly, 'I can see you are here, sir.' I felt him give me a keen look, but I dared not meet his eyes just then. He must have wondered why I had drawn the curtains of my bed before going to sleep on the couch. He went out, hooking the door open as usual.

I heard the crew washing decks above me. I knew I would have been told at once if there had been any wind. Calm, I thought, and I was doubly vexed. Indeed, I felt dual more than ever. The steward reappeared suddenly in the doorway. I jumped up from the couch so quickly that he gave a start.

'What do you want here?'

'Close your port, sir – they are washing decks.'

'It is closed,' I said, reddening.

'Very well, sir.' But he did not move from the doorway and returned my stare in an extraordinary, equivocal manner for a time. Then his eyes wavered, all his expression changed, and in a voice unusually gentle, almost coaxingly:

'May I come in to take the empty cup away, sir?'

'Of course!' I turned my back on him while he popped in and out. Then I unhooked and closed the door and even pushed the bolt. This sort of thing could not go on very long. The cabin was as hot as an oven, too. I took a peep at my double, and discovered that he had not moved, his arm was still over his eyes; but his chest heaved; his hair was wet; his chin glistened with perspiration. I reached over him and opened the port.

'I must show myself on deck,' I reflected.

Of course, theoretically, I could do what I liked, with no one to say nay to me within the whole circle of the horizon; but to lock my cabin door and take the key away I did not dare. Directly I put my head out of the companion I saw the group of my two officers, the second mate barefooted, the chief mate in long india-rubber boots, near the break of the poop, and the steward half-way down the poop-ladder talking to them eagerly. He happened to catch sight of me and dived, the second ran down on the main-deck shouting some order or other, and the chief mate came to meet me, touching his cap.

There was a sort of curiosity in his eye that I did not like. I don't know whether the steward had told them that I was 'queer' only, or downright drunk, but I know the man meant to have a good look at me. I watched him coming with a smile which, as he got into point-blank range, took effect and froze his very whiskers. I did not give him time to open his lips.

'Square the yards by lifts and braces before the hands go to breakfast.'

It was the first particular order I had given on board that ship; and I stayed on deck to see it executed, too. I had felt the need of asserting myself without loss of time. That sneering young cub got taken down a peg or two on that occasion, and I also seized the opportunity of having a good look at the face of every foremast man as they filed past me to go to the after braces. At breakfast time, eating nothing myself, I presided with such frigid dignity that the two mates were only too glad to escape from the cabin as soon as decency permitted; and all the time the dual working of my mind distracted me almost to the point of insanity. I was constantly watching myself, my secret self, as dependent on my actions as my own personality, sleeping in that bed, behind that door which faced me as I sat at the head of the table. It was very much like being mad, only it was worse because one was aware of it.

I had to shake him for a solid minute, but when at last he opened his eyes it was in the full possession of his senses, with an inquiring look.

'All's well so far,' I whispered. 'Now you must vanish into the bath-room.'

He did so, as noiseless as a ghost, and then I rang for the steward, and facing him boldly, directed him to tidy up my stateroom while I was having my bath – 'and be quick about it'. As my tone admitted of no excuses, he said, 'Yes, sir,' and ran off to fetch his dust-pan and brushes. I took a bath and did most of my dressing, splashing, and whistling softly for the steward's edification, while the secret sharer of my life stood drawn up bolt upright in that little space, his face looking very sunken in daylight, his eyelids lowered under the stern, dark line of his eyebrows drawn together by a slight frown.

When I left him there to go back to my room the steward was finishing dusting. I sent for the mate and engaged him in some insignificant conversation. It was, as it were, trifling with the terrific character of his whiskers; but my object was to give him an opportunity for a good look at my cabin. And then I could at last shut, with a clear conscience, the door of my stateroom and get my double back into the recessed part. There was nothing else for it. He had to sit still on a small folding stool, half smothered by the heavy coats hanging there. We listened to the steward going into the bath-room out of the saloon, filling the water-bottles there, scrubbing the bath, setting things to rights, whisk, bang, clatter – out again into the saloon – turn the key – click. Such was my scheme for keeping my second self invisible. Nothing better could be contrived under the circumstances. And there we sat; I at my writing-desk ready to appear busy with some papers, he behind me out of sight of the door. It would not have been prudent to talk in daytime; and I could not have stood the excitement of that queer sense of whispering to myself. Now and then, glancing over my shoulder, I saw him far back there, sitting rigidly on the low stool, his bare feet close together, his arms folded, his head hanging on his breast – and perfectly still. Anybody would have taken him for me.

I was fascinated by it myself. Every moment I had to glance over my shoulder. I was looking at him when a voice outside the door said:

'Beg pardon, sir.'

'Well!' . . . I kept my eyes on him, and so when the voice outside the door announced, 'There's a ship's boat coming our way, sir,' I saw him give a start – the first movement he had made for hours. But he did not raise his bowed head.

'All right. Get the ladder over.'

I hesitated. Should I whisper something to him? But what? His immobility seemed to have been never disturbed. What could I tell him he did not know already? . . . Finally I went on deck.

2

The skipper of the *Sephora* had a thin red whisker all round his face, and the sort of complexion that goes with hair of that colour; also the particular, rather smeary shade of blue in the eyes. He was not exactly a showy figure; his shoulders were high, his stature but middling – one leg slightly more bandy than the other. He shook hands, looking vaguely around. A spiritless tenacity was his main characteristic, I judged. I behaved with a politeness which seemed to disconcert him. Perhaps he was shy. He mumbled to me as if he were ashamed of what he was saying; gave his name (it was something like Archbold – but at this distance of years I hardly am sure), his ship's name, and a few other particulars of that sort, in the manner of a criminal making a reluctant and doleful confession. He had had terrible weather on the passage out – terrible – terrible – wife aboard, too.

By this time we were seated in the cabin and the steward brought in a tray with a bottle and glasses. 'Thanks! No.' Never took liquor. Would have some water, though. He drank two tumblerfuls. Terrible thirsty work. Ever since daylight had been exploring the islands round his ship.

'What was that for – fun?' I asked, with an appearance of polite interest.

'No!' He sighed. 'Painful duty.'

As he persisted in his mumbling and I wanted my double to hear every word, I hit upon the notion of informing him that I regretted to say I was hard of hearing.

'Such a young man, too!' he nodded, keeping his smeary blue, unintelligent eyes fastened upon me. What was the cause of it – some disease? he inquired, without the least sympathy and as if he thought that, if so, I'd got no more than I deserved.

'Yes; disease,' I admitted in a cheerful tone which seemed

to shock him. But my point was gained, because he had to raise his voice to give me his tale. It is not worth while to record that version. It was just over two months since all this had happened, and he had thought so much about it that he seemed completely muddled as to its bearings, but still immensely impressed.

'What would you think of such a thing happening on board your own ship? I've had the *Sephora* for these fifteen years. I am a well-known shipmaster.'

He was densely distressed – and perhaps I should have sympathized with him if I had been able to detach my mental vision from the unsuspected sharer of my cabin as though he were my second self. There he was on the other side of the bulkhead, four or five feet from us, no more, as we sat in the saloon. I looked politely at Captain Archbold (if that was his name), but it was the other I saw, in a grey sleeping-suit, seated on a low stool, his bare feet close together, his arms folded, and every word said between us falling into the ears of his dark head bowed on his chest.

'I have been at sea now, man and boy, for seven-and-thirty years, and I've never heard of such a thing happening in an English ship. And that it should be my ship. Wife on board, too.'

I was hardly listening to him.

'Don't you think,' I said, 'that the heavy sea which, you told me, came aboard just then might have killed the man? I have seen the sheer weight of a sea kill a man very neatly, by simply breaking his neck.'

'Good God!' he uttered, impressively, fixing his smeary blue eyes on me. 'The sea! No man killed by the sea ever looked like that.' He seemed positively scandalized at my suggestion. And as I gazed at him, certainly not prepared for anything original on his part, he advanced his head close to mine and thrust his tongue out at me so suddenly that I couldn't help starting back.

After scoring over my calmness in this graphic way he

nodded wisely. If I had seen the sight, he assured me, I would never forget it as long as I lived. The weather was too bad to give the corpse a proper sea burial. So next day at dawn they took it up on the poop, covering its face with a bit of bunting; he read a short prayer, and then, just as it was, in its oilskins and long boots, they launched it amongst those mountainous seas that seemed ready every moment to swallow up the ship herself and the terrified lives on board of her.

'That reefed foresail saved you,' I threw in.

'Under God – it did,' he exclaimed fervently. 'It was by a special mercy, I firmly believe, that it stood some of those hurricane squalls.'

'It was the setting of that sail which——' I began.

'God's own hand in it,' he interrupted me. 'Nothing less could have done it. I don't mind telling you that I hardly dared give the order. It seemed impossible that we could touch anything without losing it, and then our last hope would have been gone.'

The terror of that gale was on him yet. I let him go on for a bit, then said, casually – as if returning to a minor subject:

'You were very anxious to give up your mate to the shore people, I believe?'

He was. To the law. His obscure tenacity on that point had in it something incomprehensible and a little awful; something, as it were, mystical, quite apart from his anxiety that he should not be suspected of 'countenancing any doings of that sort'. Seven-and-thirty virtuous years at sea, of which over twenty of immaculate command, and the last fifteen in the *Sephora*, seemed to have laid him under some pitiless obligation.

'And you know,' he went on, groping shamefacedly amongst his feelings, 'I did not engage that young fellow. His people had some interest with my owners. I was in a way forced to take him on. He looked very smart, very gentlemanly, and all that. But do you know – I never liked him, somehow. I am a plain man. You see, he wasn't exactly the sort for the chief mate of a ship like the *Sephora*.'

I had become so connected in thoughts and impressions with the secret sharer of my cabin that I felt as if I, personally, were being given to understand that I, too, was not the sort that would have done for the chief mate of a ship like the *Sephora*. I had no doubt of it in my mind.

'Not at all the style of man. You understand,' he insisted, superfluously, looking hard at me.

I smiled urbanely. He seemed at a loss for a while.

'I suppose I must report a suicide.'

'Beg pardon?'

'Sui-cide! That's what I'll have to write to my owners directly I get in.'

'Unless you manage to recover him before tomorrow,' I assented, dispassionately. . . . 'I mean, alive.'

He mumbled something which I really did not catch, and I turned my ear to him in a puzzled manner. He fairly bawled:

'The land – I say, the mainland is at least seven miles off my anchorage.'

'About that.'

My lack of excitement, of curiosity, of surprise, of any sort of pronounced interest, began to arouse his distrust. But except for the felicitous pretence of deafness I had not tried to pretend anything. I had felt utterly incapable of playing the part of ignorance properly, and therefore was afraid to try. It is also certain that he had brought some ready-made suspicions with him, and that he viewed my politeness as a strange and unnatural phenomenon. And yet how else could I have received him? Not heartily! That was impossible for psychological reasons, which I need not state here. My only object was to keep off his inquiries. Surlily? Yes, but surliness might have provoked a point-blank question. From its novelty to him and from its nature, punctilious courtesy was the manner best calculated to restrain the man. But there was the danger of his breaking through my defence bluntly. I could not, I think, have met him by a direct lie, also for psychological (not moral) reasons. If he had only known how afraid I was of his putting my feeling of identity with the other to the test! But, strangely enough – (I thought of it only afterwards) – I believe that he was not a little disconcerted by the reverse side of that weird situation, by something in me that reminded him of the man he was seeking – suggested a mysterious similitude to the young fellow he had distrusted and disliked from the first.

However that might have been, the silence was not very prolonged. He took another oblique step.

'I reckon I had no more than a two-mile pull to your ship. Not a bit more.'

'And quite enough, too, in this awful heat,' I said.

Another pause full of mistrust followed. Necessity, they say, is mother of invention, but fear, too, is not barren of ingenious suggestions. And I was afraid he would ask me point-blank for news of my other self.

'Nice little saloon, isn't it?' I remarked, as if noticing for the first time the way his eyes roamed from one closed door to the other. 'And very well fitted out, too. Here, for instance,' I continued, reaching over the back of my seat negligently and flinging the door open, 'is my bath-room.'

He made an eager movement, but hardly gave it a glance. I got up, shut the door of the bath-room, and invited him to have a look round, as if I were very proud of my accommodation. He had to rise and be shown round, but he went through the business without any raptures whatever.

'And now we'll have a look at my stateroom,' I declared, in a voice as loud as I dared to make it, crossing the cabin to the starboard side with purposely heavy steps.

He followed me in and gazed around. My intelligent double had vanished. I played my part.

'Very convenient – isn't it?'

'Very nice. Very comf...' He didn't finish and went out brusquely as if to escape from some unrighteous wiles of mine. But it was not to be. I had been too frightened not to feel vengeful; I felt I had him on the run, and I meant to keep him on the run. My polite insistence must have had something menacing in it, because he gave in suddenly. And I did not let him off a single item; mate's room, pantry, storerooms, the very sail-locker which was also under the poop – he had to look into them all. When at last I showed him out on the quarter-deck he drew a long, spiritless sigh, and mumbled dismally that he must really be going back to his ship now. I desired my mate, who had joined us, to see to the captain's boat.

The man of whiskers gave a blast on the whistle which he used to wear hanging round his neck, and yelled, '*Sephora's* away!' My double down there in my cabin must have heard, and certainly could not feel more relieved than I. Four fellows came running out from somewhere forward and went over the side, while my own men, appearing on deck too, lined the rail. I escorted my visitor to the gangway ceremoniously, and nearly overdid it. He was a tenacious beast. On the very ladder he lingered, and in that unique, guiltily conscientious manner of sticking to the point:

'I say ... you ... you don't think that—'

I covered his voice loudly:

'Certainly not. ... I am delighted. Good-bye.'

I had an idea of what he meant to say, and just saved myself by the privilege of defective hearing. He was too shaken generally to insist, but my mate, close witness of that parting, looked mystified and his face took on a thoughtful cast. As I did not want to appear as if I wished to avoid all communication with my officers, he had the opportunity to address me.

'Seems a very nice man. His boat's crew told our chaps a very extraordinary story, if what I am told by the steward is true. I suppose you had it from the captain, sir?'

'Yes. I had a story from the captain.'

'A very horrible affair – isn't it, sir?'

'It is.'

'Beats all these tales we hear about murders in Yankee ships.'

'I don't think it beats them. I don't think it resembles them in the least.'

'Bless my soul – you don't say so! But of course I've no acquaintance whatever with American ships, not I, so I couldn't go against your knowledge. It's horrible enough for me. . . . But the queerest part is that those fellows seemed to have some idea the man was hidden aboard here. They had really. Did you ever hear of such a thing?'

'Preposterous – isn't it?'

We were walking to and fro athwart the quarter-deck. No one of the crew forward could be seen (the day was Sunday), and the mate pursued:

'There was some little dispute about it. Our chaps took offence. "As if we would harbour a thing like that," they said. "Wouldn't you like to look for him in our coal-hole?" Quite a tiff. But they made it up in the end. I suppose he did drown himself. Don't you, sir?'

'I don't suppose anything.'

'You have no doubt in the matter, sir?'

'None whatever.'

I left him suddenly. I felt I was producing a bad impression, but with my double down there it was most trying to be on deck. And it was almost as trying to be below. Altogether a nerve-trying situation. But on the whole I felt less torn in two when I was with him. There was no one in the whole ship whom I dared take into my confidence. Since the hands had got to know his story, it would have been impossible to pass him off for any one else, and an accidental discovery was to be dreaded now more than ever . . .

The steward being engaged in laying the table for dinner, we could talk only with our eyes when I first went down. Later in the afternoon we had a cautious try at whispering. The Sunday quietness of the ship was against us; the stillness of air and water around her was against us; the elements, the men were against us – everything was against us in our secret partnership; time itself – for this could not go on forever. The very trust in Providence was, I suppose, denied to his guilt. Shall I confess that this thought cast me down very much?

And as to the chapter of accidents which counts for so much in the book of success, I could only hope that it was closed. For what favourable accident could be expected?

'Did you hear everything?' were my first words as soon as we took up our position side by side, leaning over my bed-place.

He had. And the proof of it was his earnest whisper, 'The man told you he hardly dared to give the order.'

I understood the reference to be to that saving fore-sail.

'Yes. He was afraid of it being lost in the setting.'

'I assure you he never gave the order. He may think he did, but he never gave it. He stood there with me on the break of the poop after the maintopsail blew away, and whimpered about our last hope – positively whimpered about it and nothing else – and the night coming on! To hear one's skipper go on like that in such weather was enough to drive any fellow out of his mind. It worked me up into a sort of desperation. I just took it into my own hands and went away from him, boiling, and—— But what's the use telling you? *You* know! . . . Do you think that if I had not been pretty fierce with them I should have got the men to do anything? Not it! The bos'n perhaps? Perhaps! It wasn't a heavy sea – it was a sea gone mad! I suppose the end of the world will be something like that; and a man may have the heart to see it coming once and be done with it – but to have to face it day after day—— I don't blame anybody. I was precious little better than the rest. Only – I was an officer of that old coal-wagon, anyhow——'

'I quite understand,' I conveyed that sincere assurance into his ear. He was out of breath with whispering; I could hear him pant slightly. It was all very simple. The same strung-up force which had given twenty-four men a chance, at least, for their lives, had, in a sort of recoil, crushed an unworthy mutinous existence.

But I had no leisure to weigh the merits of the matter – footsteps in the saloon, a heavy knock. 'There's enough wind to get under way with, sir.' Here was the call of a new claim upon my thoughts and even upon my feelings.

'Turn the hands up,' I cried through the door. 'I'll be on deck directly.'

I was going out to make the acquaintance of my ship. Before I left the cabin our eyes met – the eyes of the only two strangers on board. I pointed to the recessed part where the little camp-stool awaited him and laid my finger on my lips. He made a gesture – somewhat vague – a little mysterious, accompanied by a faint smile, as if of regret.

This is not the place to enlarge upon the sensations of a man who feels for the first time a ship move under his feet to his own independent word. In my case they were not unalloyed. I was not wholly alone with my command; for there was that stranger in my cabin. Or rather, I was not completely and wholly with her. Part of me was absent. That mental feeling of being in two places at once affected me physically as if the mood of secrecy had penetrated my very soul. Before an hour had elapsed since the ship had begun to move, having occasion to ask the mate (he stood by my side) to take a compass bearing of the Pagoda, I caught myself reaching up to his ear in whispers. I say I caught myself, but enough had escaped to startle the man. I can't describe it otherwise than by saying that he shied. A grave, preoccupied manner, as though he were in possession of some perplexing intelligence, did not leave him henceforth. A little later I moved away from the rail to look at the compass with such a stealthy gait that the helmsman noticed it – and I could not help noticing the unusual roundness of his eyes. These are trifling instances, though it's to no commander's advantage to be suspected of ludicrous eccentricities. But I was also more seriously affected. There are to a seaman certain words, gestures, that should in given conditions come as naturally, as instinctively as the winking of a menaced eye. A certain order should spring on to his lips without thinking; a certain sign should get itself made, so to speak, without reflection. But all unconscious alertness had abandoned me. I had to make an effort of will to recall myself back (from the cabin) to the conditions of the moment. I felt that I was appearing an irresolute commander to those people who were watching me more or less critically.

And, besides, there were the scares. On the second day out, for instance, coming off the deck in the afternoon (I had straw slippers on my bare feet) I stopped at the open pantry door and spoke to the steward. He was doing something there with his back to me. At the sound of my voice he nearly jumped out of his skin, as the saying is, and incidentally broke a cup.

'What on earth's the matter with you?' I asked, astonished.

He was extremely confused. 'Beg your pardon, sir. I made sure you were in your cabin.'

'You see I wasn't.'

'No, sir. I could have sworn I had heard you moving in there not a moment ago. It's most extraordinary . . . very sorry, sir.'

I passed on with an inward shudder. I was so identified with my secret double that I did not even mention the fact in those scanty, fearful whispers we exchanged. I suppose he had made some slight noise of some kind or other. It would have been miraculous if he hadn't at one time or another. And yet, haggard as he appeared, he looked always perfectly self-controlled, more than calm – almost invulnerable. On my suggestion he remained almost entirely in the bathroom, which, upon the whole, was the safest place. There could be really no shadow of an excuse for any one ever wanting to go in there, once the steward had done with it. It was a very tiny place. Sometimes he reclined on the floor, his legs bent, his head sustained on one elbow. At others I would find him on the camp-stool, sitting in his grey sleeping-suit and with his cropped dark hair like a patient, unmoved convict. At night I would smuggle him into my bed-place, and we would whisper together, with the regular footfalls of the officer of the watch passing and repassing over our heads. It was an infinitely miserable time. It was lucky that some tins of fine preserves were stowed in a locker in my stateroom; hard bread I could always get hold of; and so he lived on stewed chicken, paté de foie gras, asparagus, cooked oysters, sardines – on all sorts of abominable sham delicacies out of tins. My early morning coffee he always drank; and it was all I dared do for him in that respect.

Every day there was the horrible manoeuvring to go through so that my room and then the bath-room should be done in the usual way. I came to hate the sight of the steward, to abhor the voice of that harmless man. I felt that it was he who would bring on the disaster of discovery. It hung like a sword over our heads.

The fourth day out, I think (we were then working down the east side of the Gulf of Siam, tack for tack, in light winds and smooth water) – the fourth day, I say, of this miserable juggling with the unavoidable, as we sat at our evening meal, that man, whose slightest movement I dreaded, after putting down the dishes ran up on deck busily. This could not be dangerous. Presently he came down again; and then it appeared that he had remembered a coat of mine which I had thrown over a rail to dry after having been wetted in a shower which had passed over the ship in the afternoon. Sitting stolidly at the head of the table I became terrified at the sight of the garment on his arm. Of course he made for my door. There was no time to lose.

'Steward,' I thundered. My nerves were so shaken that I could not govern my voice and conceal my agitation. This was the sort of thing that made my terrifically whiskered mate tap his forehead with his forefinger. I had detected him using that gesture while talking on deck with a confidential air to the carpenter. It was too far to hear a word, but I had no doubt that his pantomime could only refer to the strange new captain.

'Yes, sir,' the pale-faced steward turned resignedly to me. It was this maddening course of being shouted at, checked without rhyme or reason, arbitrarily chased out of my cabin, suddenly called into it, sent flying out of his pantry on incomprehensible errands, that accounted for the growing wretchedness of his expression.

'Where are you going with that coat?'

'To your room, sir.'

'Is there another shower coming?'

'I'm sure I don't know, sir. Shall I go up again and see, sir?'

'No! never mind.'

My object was attained, as of course my other self in there would have heard everything that passed. During this interlude my two officers never raised their eyes off their respective plates; but the lip of that confounded cub, the second mate, quivered visibly.

I expected the steward to hook my coat on and come out at once. He was very slow about it; but I dominated my nervousness sufficiently not to shout after him. Suddenly I became aware (it could be heard plainly enough) that the fellow for some reason or other was opening the door of the bath-room. It was the end. The place was literally not big enough to swing a cat in. My voice died in my throat and I went stony all over. I expected to hear a yell of surprise and terror, and made a movement, but had not the strength to get on my legs. Everything remained still. Had my second self taken the poor wretch by the throat? I don't know what I could have done next moment if I had not seen the steward come out of my room, close the door, and then stand quietly by the side-board.

'Saved,' I thought. 'But, no! Lost! Gone! He was gone!'

I laid my knife and fork down and leaned back in my chair. My head swam. After a while, when sufficiently recovered to speak in a steady voice, I instructed my mate to put the ship round at eight o'clock himself.

'I won't come on deck,' I went on. 'I think I'll turn in, and unless the wind shifts I don't want to be disturbed before midnight. I feel a bit seedy.'

'You did look middling bad a little while ago,' the chief mate remarked without showing any great concern.

They both went out, and I stared at the steward clearing the table. There was nothing to be read on that wretched man's face. But why did he avoid my eyes I asked myself. Then I thought I should like to hear the sound of his voice.

'Steward!'

'Sir!' Startled as usual.

'Where did you hang up that coat?'

'In the bath-room, sir.' The usual anxious tone. 'It's not quite dry yet, sir.'

For some time longer I sat in the cuddy. Had my double vanished as he had come? But of his coming there was an explanation, whereas his disappearance would be inexplicable. ... I went slowly into my dark room, shut the door, lighted the lamp, and for a time dared not turn round. When at last I did I saw him standing bolt-upright in the narrow recessed part. It would not be true to say I had a shock, but an irresistible doubt of his bodily existence flitted through my mind. Can it be, I asked myself, that he is not visible to other eyes than mine? It was like being haunted. Motionless, with a grave face, he raised his hands slightly at me in a gesture which meant clearly, 'Heavens! what a narrow escape!' Narrow indeed. I think I had come creeping quietly as near insanity as any man who has not actually gone over the border. That gesture restrained me, so to speak.

The mate with the terrific whiskers was now putting the ship on the other tack. In the moment of profound silence which follows upon the hands going to their stations I heard on the poop his raised voice: 'Hard alee!' and the distant shout of the order repeated on the maindeck. The sails, in that light breeze, made but a faint fluttering noise. It ceased. The ship was coming round slowly; I held my breath in the renewed stillness of expectation; one wouldn't have thought that there was a single living soul on her decks. A sudden brisk shout, 'Mainsail haul!' broke the spell, and in the noisy cries and rush overhead of the men running away with the main-brace we two, down in my cabin, came together in our usual position by the bed-place.

He did not wait for my question. 'I heard him fumbling here and just managed to squat myself down in the bath,' he whispered to me. 'The fellow only opened the door and put his arm in to hang the coat up. All the same——'

'I never thought of that,' I whispered back, even more appalled than before at the closeness of the shave, and marvelling at that something unyielding in his character which was carrying him through so finely. There was no agitation in his whisper. Whoever was being driven distracted, it was not he. He was sane. And the proof of his sanity was continued when he took up the whispering again.

'It would never do for me to come to life again.'

It was something that a ghost might have said. But what he was alluding to was his old captain's reluctant admission of the theory of suicide. It would obviously serve his turn – if I had understood at all the view which seemed to govern the unalterable purpose of his action.

'You must maroon me as soon as ever you can get amongst these islands off the Cambodje shore,' he went on.

'Maroon you! We are not living in a boy's adventure tale,' I protested. His scornful whispering took me up.

'We aren't indeed! There's nothing of a boy's tale in this. But there's nothing else for it. I want no more. You don't suppose I am afraid of what can be done to me? Prison or gallows or whatever they may please. But you don't see me coming back to explain such things to an old fellow in a wig and twelve respectable tradesmen, do you? What can they know whether I am guilty or not – or of *what* I am guilty, either? That's my affair. What does the Bible say? "Driven off the face of the earth." Very well. I am off the face of the earth now. As I came at night so I shall go.'

'Impossible!' I murmured. 'You can't.'

'Can't? . . . Not naked like a soul on the Day of Judgment. I shall freeze on to this sleeping-suit. The Last Day is not yet – and . . . you have understood thoroughly. Didn't you?'

I felt suddenly ashamed of myself. I may say truly that I understood – and my hesitation in letting that man swim away from my ship's side had been a mere sham sentiment, a sort of cowardice.

'It can't be done now till next night,' I breathed out. 'The ship is on the off-shore tack and the wind may fail us.'

'As long as I know that you understand,' he whispered. 'But of course you do. It's a great satisfaction to have got somebody to understand. You seem to have been there on purpose.' And in the same whisper, as if we two whenever we talked had to say things to each other which were not fit for the world to hear, he added, 'It's very wonderful.'

We remained side by side talking in our secret way – but sometimes silent or just exchanging a whispered word or two at long intervals. And as usual he stared through the port. A breath of wind came now and again into our faces. The ship might have been moored in dock, so gently and on an even keel she slipped through the water, that did not murmur even at our passage, shadowy and silent like a phantom sea.

At midnight I went on deck, and to my mate's great surprise put the ship round on the other tack. His terrible whiskers flitted round me in silent criticism. I certainly should not have done it if it had been only a question of getting out of that sleepy gulf as quickly as possible. I believe he told the second mate, who relieved him, that it was a great want of judgment. The other only yawned. The intolerable cub shuffled about so sleepily and lolled against the rails in such a slack, improper fashion that I came down on him sharply.

'Aren't you properly awake yet?'

'Yes, sir! I am awake.'

'Well, then, be good enough to hold yourself as if you were. And keep a look-out. If there's any current we'll be closing with some islands before daylight.'

The east side of the gulf is fringed with islands, some solitary, others in groups. On the blue background of the high coast they seem to float on silvery patches of calm water, arid and grey, or dark green and rounded like clumps of evergreen bushes, with the larger ones, a mile or two long, showing the outlines of ridges, ribs of grey rock under the dank mantle of matted leafage. Unknown to trade, to travel, almost to geography, the manner of life they harbour is an unsolved secret.

There must be villages – settlements of fishermen at least – on the largest of them, and some communication with the world is probably kept up by native craft. But all that forenoon, as we headed for them, fanned along by the faintest of breezes, I saw no sign of man or canoe in the field of the telescope I kept on pointing at the scattered group.

At noon I gave no orders for a change of course, and the mate's whiskers became much concerned and seemed to be offering themselves unduly to my notice. At last I said:

'I am going to stand right in. Quite in – as far as I can take her.'

The stare of extreme surprise imparted an air of ferocity also to his eyes, and he looked truly terrific for a moment.

'We're not doing well in the middle of the gulf,' I continued, casually. 'I am going to look for the land breezes tonight.'

'Bless my soul! Do you mean, sir, in the dark amongst the lot of all them islands and reefs and shoals?'

'Well – if there are any regular land breezes at all on this coast one must get close inshore to find them, mustn't one?'

'Bless my soul!' he exclaimed again under his breath. All that afternoon he wore a dreamy, contemplative appearance which in him was a mark of perplexity. After dinner I went into my stateroom as if I meant to take some rest. There we two bent our dark heads over a half-unrolled chart lying on my bed.

'There,' I said. 'It's got to be Koh-ring. I've been looking at it ever since sunrise. It has got two hills and a low point. It must be inhabited. And on the coast opposite there is what looks like the mouth of a biggish river – with some town, no doubt, not far up. It's the best chance for you that I can see.'

'Anything. Koh-ring let it be.'

He looked thoughtfully at the chart as if surveying chances and distances from a lofty height – and following with his eyes his own figure wandering on the blank land of Cochin-China, and then passing off that piece of paper clean out of sight into uncharted regions. And it was as if the ship had two captains to plan her course for her. I had been so worried and restless running up and down that I had not had the patience to dress that day. I had remained in my sleeping-suit, with straw slippers and a soft floppy hat. The closeness of the heat in the gulf had been most oppressive, and the crew were used to see me wandering in that airy attire.

'She will clear the south point as she heads now,' I whispered into his ear. 'Goodness only knows when, though, but certainly after dark. I'll edge her in to half a mile, as far as I may be able to judge in the dark—'

'Be careful,' he murmured, warningly – and I realized suddenly that all my future, the only future for which I was fit, would perhaps go irretrievably to pieces in any mishap to my first command.

I could not stop a moment longer in the room. I motioned him to get out of sight and made my way on the poop. That unplayful cub had the watch. I walked up and down for a while thinking things out, then beckoned him over.

'Send a couple of hands to open the two quarter-deck ports,' I said, mildly.

He actually had the impudence, or else so forgot himself in his wonder at such an incomprehensible order, as to repeat:

'Open the quarter-deck ports! What for, sir?'

'The only reason you need concern yourself about is because I tell you to do so. Have them open wide and fastened properly.'

He reddened and went off, but I believe made some jeering remark to the carpenter as to the sensible practice of ventilating a ship's quarter-deck. I know he popped into the mate's cabin to impart the fact to him because the whiskers came on deck, as it were by chance, and stole glances at me from below – for signs of lunacy or drunkenness, I suppose.

A little before supper, feeling more restless than ever, I rejoined, for a moment, my second self. And to find him sitting so quietly was surprising, like something against nature, in-human.

I developed my plan in a hurried whisper.

'I shall stand in as close as I dare and then put her round. I will presently find means to smuggle you out of here into the sail-locker, which communicates with the lobby. But there is an opening, a sort of square for hauling the sails out, which gives straight on the quarter-deck and which is never closed in fine weather, so as to give air to the sails. When the ship's way is deadened in stays and all the hands are aft at the main-braces you will have a clear road to slip out and get overboard through the open quarter-deck port. I've had them both fastened up. Use a rope's end to lower yourself into the water so as to avoid a splash – you know. It could be heard and cause some beastly complication.'

He kept silent for a while, then whispered, 'I understand.'

'I won't be there to see you go,' I began with an effort. 'The rest . . . I only hope I have understood, too.'

'You have. From first to last' – and for the first time there seemed to be a faltering, something strained in his whisper. He caught hold of my arm, but the ringing of the supper bell made me start. He didn't, though; he only released his grip.

After supper I didn't come below again till well past eight o'clock. The faint, steady breeze was loaded with dew; and the wet, darkened sails held all there was of propelling power in it. The night, clear and starry, sparkled darkly, and the opaque, lightless patches shifting slowly against the low stars were the drifting islets. On the port bow there was a big one more distant and shadowily imposing by the great space of sky it eclipsed.

On opening the door I had a back view of my very own self looking at a chart. He had come out of the recess and was standing near the table.

'Quite dark enough,' I whispered.

He stepped back and leaned against my bed with a level, quiet glance. I sat on the couch. We had nothing to say to each other. Over our heads the officer of the watch moved here and there. Then I heard him move quickly. I knew what that meant. He was making for the companion; and presently his voice was outside my door.

'We are drawing in pretty fast, sir. Land looks rather close.'

'Very well,' I answered. 'I am coming on deck directly.'

I waited till he was gone out of the cuddy, then rose. My double moved too. The time had come to exchange our last whispers, for neither of us was ever to hear each other's natural voice.

'Look here!' I opened a drawer and took out three sovereigns. 'Take this anyhow. I've got six and I'd give you the lot, only I must keep a little money to buy some fruit and vegetables for the crew from native boats as we go through Sunda Straits.' He shook his head.

'Take it,' I urged him, whispering desperately. 'No one can tell what——'

He smiled and slapped meaningly the only pocket of the sleeping-jacket. It was not safe, certainly. But I produced a large old silk handkerchief of mine, and tying the three pieces of gold in a corner, pressed it on him. He was touched, I suppose, because he took it at last and tied it quickly round his waist under the jacket, on his bare skin.

Our eyes met; several seconds elapsed, till, our glances still mingled, I extended my hand and turned the lamp out. Then I passed through the cuddy, leaving the door of my room wide open ... 'Steward!'

He was still lingering in the pantry in the greatness of his zeal, giving a rub-up to a plated cruet stand the last thing before going to bed. Being careful not to wake up the mate, whose room was opposite, I spoke in an undertone.

He looked round anxiously. 'Sir!'

'Can you get me a little hot water from the galley?'

'I am afraid, sir, the galley fire's been out for some time now.'

'Go and see.'

He flew up the stairs.

'Now,' I whispered, loudly, into the saloon – too loudly, perhaps, but I was afraid I couldn't make a sound. He was by my side in an instant – the double captain slipped past the stairs – through a tiny dark passage ... a sliding door. We were in the sail-locker, scrambling on our knees over the sails. A sudden thought struck me. I saw myself wandering barefooted, bareheaded, the sun beating on my dark poll. I snatched off my floppy hat and tried hurriedly in the dark to ram it on my other self. He dodged and fended off silently. I wonder what he thought had come to me before he understood and suddenly desisted. Our hands met gropingly, lingered united in a steady, motionless clasp for a second ... No word was breathed by either of us when they separated.

I was standing quietly by the pantry door when the steward returned.

'Sorry, sir. Kettle barely warm. Shall I light the spirit-lamp?'

'Never mind.'

I came out on deck slowly. It was now a matter of conscience to shave the land as close as possible – for now he must go overboard whenever the ship was put in stays. Must! There could be no going back for him. After a moment I walked over to leeward and my heart flew into my mouth at the nearness of the land on the bow. Under any other circumstances I would not have held on a minute longer. The second mate had followed me anxiously.

I looked on till I felt I could command my voice.

'She may weather,' I said then in a quiet tone.

'Are you going to try that, sir?' he stammered out incredulously.

I took no notice of him and raised my tone just enough to be heard by the helmsman.

'Keep her good full.'

'Good full, sir.'

The wind fanned my cheek, the sails slept, the world was silent. The strain of watching the dark loom of the land grow bigger and denser was too much for me. I had shut my eyes – because the ship must go closer. She must! The stillness was intolerable. Were we standing still?

When I opened my eyes the second view started my heart with a thump. The black southern hill of Koh-ring seemed to hang right over the ship like a towering fragment of the ever-lasting night. On that enormous mass of blackness there was not a gleam to be seen, not a sound to be heard. It was gliding irresistibly towards us and yet seemed already within reach of the hand. I saw the vague figures of the watch grouped in the waist, gazing in awed silence.

'Are you going on, sir?' inquired an unsteady voice at my elbow.

I ignored it. I had to go on.

'Keep her full. Don't check her way. That won't do now,' I said, warningly.

'I can't see the sails very well,' the helmsman answered me, in strange, quavering tones.

Was she close enough? Already she was, I won't say in the shadow of the land, but in the very blackness of it, already swallowed up as it were, gone too close to be recalled, gone from me altogether.

'Give the mate a call,' I said to the young man who stood at my elbow as still as death. 'And turn all hands up.'

My tone had a borrowed loudness reverberated from the height of the land. Several voices cried out together: 'We are all on deck, sir.'

Then stillness again, with the great shadow gliding closer, towering higher, without light, without a sound. Such a hush had fallen on the ship that she might have been a bark of the dead floating in slowly under the very gate of Erebus.

'My God! Where are we?'

It was the mate moaning at my elbow. He was thunderstruck, and as it were deprived of the moral support of his whiskers. He clapped his hands and absolutely cried out, 'Lost!'

'Be quiet,' I said, sternly.

He lowered his tone, but I saw the shadowy gesture of his despair. 'What are we doing here?'

'Looking for the land wind.'

He made as if to tear his hair, and addressed me recklessly. 'She will never get out. You have done it, sir. I knew it'd end in something like this. She will never weather, and you are too close now to stay. She'll drift ashore before she's round. O my God!'

I caught his arm as he was raising it to batter his poor devoted head, and shook it violently.

'She's ashore already,' he wailed, trying to tear himself away.

'Is she? . . . Keep good full there!'

'Good full, sir,' cried the helmsman in a frightened, thin, child-like voice.

I hadn't let go the mate's arm and went on shaking it. 'Ready about, do you hear? You go forward' – shake – 'and stop there' – shake – 'and hold your noise' – shake – 'and see these head-sheets properly overhauled' – shake, shake – shake.

And all the time I dared not look towards the land lest my heart should fail me. I released my grip at last and he ran forward as if fleeing for dear life.

I wondered what my double there in the sail-locker thought of this commotion. He was able to hear everything – and perhaps he was able to understand why, on my conscience, it had to be thus close – no less. My first order 'Hard alee!' re-echoed ominously under the towering shadow of Koh-ring as if I had shouted in a mountain gorge. And then I watched the land intently. In that smooth water and light wind it was impossible to feel the ship coming-to. No! I could not feel her. And my second self was making now ready to slip out and lower himself overboard. Perhaps he was gone already . . . ?

The great black mass brooding over our very mastheads began to pivot away from the ship's side silently. And now I forgot the secret stranger ready to depart, and remembered only that I was a total stranger to the ship. I did not know her. Would she do it? How was she to be handled?

I swung the mainyard and waited helplessly. She was perhaps stopped, and her very fate hung in the balance, with the black mass of Koh-ring like the gate of the everlasting night towering over her taffrail. What would she do now? Had she way on her yet? I stepped to the side swiftly, and on the shadowy water

I could see nothing except a faint phosphorescent flash revealing the glassy smoothness of the sleeping surface. It was impossible to tell – and I had not learned yet the feel of my ship. Was she moving? What I needed was something easily seen, a piece of paper, which I could throw overboard and watch. I had nothing on me. To run down for it I didn't dare. There was no time. All at once my strained, yearning stare distinguished a white object floating within a yard of the ship's side. White on the black water. A phosphorescent flash passed under it. What was that thing? . . . I recognized my own floppy hat. It must have fallen off his head . . . and he didn't bother. Now I had what I wanted – the saving mark for my eyes. But I hardly thought of my other self, now gone from the ship, to be hidden for ever from all friendly faces, to be a fugitive and a vagabond on the earth, with no brand of the curse on his sane forehead to stay a slaying hand . . . too proud to explain.

And I watched the hat – the expression of my sudden pity for his mere flesh. It had been meant to save his homeless head from the dangers of the sun. And now – behold – it was saving the ship, by serving me for a mark to help out the ignorance of my strangeness. Ha! It was drifting forward, warning me just in time that the ship had gathered sternway.

'Shift the helm,' I said in a low voice to the seaman standing still like a statue.

The man's eyes glistened wildly in the binnacle light as he jumped round to the other side and spun round the wheel.

I walked to the break of the poop. On the overshadowed deck all hands stood by the forebraces waiting for my order. The stars ahead seemed to be gliding from right to left. And all was so still in the world that I heard the quiet remark 'She's round,' passed in a tone of intense relief between two seamen.

'Let go and haul.'

The foreyards ran round with a great noise, amidst cheery cries. And now the frightful whiskers made themselves heard giving various orders. Already the ship was drawing ahead. And I was alone with her. Nothing! no one in the world should stand now between us, throwing a shadow on the way of silent knowledge and mute affection, the perfect communion of a seaman with his first command.

Walking to the taffrail, I was in time to make out, on the very edge of a darkness thrown by a towering black mass like the very gateway of Erebus – yes, I was in time to catch an evanescent glimpse of my white hat left behind to mark the spot where the secret sharer of my cabin and of my thoughts, as though he were my second self, had lowered himself into the water to take his punishment: a free man, a proud swimmer striking out for a new destiny.

COMMENTARY

The Secret Sharer was completed in two months at the end of 1909, during a period when Conrad was much preoccupied with justifying to himself and others the decision he had taken many years earlier to leave Poland for good and to settle, both as a man and as a writer, firmly on English soil. He was anxious that his action should not be interpreted as a desertion of his native land and her cultural heritage: he wanted people to accept that he had been prompted by the best motives and that he had behaved in no way dishonourably. Not surprisingly, honourable behaviour is an important theme in this story, which was first published as a serial in Harper's Magazine during the autumn of 1910 and appeared in book form two years later. Conrad himself characterized *The Secret Sharer* as one of his two 'calm-pieces' (the other being *The Shadow Line*) and thus contrasted it directly with *Typhoon* and *The Nigger of the 'Narcissus'*, his so-called 'storm-pieces'. We should not, however, be misled by this appellation. In no sense does the story lack bite or excitement. Calm conditions in the days of sail were seldom comfortable or convenient. It is an ominous, brooding serenity which hangs about the events of *The Secret Sharer* − one which conceals the eddies and currents lying beneath the surface and exaggerates the tension engendered by the association between Leggatt and the narrator. There is considerable significance in the fact that it is the treacherousness of a calm spell that nearly brings about the destruction of ship and crew in the closing pages of the story.

The story itself is based on actual events which took place in 1880 on the famous clipper *Cutty Sark*, whose chief mate, having accidentally killed a truculent seaman and subsequently, with the help of his captain, escaped from the ship, was recaptured and sentenced to seven years imprisonment for manslaughter. As Conrad admits, the story was common currency among 'the whole fleet of merchant ships trading to India, China, and Australia' and it even reached the English newspapers during the mid-eighties. When he came at last to use these events in *The Secret Sharer* he adapted and integrated them into what is much more than a simple tale of adventure. They are merely the bare bones that he clothes with the living flesh of everyday experience – the problems confronting a young man undertaking a new and untried enterprise; the development of his self-confidence; the way in which physical danger can act as a yard-stick to a man's true character (a theme shared with *Typhoon*); the matter of behaving in accordance with one's honour; and the fact, highlighted by the central relationship of the story, that a single disaster may lead to any man, whatever his background or standing, becoming 'a fugitive and a vagabond on the earth'.

The Secret Sharer falls into two parts, the first being concerned with setting the scene, determining the background events and establishing the central situation and character relationships, while the second deals with the development of both situation and relationships under the pressure of further events, and with the final resolution of the various problems with which the tale has been concerned.

The narrator here, unlike in *Typhoon* or *The Black Mate*, is one of the chief protagonists, intimately involved in events and relationships on which he is looking back after many years. He is, in fact, the most important character. It is what happens to him as a result of the adventure he recounts that most concerns us as we read the story. We see him at the outset as a young captain taking his first command. He is the only newcomer to a crew that has been together for eighteen months, 'the only stranger on board'. But, perhaps more important, he is untried. As he waits with his ship in the estuary for the breeze that is to take them to the open sea, he is deeply conscious of the fact that he has not yet given his first order. He is unsure of how either ship or crew will respond: 'what I felt most was my being a stranger to the ship.' It is this sensation of strangeness that prompts his arrangement of the anchor-watch, his decision to stay on deck alone 'as if I had expected . . . to get on terms with the ship of which I knew nothing'. These feelings are heightened for him by the immense pervasive calm. It is not merely a stillness – there is a sort of deadness about everything, an emptiness, a barrenness, something akin to hostility. There is no sound in the ship 'and around us nothing moved, nothing lived, not a canoe on the water, not a bird in the air, not a cloud in the sky'.

Having established both mood and setting in this way, Conrad now presents a typical contrast – a narrative technique employed to similar effect both in *Typhoon* and *The Black Mate*. From the eerie stillness of the deck, we are introduced to the very different world of the cuddy where the officers share their meals: to the 'painstaking' chief mate whose dominant trait is 'to take all things into earnest consideration' and who is caricatured by means of his bushy whiskers (referred to by turns as 'absurd', 'terrible', 'frightful') and to the enigmatic second mate, outwardly 'grave beyond his years' but capable of satirical humour at the expense of his superiors, as we see from his allowing captain and first mate to indulge in fruitless conjecture about the *Sephora* throughout the meal without letting on that he knows the facts all the time. Thus from the sombre stillness of the deck and from the captain's loneliness we are brought to the casual conversation of mealtime in the cuddy and the feeling of human beings reacting to each other. We are even invited to smile at the business of the first mate and the scorpion. What we are perhaps unaware of is that Conrad is relaxing us so that the impact of the coming drama will be all the greater.

In the moments before the first encounter between the captain and his secret sharer we are diverted in another manner. We begin to notice small details about the narrator – features that, as a commander, he shares with men like MacWhirr and even Johns, and which perhaps demonstrate some of Conrad's own feelings about what sort of men are best suited to this great responsibility. The rope side-ladder has been left out from when the master of the tug departed. The captain is irritated. 'Exactitude in small matters,' he tells us, just as MacWhirr might have done had he been writing, 'is the very soul of discipline.' Then he realizes that the fault is likely his, that had he not altered the watch arrangements the men would have stowed the ladder away in the normal course of things; and we are treated to a little more of the philosophy of experienced command as he questions whether it is ever wise to interfere with routine.

If he can hold off the next stage of his narrative – the encounter itself – no longer, Conrad can and does present it in a far from conventional manner. Where a lesser writer might have wrung from the situation the last drop of tension and mystery, *he* tantalizes by evoking in us a subtle blend of emotional responses. Certainly there is mystery – the uncanny phosphorescence of the 'sleeping water' or the sea-lightning that makes Leggatt appear 'ghastly, silvery, fish-like'; certainly there is too a gulping horror as we witness with the narrator the naked body of a man at the foot of the ladder – a corpse? headless? What we don't expect, however, is a lightness almost approaching humour in the narrator's attention to the detail of his cigar entering the water with a 'tiny plop and a short hiss', in the visitor's enquiry as to what time it is or in his apparent intention to swim off once more into the night. For those who by now are beginning to know and enjoy their Conrad, moreover, there is another feature worth noticing in this episode. Listen to Leggatt's voice. It is 'calm and resolute', 'a good voice'. There is a revealing superiority in the way he unknowingly addresses the narrator as 'my man'. If we notice these details now, we will not be too surprised when in the second part of the story the fugitive's captain describes him as being not the right sort for chief mate of a ship like the *Sephora*. Too gentlemanly! Echoes of the unpleasant Captain Johns of the *Sapphire* (uncanny similarity of names for the two ships as well!) and his declaration that after Bunter there were to be no more 'gentleman mates' for him. Echoes of Conrad's own career maybe: he was after all a gentleman by birth and he does seem to have parted company with a number of ships during his early career as a result of arguments with their masters. It may be worth making a mental note at this stage, therefore, to watch the relationship of Leggatt and his captain for signs of strain.

But that need not concern us now. Conrad, with considerable skill, avoids the danger of narrative anticlimax once Leggatt has climbed aboard by two distinct means: first, by establishing the eerie relationship between the visitor and his host; second, by turning to Leggatt's story of the events which led eventually to his dramatic escape from the *Sephora*.

The relationship seems at first to be on the level merely of superficial appearances. Indeed, the narrator dwells on this idea at one point, saying that they share certain likenesses only because of the night and the circumstances in which they find themselves. Both men are young, with only a few years between them; they are similar in size, build and complexion – the narrator notices Leggatt's 'shadowy, dark head' to be like his own. Soon they are dressed in identical sleeping-suits, so that the one follows the other on the poop like his double. They stand whispering, each with a hand on the skylight. Then the texture begins to thicken: they were both Conway boys, they discover, from similar backgrounds. We begin to feel perhaps that the narrator, too, is of a 'gentlemanly' disposition and that he is unlikely to see eye to eye with the master of the *Sephora*. It is not surprising that when it comes to his listening to Leggatt's account of what happened aboard that ship during the storm he grasps the situation very rapidly; his is sympathy in its fullest sense: 'I saw it all going on as though I were myself inside that other sleeping-suit.' Thus, a more mystical association develops between the two men, who begin to find that they can understand each other's feelings without the need for words. They discover that they have even deeper experiences in common – not the least being that of loneliness and isolation, engendered in the one by his having killed a man and in the other by the responsibilities of his command.

The captain soon becomes all too well aware of the implications for himself of Leggatt's continuing presence in his quarters. In private he is able – albeit with some effort – to adjust his habits, his movements, his way of speaking in order to accommodate the secret sharer of his life; but in public he has to carry on in his customary manner as if nothing untoward has occurred. New tensions arise in the narrative with the chances of their being discovered either as a result of some slip on the captain's part or else because of the watchfulness of his crew. Such is the degree of mutual understanding between him and Leggatt that when the boat arrives from the *Sephora* the captain does not need to explain the danger – 'What could I tell that he did not know already?' The question is, however, one which sums up the whole relationship of the two men.

Leggatt's account of the events surrounding his accidental killing of one of his *Sephora* shipmates is important not only because it extends the narrative scope of the story by the introduction of a new setting and characters and of a further source of suspenseful excitement, but also because it provides a study of men under stress closely similar to that which Conrad created in *Typhoon*. On this latter score, there are indeed several marked parallels. We have already seen in our examination of *Typhoon* that Conrad shows particular interest in the different ways men react to moments of high crisis and the manner in which they relate to one another in such circumstances. Though his portrayal of the 'terrific weather' encountered by the *Sephora* is by no means as detailed as his orchestration of the hurricane in *Typhoon*, he undoubtedly intends us to see it as a test of man's willpower and courage. The man whom Leggatt has killed, we ought not to be surprised to learn, was 'one of those creatures that are just simmering all the time with a silly sort of wickedness'. He wouldn't do his own duty, nor would he allow others to get on with theirs. Obstructive in his insolence. When it comes to the crisis, not unlike the second mate of the *Nan-Shan*, he was 'half crazed with funk'. Leggatt is forced by circumstance to act swiftly and decisively: there is something of the matter-of-fact style with which MacWhirr knocks down his second in Leggatt's assertion that there was 'no time for gentlemanly reproof, so I turned and felled him like an ox'. Something too of MacWhirr's dogged perseverance in Leggatt's decision, once free of the *Sephora*, to swim till he sank – to go on as long as humanly possible and only then to die if it must be. If Leggatt has qualities in common with the captain of the *Nan-Shan*, however, his own skipper certainly has not. We can't imagine MacWhirr 'raving' like the rest of the crew when told of the accident, or allowing the piled up stresses of a sleepless week of gales to drive him nearly out of his mind. Captain Archbold, according to his chief mate, is a very different sort of man. Afraid of his crew, dominated by his second mate and steward, shadowed by his wife, he seems frightened of his own responsibilities. He looks sick when obliged to confront his prisoner; he shakes like a leaf as he refuses to let him escape, even though he knows that his own survival and that of his ship was entirely due to Leggatt's setting of the reefed foresail. The description of him given at this point whets our anticipation for the encounter with him later in the story.

2

The care which Conrad demonstrates in the first part of *The Secret Sharer* to present a balanced structure while at the same time holding the reader's interest is once again apparent when we come to the second. The stillness of the setting continues to be relieved by references to the havoc of the hurricane which all but finished the *Sephora* and we are treated to two periods of exquisite tension – the one concerned with Captain Archbold's exploratory 'visit', the other with the extreme danger in which the narrator places his ship in an effort to ensure Leggatt's safe escape. It is at this stage, too, that the theme of honour begins to assert itself – Archbold's lack of honour (already implied in part one) in his pursuit of Leggatt; the narrator's counterpoised preoccupation with not telling an outright lie to his fellow-captain; and his final achievement of an honourable solution by jeopardizing his own career in order to help his 'second self' to a new destiny. By the time all these matters have been worked through, the young captain, in throwing himself into what another of Conrad's characters, Nostromo, would clearly have recognized as a most desperate affair, has acquired what he so patently lacked at the outset, the confidence of command.

When we meet Captain Archbold at the beginning of the second part of the story, we see at once that Leggatt's assessment of him was fundamentally accurate. He carries his character carefully: he has spent thirty-seven 'virtuous' years at sea, of which twenty have seen him in positions of 'immaculate' command. Such is his awareness of his own moral worth and reputation, we are scarcely surprised that he should only drink water. The narrator notes, on the other hand, a confusion, a mumbling quality as the man gropes 'shamefacedly amongst his feelings' over the matter of Leggatt. He is 'densely distressed' as to what has occurred, though his image of the details has become muddled. His tenacity in pursuing his objective is 'spiritless'; he has the courage to probe only by means of oblique references. Indeed, the narrator is only prevented from feeling a perverse sympathy for his visitor by his awareness, his 'mental vision', of Leggatt and everything he has been through. He observes that 'the terror of that gale' was on Archbold even now. What, we wonder, would this man who, in his chief mate's words, whimpered with fear at the onset of the storm, have done had he been like MacWhirr on the bridge of the *Nan-Shan* as that appalling 'running wall' of water raced to meet the ship? No doubt he would have given himself up to despair (like Jukes when at his lowest ebb in *Typhoon*), justifying his doing so with the conviction that he was in the hands of God or destiny and that there was nothing to be done about it. By contrast, we learn later how Leggatt had felt that as an officer there was an obligation on him to mobilize the crew into action in the face of the storm – a sentiment shared by Jukes when, with the aid of MacWhirr, he has recovered his equilibrium.

It is not to be wondered at that Archbold's blatant antipathy towards Leggatt causes the narrator to feel that he himself would not have been considered a suitable chief mate for the *Sephora*. He senses that his visitor distrusts him, even as an equal, because of his 'mysterious similitude to the young fellow he had distrusted from the first'. The prevailing tone is, however, by no means one of unrelieved moral outrage at Archbold's expense; as elsewhere in *The Secret Sharer*, Conrad touches the situation with ironic humour and thus produces in the reader a nicely ambiguous reaction to his narrative. The humour here derives from the manner in which the young captain, by feigning deafness, causes his older colleague to shout at him, in stark contrast to the conversation of whispers that he has been obliged to conduct with Leggatt since the beginning of their relationship. It is with some regret that he realizes that he will never know what his double's normal voice really sounds like.

After the departure of Archbold, the narrator still has to contend with the problems raised by Leggatt's presence. There continue to be anxious moments, as when the steward without warning takes the captain's coat to his room and all but discovers the fugitive. There are still the guardedly apprehensive reactions of the crew to their captain's odd behaviour. So identified does he feel with his secret double that he does not need to mention to him the close shaves, the scares that are taking place. As, for the first momentous time, he takes his ship out to sea, he is naggingly aware that he is not alone in his command, that he cannot devote his whole attention to the concerns of his ship. His mind is so much on the occupant of his cabin that he has to make a conscious effort to recall himself to the 'conditions of the moment'. Nonetheless, his experiences to date are already helping build up a sense of self-reliance in him. We notice the confident firmness of his tone in the conversation he has with his first mate as soon as Captain Archbold has left. When he remarks on the 'something un-yielding' in Leggatt's character which is carrying him through so finely – that MacWhirr quality, the spirit that made the chief mate of the *Sephora* determined to keep swimming as long as he could – we realize that something similar has fast been developing in him. Certainly he derives inspiration from his guest's example, but it is worth remembering that Leggatt also seems to benefit from his: 'It's a great satisfaction,' he tells the narrator, 'to have got somebody to understand' his situation. 'You seem to have been there on purpose.'

As the tale draws to a close, Conrad heightens the tension of situation and relationship alike as well as playing fully on their joint significance. In a story that has been crammed with suspense and incident, the final pages of *The Secret Sharer* rise to a pitch of overwhelming excitement. The thematic strands which we have been following individually up to this point now come together in a final, securely tied knot. To begin with, the captain asserts his authority in the most unequivocal fashion possible: he announces his decision to seek the land breezes in spite of the danger to his ship of the islands and shoals that lie close inshore. In doing so for Leggatt's sake he is not only putting his career and future in jeopardy, he is also risking his life as well as those of his men. He is, furthermore, behaving in much the same way as Leggatt did when he was faced by the insubordinate seaman aboard the *Sephora*: one simple decision, one simple action, Conrad seems to be saying, can have earth-shattering repercussions. A fine, upstanding young man with his whole life before him, because of one accident, one error of judgment, may well end as an outcast, wandering the earth, branded with the mark of Cain. Yet the decision must be taken, the action, if we are truly men, must be performed. As the ship moves in the darkness under the shadow of Koh-ring, the only member of the crew whose nerve does not give is the captain himself. Even the chief mate believes they are all lost, while the helmsman is utterly overawed. There *are* anxieties in the master's mind as he peers out into the gloom in order to establish whether or not his vessel has come round and will clear the shoreline, but it would be unnatural if there were not. By happy coincidence it is the white hat he gave to Leggatt, as a gesture of friendship, to protect him from the sun, that he is able to use as the necessary marker that tells him all is well. The symbolism is obvious: what we give of ourselves to other men will in good time return to benefit us. The narrator no longer feels there are 'two captains' on his ship. He is no longer in any doubt as to how she will respond to his handling. 'I was alone with her. Nothing! no one in the world should stand now between us, throwing a shadow on the way of silent knowledge and mute affection, the perfect communion of a seaman with his first command.' In the final moments of the story, however, Leggatt and he are still united in some senses by a common destiny: both are now 'free men', both heading for a new life, both – their honour satisfied – with head held high.

In the closing months of 1909 it was a destiny which Joseph Conrad, English author, was anxious to claim as his own.

NOTES

The notes in this edition are intended to serve the needs of overseas students as well as those of British-born users.

First, some general points.

The stories in this collection were written about the period when sailing ships, though still common, were beginning to give way to steam. This means that they contain a large number of technical terms relating not only to navigation but also to the structure and working of both types of vessel. The notes which follow are chiefly concerned with examining and explaining these terms. Conrad is, however, too fine a craftsman to allow technical language or the need for his readers to turn for help to a glossary to hold up or spoil his narrative. He uses nautical terms pre-eminently in order to build up the feeling and atmosphere of being aboard and familiar with a working ship. It does not really matter if there are details which we do not quite understand, so long as the principal ideas and events, the human motives and actions and aspirations are clear to us. Look at the following passage, for instance:

> A cross swell had set in from the direction of Formosa Channel about ten o'clock, without disturbing these passengers much, because the *Nan-Shan*, with her flat bottom, rolling chocks on bilges, and great breadth of beam, had the reputation of an exceptionally steady ship in a sea-way.

There are several terms here which will likely send the average reader thumbing through the notes (cross-swell, rolling chocks on bilges, breadth of beam, seaway), but they do not in fact hinder his understanding of the main gist of the sentence, that is, that the *Nan-Shan* was regarded as being a steady vessel in heavy seas.

A second feature of these stories is the way Conrad refers to places and geographical features such as islands and rivers by names which are not exactly those by which they are known today. There are two main reasons for this: the first is that in some cases the actual names have changed with the emergence of new states or political regimes (what Conrad knew as Siam has now long been referred to as Thailand); the second is that we now spell the names rather differently (Fo-kien has turned into Fukien), though it is worth noting in this connection that some of Conrad's names may not be quite what we expect because they are approximations by which British sailors knew places rather than the precise names used by their inhabitants.

Finally, to avoid the need to repeat explanations of the different ranks of officers mentioned in all three stories, let us begin with a survey of the most important:

captain, master: commander of a ship, responsible for all officers and crew (both deck hands and, on steam ships, engineers)

first (chief) mate: chief deck officer, second in command to the captain but equal in rank with the chief engineer on a steamship

second mate: deputy to the chief mate

boatswain (bos'n): foreman, chief petty (non-commissioned) officer

first (chief) engineer: (on steam ships only) principal officer, under the captain, responsible for the engines of the vessel

second engineer: deputy to the first engineer

third engineer: deputy to the second engineer

TYPHOON

Page

1   *typhoon:* fierce cyclonic storm in which the winds blow spirally inwards towards a centre of low barometric pressure

2   *gamp:* umbrella

208

chronometer: an instrument for the accurate measurement of time

whip-saw: frame saw with a narrow blade, used especially for cutting round curves

petty: small-time, of little consequence

Talcahuano: a Pacific port in central Chile

3   *chart-room:* room where a ship's maps (charts) are stored and where her course is plotted

4   *treaty port:* a port which has been granted or rented by the Chinese government to some other nation for a fixed period (Hong Kong is a contemporary example)

Fu-chau: (Fu-chou) a port in southeast China

coolies: Chinese peasants

Fo-kien: (Fukien) a province of southeast China opposite Taiwan

fore-deck: deck in the front part of the ship

hatches: openings in a ship's deck (covered by trap doors) through which cargo is lowered into the holds

Celestial: inhabitant of China (from a translation of one of the native names for China)

cross swell: strong movement of waves across the direction in which a ship is moving

Formosa Channel: strait of sea between mainland China and the island of Formosa (now Taiwan)

rolling chocks: blocks fixed to the hull to offset the effects of a ship's rolling movement in heavy seas

bilges: the lowest internal part of a ship's hull or (here) the hull itself

beam: width

sea-way: open water

Dumbarton: a Scottish shipbuilding town on the River Clyde

Siam: modern Thailand

5   *stem to stern:* from the front of a ship to its rear

keelson: line of timbers fastening the floor-timbers to the keel of a ship

trucks: flat discs of elmwood fixed to the tops of masts or flagstaffs

polemasts: masts made each from a single spar

steam windlass: machine, operated by steam, used for raising heavy loads by means of a rope or chain

purblind: short sighted

6 *a British register:* most maritime nations keep a register or list of shipping (containing details of construction, size and owner-ship of individual vessels) accredited to them and flying their flag. The *Nan-Shan* started life on the British register but later changed to the Siamese

throw up the billet: give notice, give up one's place in the crew of a ship

bridge: platform in the middle of a vessel used by the com-manding and other officers

7 *deck locker:* a cupboard on deck in which ropes and other tackle may be stored

lead line: line or string (weighted with a piece of lead) used for ascertaining the depth of water through which a ship is passing

8 *friction winches:* similar to windlasses, machines used for raising heavy loads only – in this case – operated by friction

derricks: cranes for lifting cargo

gins: machines or hoists used for raising

coamings: raised border round the edge of hatches, designed to prevent water entering them

bulkhead: partition separating one part of a ship's interior from another

9 *forward 'tween-deck:* space between decks in the front part of the vessel

sampan: Chinese sailing vessel

seven-years'-men: men contracted to work for their employer for a term of seven years

battens: wooden bars (generally used in flooring) about two metres in length (and in this case 7.5 cm thick)

fore and aft: to the front and rear (of the ship)

pidgin-English: a mixture of English and other languages used for general communication in the Far East

topside: on deck

gunny-bags: sacks made of coarse jute material

state-room: private cabin

indited: composed, wrote

Teddington: a residential suburb of London, on the River Thames

Solomon says: Mrs Rout likens the wisdom of her husband's views on men and ships to the wisdom of King Solomon in the Bible. However, his parody of 'They that go down to the sea in ships; and occupy their business in great waters; these men see the works of the Lord, and his wonders in the deep' misses the mark because it comes not from any of Solomon's writings but from Psalm 107.

Western ocean service: shipping routes in the Atlantic Ocean

brass-bound: covered with braid, thus emphasizing differences in rank

mess: eat

black-squad: apparently a reference to the engineers as opposed to the deck officers

dry stick: dour, laconic person

sidelights: lights carried on either side of a ship under way during the night

port alleyway: passageway running along the port side of a ship

starboard: the righthand side of a ship as one faces the front

dodger: screen on bridge erected as a protection from the spray

port: the lefthand side of a ship as one faces the front

cataclysms: disasters

herculean: immensely strong

sail-needle: a stout needle used for stitching sail canvas

whipping up coals: hoisting coal on board by means of a whip, a kind of pulley

coaling: taking on coal as fuel to fire the ship's boilers

glass: barometer

fiddle: usually called the 'fiddley' – an iron framework round a hatchway opening (at the top of stairs leading up from the stokehold in this case)

stokehold: furnace room where the ship's boilers are located

not trimming properly the stokehold ventilators: not adjusting the cowls on top of the ventilating shafts leading down to the stokehold in order to give an adequate supply of fresh air

blanked ... blank ... condemned (also *unmentionable ... gory ... crimson* later in the text): Conrad lived in an age when it was considered improper to write or print the sort of swear words which he must have encountered frequently during his life at sea. So he sometimes substitutes words like these instead by way of compromise

swab-headed deck hand: a swab is a ship's mop made of rope yarn; 'swab-headed' is clearly thus an insult, illustrating here the second engineer's contempt for deck-officers

steam-gauge: instrument for measuring the pressure of steam in the boilers

18   *cowl:* hood-shaped cover on the top of ventilator shafts which may be adjusted according to the direction of the wind in order to increase or decrease the supply of fresh air to the rooms below deck

wheel-house: the sheltered room from which the ship is steered

firemen: stokers, those who keep the boiler fires supplied with fuel

19   *awning stanchion:* upright post used as a support for the covering rigged up on ships to keep off the sun's rays or the rain

20   *ship's log:* book in which is kept a daily record of the ship's progress as well as events occurring during the voyage

jambs: side posts of a doorway

battened: fastened down

21   *Shanghai:* a Chinese port several hundred kilometres further north than Fu-chou

coal-lighter: small vessel which carries supplies of coal out to larger ships to save their coming into dock

22   *West Hartlepool:* a town in northeast England

sea-chest: chest or box in which seamen keep their possessions while afloat *gimbals:* device for keeping a hanging object (for instance, a lamp or a compass box) horizontal

head on: sailing directly into the heavy seas

four points off her course: four degrees (by the compass) off the course she ought to be sailing

tack: if sailing ships want to travel in the direction from which the wind is coming, they have to proceed in a zig-zag path (tack) to catch the wind in the sails.

oilcloth: linoleum, waterproof floorcovering

sea-boots: thigh length waterproof boots

oilskin coat: waterproof coat

semi-circles . . . quadrants . . . curves: geometrical figures used in the calculation of the tracks of storms in the book to which MacWhirr is referring

bearing of the centre: position of the eye (centre) of the storm

get behind the weather: keep out of the track of the typhoon while it passes

come booming down: arrive in great haste

the centre of them things bears eight points off the wind: the direction in which the eye of a typhoon lies is eight degrees different from that from which the wind is coming

watch below: off-duty period

sou'wester: waterproof hat with flap at the back to cover neck

beam: side

weather-cloth: canvas or tarpaulin covering to protect men from wind and spray

head sea: the swell or movement of waves coming head-on

stentorian: full and loud

rail-stanchions: upright posts supporting the guard-rail

mite: small amount (as compared with the 'tremendous uproar raging around')

taking a header: diving headfirst

companions: staircases leading from the deck to the cabins below

half-tide rock: a rock which becomes exposed only when the tide drops to point midway between high and low

trysails: small sails used on steamships during bad weather in

Conrad's time

gaskets: cords for securing a sail to the beam (yard) along which it is stretched when in use

double-lashed awnings: awnings that have been tied down especially securely

light-screens: screens protecting the ship's lights

amidships: towards the midpoint of the ship's length

davits: pairs of cranes for raising and lowering lifeboats from the sides of a ship

fall: the load-bearing rope in hoisting gear

block: pulley

36   *overture:* gesture

       hands: crew, seamen

39   *petty officer:* non-commissioned officer

40   *fetched away:* the battens nailed into the deck to secure the coolies' chests have broken away

       leeward: on the opposite side (of the speakers) from that from which the wind is blowing

41   *game of nap:* a card game (properly called Napoleon)

       Table Bay: large bay just north of the South African port of Cape Town

43   *hooker:* small ship

       patent: obvious

       lamp-room: the room in which lamps are overhauled and stored

       athwartship coal-bunker: hold for storing coal which occupies the whole width of part of the vessel

44   *coal-trimmer's slice:* tool for breaking coal used by the men responsible on board ship for storing and shifting the fuel

       'taking charge': falling and losing control

46   *ring-bolt:* bolt with a ring through a hole at one end

47   *engine-room telegraph:* mechanical apparatus by which captain transmits from the bridge to the engine-room his instructions about the speed the ship should be moving

       engine-room tube: speaking tube linking the engine-room with the bridge

       in chancery: in wrestling, the position in which the head of one wrestler is held firmly under the arm of the other

smoke-stack: funnel

binnacle: box in which ship's compass is kept, illuminated at
night for easy reference

lanyard: short rope

man at the helm: helmsman, seaman responsible for steering the
ship

gear-casing: protective case covering steering equipment in the
wheelhouse

the bells had not been struck: bells are usually rung in order to
mark the beginnings and ends of watches (duties) on board
ship

gone down wind: disappeared, come to nothing

donkey-man: seaman responsible for operating the hoisting
(donkey) engine on a ship's deck

firing-up: stoking the fires to keep them going

crank-heads . . . crossheads: parts of a steam engine

low-pressure cylinder: part of a steam engine

Tophet: Hell

keeping a full head of steam: not allowing the steam pressure to
drop

blowing off: giving off steam

Hades: Hell

a heavy crank arrested on the cant: the crank of the engine stopped
in mid-stroke

piston-rods: parts of a steam engine

slush-slingers: the second engineer's scathing reference to the
deck-crew (possibly from their job of clearing out the slush
from the coal-bunkers)

wind up: hoist by means of a pulley

articles: rules laid down for the running of a ship

brooked no delay: would tolerate no delay

pitches: the stem to stern plunges of a ship in heavy sea (as
opposed to the side-to-side rolls)

scrimmage: tussle, scrum

life-lines: ropes stretched at all angles across the open space, to which the coolies may cling as the ship pitches and rolls

ruck: heap, mass of people

setting taut and hitching: tightening and securing

64   *gleaners*: those who gather up what is left behind the reapers in a cornfield. Conrad uses the word to suggest the stooping of the seamen in their search for anything of value on the floor.

polls: heads

salient: prominent

65   *shot the bolt*: to secure the door

67   *look out for her*: take over control of the ship

68   *the oracle of a Joss*: altar of a Chinese idol

aneroid glass: type of barometer which, unlike the conventional sort, works without the use of mercury

pshawed: uttered an expression of contempt or impatience

70   *had the wheel relieved*: ordered another man to take the wheel from the helmsman who had seen the ship through the storm

72   *run with the wind*: move in the same direction as the wind

shirt of mail: type of medieval armour composed of closely linked and woven chains

point: of a sword or spear

on the bow: at the front of the ship

73   *unwonted*: unusual

running target: a target towed at speed for gunnery practice

secondary batteries of a cruiser: reserve guns on board a fast warship

salvage: compensation made by the owner of a wrecked or damaged vessel to those (other than her own crew) who have preserved her and her cargo from loss

74   *Foreign Concession*: the area of Fu-chou then under the control of a foreign government

incontinently: immediately

scow: flat-bottomed boat

manila line: thick rope of very strong fibre, originating in the Philippine Islands

75   *bummer*: someone who drifts from place to place scrounging

off others

prosy: dull, tedious

the Pond: the Atlantic Ocean

consuls: agents of one country living in another

gunboats: small warship with heavy guns

Mandarin or Taotai: officials of the Chinese Empire

goggles: spectacles

sedan-chairs: covered chairs carried by means of two poles held horizontally

sanguine: confident, optimistic

abaft: behind

Bedlam: madhouse

Hong Kong: a Chinese treaty port leased to Great Britain, southwest along the coast from Fu-chou

turned-to: got to work

mail-boat: fast boat which carries the mail

THE BLACK MATE

London Dock: the group of docks immediately downstream from Tower Bridge

lumpers: labourers employed in loading and unloading ships, stevedores

foreman stevedore: chief 'lumper'

poop: high deck in the stern (rear) part of a ship

clipper ship: sleek-lined, fast sailing ship

sack-coat: short, loose coat worn by men

small potatoes: insignificant person, thing or event

Fenchurch Street: street in the city of London, not far from Tower Bridge

berth: sleeping-place on a ship, hence, a place in her crew

birds'-eye: a type of tobacco

Western Ocean trade: shipping routes in the Atlantic Ocean

mediums: people through whom spirits of the dead are said to communicate with the material world

Leytonstone: an inner suburb of north-east London

virago: an amazon, a woman with manly qualities

118   *Calcutta:* important sea-port in India

     berthing-master: dock officer responsible for allocating to ships their places in harbour or at a wharf

119   *dock walloper:* someone who carries out heavy manual labour in a dock

     brass-bound: officers are distinguished by the braid on their uniform

     Paul Pry: a nosey person

     mooring post: a fixed post on the jetty to which ships are secured when in harbour

     portholes: reinforced windows in the sides of ships

     bread-locker: place where bread is stored on board ship

     mizzen-rigging: rigging attached to the mizzen-mast, that nearest the stern of the ship

120   *skeletons in . . . cupboards:* secrets in people's past lives

121   *mud-pilot:* man whose job it is to guide a ship among the mud-banks of the upper reaches of a river on its way to or from a port or dock

     river man: pilot responsible for guiding a ship through a river estuary

     five-inch manila: thick rope made of very strong fibre, originating in Philippine Islands

     check-rope: rope attached to the shore and used to stabilize ship while it is negotiating narrow channels

     sea-pilot: man responsible for navigating a ship through tricky sea-channels

     down Channel off Dover: heading westwards down the English Channel towards the Atlantic, in the region of the cross-channel port of Dover

122   *Cape of Good Hope:* headland south of Cape Town (South Africa), a notable landmark for ships making for the Indian Ocean

     staterooms: private cabins

     cuddy: officers' cabin under the poop deck

123   *second dog-watch:* unlike most watches (duties) on board ship,

which are of four-hour duration, the dog-watches last only two hours; the first dog-watch is from 4 to 6pm, and the second from 6 to 8pm

sleeping-suit: pyjama suit, usually of flannelette, worn for sleeping on board ship

sensitized plate: photographic plate, one which responds to the action of light

taffrail: rail round the stern end of a ship, the upper portion of a ship's stern timbers

wake: area of foamy water left behind a moving ship

astern: behind the ship as it travels on its way

utilitarianism: the attitude which evaluates ideas and actions according to their usefulness

pooh-pooh: make light of, dismiss as unimportant

starboard: the righthand side of a ship as one faces the front

clew: tackle for rolling and securing sails to the yards

mainsail: principal sail of a ship, attached to the mainmast

yards: the horizontal beams on the masts of a ship along which the sails are stretched

dead square: exactly at right-angles to the mast

nearly right aft: coming pretty well from directly behind the ship

well out on the quarter: coming plainly from the side rather than from the rear of the vessel

companion-steps: staircase from the deck to the cabins below

trimming: having balance of the sails adjusted

helmsman: seaman responsible for steering the ship

wheel: for steering the ship

port: the lefthand side of a ship as one faces the front

poop-ladder: ladder down from the poop to the main deck

mainmast: principal mast of a ship, usually second from the prow (front) of the vessel

a rum go: a strange affair

grog: alcoholic drink, usually a mixture of rum or whisky and water

quarter-deck mooring-bits: the posts to which mooring ropes are secured, in this case situated on that part of the deck immediately behind the mainmast and reserved for passengers and superior officers

130 *falling sickness*: epilepsy

132 *pitch-and-toss*: game played by throwing coins at a marker, here it stands for something of no consequence

134 *Gulf of Bengal*: that part of the Indian Ocean to the east of India itself and to the west of Burma

135 *hard packets*: vessels which keep generally to a particular route between one port and another, on which life is often uninspiring and unpleasant

136 *curmudgeon*: mean, ill-natured person

intestate: without having made a will

'Gazette': a newspaper in which the inward and outward sailings of ships is listed

in the chops of the Channel: at the mouth of the English Channel

Dunkirk: a port in north-east France, close to the Belgian border

137 *dunnage*: sailor's baggage

gangway: walkway used for access between ship and shore when a vessel is in dock

139 *bulled*: plunged hastily (without careful planning)

to make a 'seance': to try to communicate with the spirits of the dead

THE SECRET SHARER

151 *bar*: sandbank or area of shallow water at the mouth of a river or harbour

River Meinam: This seems to be an error on Conrad's part. The setting for *The Secret Sharer* is generally taken to be the estuary of the river on which Bangkok (the capital of Siam, now Thailand) stands. But Bangkok is on the River Chao Phraya. The answer to the riddle lies in the fact that 'mae nam' in Thai means 'river'. It is amusing to think, perhaps, of Conrad as a young officer on board a ship calling in at

Bangkok, hearing the local people refer to the 'mae nam' and thinking that they were telling him the *name* of the river. He was apparently none the wiser when, in 1909, he sat down to write his story.

Paknam pagoda: Bangkok has today well over 300 pagodas or temples. Pagodas are striking on account of their characteristic tapered or tiered towers.

Gulf of Siam: a vast leg of the South China Sea which separates Thailand on the west from Kampuchea (Cambodia) on the east

spars: the masts of a sailing ship, together with the yards (beams) along which its sails are stretched

poop-deck: high deck in the stern (rear) part of a ship

cuddy: officers' cabin under the poop deck

hands forward: members of the crew, the ordinary seamen, whose quarters were in the fo'c'sle, the forepart of the ship under the main deck

drew too much water: whose displacement was too great, her hull – that is to say – floating too deeply in the water

spring tides: tides which coincide with the new and full moons at which the water rises to its greatest depth. The ship, according to the chief mate's theory, is of too great a displacement to cross over the sandbank except when the tides are at their fullest.

roadstead: channel close to the shore in which ships may ride at anchor

waist: the middle section of a ship

Malay Archipelago: the group of islands which makes up the Malay States. The ship will need to sail about a thousand miles (1500 km) in a south-south-easterly direction in order to round it and then be in a position to sail westwards through the Malacca Strait into the Indian Ocean

quarter-deck: that part of the deck immediately behind the mainmast and reserved for passengers and superior officers. It is saluted on warships

sleeping-suit: pyjama suit, usually of flannelette, worn for sleeping on board ship

forecastle: fo'c'sle, forepart of a ship under the main deck

riding-light: light hung out in the rigging at night when a ship is riding at anchor

fore-rigging: the rigging is the system of ropes and cables supporting a ship's masts and by means of which the sails are extended along the yards. The fore-rigging is the tackle which occupies the front part of the ship.

156 *side-ladder:* a ladder of rope and wood which can be thrown over the side of a ship to afford access to visitors

157 *spare spar:* a spar kept for use in emergencies

158 *main-hatch:* a hatch is a half-door covering a stairway to quarters below deck: the main hatch is the hatch at the head of the main stairway.

159 *right aft:* to the very rear of the ship

binnacle: box in which ship's compass is kept, illuminated at night for easy reference

Conway boy: the *Conway* was a training ship for boys intending to become officers in the merchant navy

160 *setting a reefed foresail:* the foresail is the principal and lowest square sail on the fore (front) mast of a ship; a reefed sail is one of which a part has been rolled or folded up so that it catches less wind and is therefore less dangerous in high winds. To set a sail is to adjust it according to the position of the wind.

sheet: rope attached to a sail and used to adjust it

161 *forebits:* the posts at the front of a ship on which cables are secured

sou'wester: waterproof hat with flap at the back to cover neck

companion: staircase from the deck to the cabins below

wheel: for steering the ship

162 *stateroom:* private cabin

ratlines: small ropes which form horizontal steps in the rigging of a ship

mizzen-rigging: rigging attached to the mizzen-mast, that nearest the stern of the ship *rudder-casing:* the casing enclosing the ship's steering mechanism

chronometer: an instrument for accurate measurement of time

oilskin coat: waterproof coat

bulkhead: partition separating one part of a ship's interior from another

gimbals: device for keeping a hanging object horizontal

Java Head: headland forming the western tip of Java

port: porthole, reinforced window in the side of a ship

too deep to have run long under bare poles: had too deep a draught to be able to survive in such weather without sails on her masts

halter: rope (suggesting that he was bound to be hanged for his unfortunate accident)

Sunda Straits: the stretch of sea between the Indonesian islands of Sumatra and Java

Angier Point: a headland in northwest Java

scrimmage: tussle, scrum

'brand of Cain': Cain, one of Adam's two sons (in the Bible), killed his brother Abel and in so doing committed the first murder. The 'brand of Cain' is thus the mark of a murderer. Cain's punishment was to be forced to wander the earth for the rest of his days.

Java Sea: the sea between Borneo (to the north) and Java (to the south)

Carimata: the Selat Karimata is a strait between Borneo (to the east) and Sumatra (to the west)

consul: an agent of one country (here presumably Great Britain) living in another

hullabaloo: racket, hue-and-cry

glass: telescope

rudder-chains: the chains by which the rudder is operated in order to steer the vessel in the required direction

break of the poop: the gap in the rail round the poop deck at the top of the poop-ladder

poop-ladder: ladder down from the poop deck to the main deck of a ship

170 *square the yards by lifts and braces:* square off, set yards at right angles to the masts by use of lifts and braces (ropes). Lifts are special ropes running from the top of a mast to the ends of its yards, used for steadying them

foremast man: any sailor below the rank of petty officer (those whose quarters were 'before the mast' in the fo'c'sle of a ship)

174 *bunting:* small flags made of thin cloth

176 *starboard:* the righthand side of a ship as one faces the front

177 *sail-locker:* the locker in which sails were stored when not in use

179 *main topsail:* the sail nearest but one to the deck on the mainmast of a ship

180 *helmsman:* seaman responsible for steering the ship

182 *tack for tack:* to tack is to change the course of a sailing ship by altering the position of its sails. Proceeding 'tack for tack' means employing this technique continuously.

184 *hard alee:* an order to steer the ship hard (sharply) into the direction in which the wind is blowing

main-brace: the brace attached to the mainyard (which is the lower yard of the mainmast)

185 *maroon:* abandon

Cambodje shore: the coast of Cambodia (Kampuchea)

old fellow in a wig and twelve respectable tradesmen: judge and jury

186 *off-shore tack:* a course away from the coast

the other tack: course heading towards the coastline

187 *stand right in:* go close inshore

land breezes: breezes blowing off the land

shoals: shallow water

Koh-ring: Kaoh Rung is a large island off the coast of Kampuchea

Cochin China: the old name for the southernmost part of Vietnam

188 *had the watch:* was on duty on deck

quarter-deck ports: portholes in the quarter-deck

189 *put her round:* change course (back on to an off-shore tack)

the ship's way is deadened in stays: the vessel has slowed down to a standstill

poll: head

weather: sail straight into the direction from which the wind is coming

good full: going firmly in the same direction

don't check her way: don't slow her speed

Erebus: Hell

ready about: get ready to change course

head-sheets properly overhauled: the frontmost sails on the ship properly hauled over

coming-to: pointing into wind before moving on to the new tack

mainyard: the lower yard (beam) carrying the sails on the mainmast

taffrail: rail round the stern end of ship, the upper portion of a ship's stern timbers

gathered sternway: was moving backwards

shift the helm: move the rudder (to change the direction of the ship)

forebraces: ropes attached to the foreyard used for setting the foresail

she's round: the ship has now changed course and is moving clear of the land

foreyards: the beams which carry the sails on the foremast

drawing ahead: moving off on her new tack

FURTHER READING

If you have enjoyed this collection you may like to investigate some of the following stories and novels by Conrad. They are among his best and most immediately appealing work and most of them are currently available in paperback as well as hard cover editions:

SHORT STORIES
Amy Foster
The Duel
The End of the Tether
Heart of Darkness
The Idiots
The Inn of the Two Witches
The Nigger of the 'Narcissus'
An Outpost of Progress
The Shadow-Line
Youth

NOVELS
Lord Jim
Nostromo
The Secret Agent
Under Western Eyes
Victory

For those who are interested by and wish to find out more about Conrad's life and times, two books stand out:

JOCELYN BAINES, *Joseph Conrad: a critical biography*, Weidenfeld & Nicolson. NORMAN SHERRY, *Conrad and His World*, Thames & Hudson. This includes a fascinating selection of photographs of ships, places and people with whom Conrad was associated.